I0675739

Readers love
The Warlock Brothers of Havenbridge series
by JACOB Z. FLORES

Spell Bound

"…this was a fun, fast-paced and exciting book… once I started, I was immediately pulled into the story."

—The Blogger Girls

Blood Tied

"The writing is supreme, the story is an intricately woven idea that intrigued me, brought me in from the beginning."

—On Top Down Under

Soul Struck

"I am loving this world. The magic, this shifters, the mystery, all these elements were just so well done and interesting."

—Prism Book Alliance

Spell Fall

"*Spell Fall* is an excellent addition to The Warlocks of Havenbridge series. It has danger, intrigue, and a heartfelt romance that readers will love."

—Joyfully Jay

By Jacob Z. Flores

3
Being True
The Gifted One
Please Remember Me

DREAMSPUN DESIRES
ONE FINE DAY
#18 – Suddenly Yours

PROVINCETOWN
When Love Takes Over
Chasing the Sun
When Love Gets Hairy
When Love Comes to Town

THE WARLOCK BROTHERS OF HAVENBRIDGE
Spell Bound
Blood Tied
Soul Struck
Spell Fall
Blood Drop

Published by Dreamspinner Press
www.dreamspinnerpress.com

JACOB Z. FLORES

BLOOD DROP

Published by
DREAMSPINNER PRESS

5032 Capital Circle SW, Suite 2, PMB# 279, Tallahassee, FL 32305-7886 USA
www.dreamspinnerpress.com

This is a work of fiction. Names, characters, places, and incidents either are the product of author imagination or are used fictitiously, and any resemblance to actual persons, living or dead, business establishments, events, or locales is entirely coincidental.

Blood Drop
© 2017 Jacob Z. Flores.

Cover Art
© 2017 Paul Richmond.
http://www.paulrichmondstudio.com
Cover content is for illustrative purposes only and any person depicted on the cover is a model.

All rights reserved. This book is licensed to the original purchaser only. Duplication or distribution via any means is illegal and a violation of international copyright law, subject to criminal prosecution and upon conviction, fines, and/or imprisonment. Any eBook format cannot be legally loaned or given to others. No part of this book may be reproduced or transmitted in any form or by any means, electronic or mechanical, including photocopying, recording, or by any information storage and retrieval system, without the written permission of the Publisher, except where permitted by law. To request permission and all other inquiries, contact Dreamspinner Press, 5032 Capital Circle SW, Suite 2, PMB# 279, Tallahassee, FL 32305-7886, USA, or www.dreamspinnerpress.com.

ISBN: 978-1-64080-039-7
Digital ISBN: 978-1-64080-040-3
Library of Congress Control Number: 2017949838
Published November 2017
v. 1.0

Printed in the United States of America
∞
This paper meets the requirements of
ANSI/NISO Z39.48-1992 (Permanence of Paper).

To my readers,

Thank you for your never-ending love and support.
Without you, this book wouldn't be possible.

To Lara,

Your assistance on this journey has been invaluable.
I love you so much!

INTRODUCTION AND DRAMATIS PERSONAE

MAGIC HAS existed since the dawn of mankind. Its source is the Gate, a portal to the astral plane that powers the wonders of the world. From this Gate, a new species—the *homo magus*—evolved from humans and divided into three different subspecies: *homo ater magus* or warlocks, *homo albus magus* or witches, and *homo neuter magus* or wizards.

From the first moment the humans witnessed the power of this new species, homo magus were hunted without mercy and brought to the brink of extinction.

But the homo magus survived by forming a secret society that lives amid humans.

The witch hunters still exist today, continuing their pursuit of eradicating magic. As long as they are hunted, warlocks, witches, and wizards will continue to live in secret, protecting themselves from extinction while saving humans from the new enemies and ancient threats they know nothing about.

THE BLACKMOORS (WARLOCKS)

Pierce Blackmoor is the oldest of his siblings and the future High Priest of his coven, a duty he now takes seriously. After Pierce suffered through a brief period where his brothers possessed more power than he did, his command over lightning has evolved. He can now see energy auras and transform his body into living lightning.

Thad Blackmoor is the middle child. He is coolly logical and often aloof. He uses his ice abilities to strategic advantage. His powers have grown as well. He can now create snowstorms and call forth a blizzard. Knowledge is far more important to Thad than defeating his enemies.

Mason Blackmoor is the youngest of his siblings, who initially had trouble controlling his magic or accessing his active power. Mason has since learned he is a shadow weaver, which means he can bend the darkness to his will. This is a rare and powerful warlock ability that has led to the corruption of every warlock who has ever wielded it, and Mason's abilities continue to grow more powerful.

Drake Carpenter, the human boyfriend of Mason, has been an honorary member of the Blackmoor coven ever since his aunt Millie was murdered and turned into a vampyre. Despite recently learning he is also a witch hunter, which makes him a natural enemy to the *homo magus*, Drake continues to use his immunity to magic to protect those he loves from vengeful shadow weavers, psychotic sorcerers, and mysterious magical foes.

Aiden Teine joined the Blackmoor family after being cast out of Otherworld, the land of the fairies, by his father. King Oberon and the fae rejected Aiden when he was turned into the first vampyre fae. As a fire fae and former prince of his realm, Aiden struggles with balancing his conflicting fae and vampyren tendencies. His love for Thad continues to keep his more dangerous instincts at bay.

Kale Aquilo is a shifter and the most recent addition to the Blackmoor family. When he first arrived from the shifters' magically shrouded island, Aeaea, Kale was as timid and docile as the dove he turned into. However, his love for Pierce and the devastation brought to his home by shadow weaver Ben Crane and the mad sorcerer Sersie gave Kale the ability to transform into an eagle. Kale now serves as the Chief Advisor to Caspian, the Beast King who rules over all shifters. Kale serves as a liaison between his people and the rest of the magical community.

Oliver Blackmoor is the head of his family and the High Priest of his coven. Although many still consider him the most powerful warlock in the family, since he turns his entire body to stone, his sons' growing magical abilities have begun to eclipse his own. He is often distant and irritable, but Oliver loves his sons and his ever-growing family. He also still grieves for his wife.

Priscilla Blackmoor was Oliver's wife and mother to Pierce, Thad, and Mason. She died from breast cancer over one year ago.

THE PROCTORS (WITCHES)

Charles and Camille Proctor are the High Priests of their coven. Charles, who works for the Havenbridge Police Department as a detective, is capable of commanding fire, while Camille has dominion over plants. The Proctors pride themselves on the white magic they practice, which connects them to the spiritual forces of the universe.

Adam Proctor is the oldest of his siblings and the future High Priest of his coven. His guiding element of magic is air, which allows him to use it as an offensive or defensive ability. Adam's rocky past with Pierce Blackmoor has been resolved, and he no longer nurses his previous wounds for the unrequited feelings he once had for Mason Blackmoor.

Charlotte Proctor finds herself bookended by two strong-willed siblings. She is the peacemaker in the family, and this characteristic manifests itself in her powers. Charlotte taps into the element of water, which grants her astounding healing abilities. She is also a staunch supporter of the Conclave.

Miranda Proctor fancies herself the rebel in her family. She is loud and opinionated, which often gets her in trouble and sets her at odds with her family. This likely explains why Miranda and Mason Blackmoor do not get along; they are two peas in a pod. Miranda's active ability derives from the spirit element, which grants her a unique ability to teleport objects and people at will.

THE STONEWALLS (WIZARDS)

Lawrence and Rachel Stonewall are the High Priests of their coven. The gray magic of wizards gives them direct access to the spirit element, which allows them to tap into powerful abilities that are kept in check by their logical ways. Lawrence is able to control minds while Rachel can cast illusions.

Edith Stonewall is the eldest of her siblings. She is the future High Priest of her coven and can erect invisible force fields for protection. She is also the most like her parents. She rarely engages with others outside her coven, although she does share a friendship with Pierce. She is closest, however, with her twin brother, Elliot.

Elliot Stonewall is Edith's younger twin brother by three minutes. He is mute and cannot access his magic like others in the community. He does, however, have the ability to speak to others telepathically.

Kate and Keaton Stonewall are the youngest members of the family, and they are also twins. Neither of them has tapped into their active powers because they are still too young. Once they turn sixteen, they will learn what ability they will have at their disposal.

OTHER CHARACTERS AND ENTITIES

The Conclave is the governing body of the magical community. The nine most powerful warlocks, witches, and wizards serve on the

Conclave. They are charged with making and enforcing magical laws as well as ensuring the Gate is protected from all threats. The word of the Conclave is absolute, and their power is feared across the magical community. Recently, the Conclave has removed the Blackmoors as one of the protector covens guarding the Gate.

Gerald Wa, a wizard and the only identified member of the Conclave, acts as an advisor to the protector covens. He was believed to be dead, but his death was staged to hide his ascension to the Conclave. Prior to this "death," Gerald was romantically involved with Drake's aunt Millie. The information Gerald provides to the protector covens and more specifically to the Blackmoors is a bone of contention between him and the rest of the governing body.

The Warlock Hag is a member of the Conclave. Although her identity is unknown, she has made her dislike of the Blackmoors evident. Her animosity toward the Blackmoors places her and Gerald at odds, especially since she led the charge to replace the Blackmoors with the Edwells as the protector coven for the Order of the Black.

The Edwells consist of Leopold and Agnes and their teenage daughter, Charity. Although the Proctors and the Stonewalls do not like them, they put up with the Edwells in their role as the new protector coven. The Blackmoors, however, display open hostility for the coven they consider to be made of opportunistic weasels.

Sersie was a sorcerer, a magical species that resulted from humans and magical beings interbreeding. During 700 B.C., Sersie led a rebellion, along with other sorcerers, against the magical community. She cast a spell that turned humans into the first shifters. To escape death at the conclusion of the Sorcerer Wars, Sersie transformed her soul into a wraith. With the help of Ben Crane, Sersie possessed the body of a young sorcerer named Chloe and came back to exact her revenge until she was killed by Pierce.

Bartram Kane lived during the Salem witch trials. Bartram was a powerful member of the Conclave of his time. He was also the last warlock to possess the abilities of a shadow weaver. When his son Ebenezer was burned at the stake, Bartram went mad. He spoke the forbidden immortalitas spell to resurrect his son, but turned him into a vampyre instead.

Ebenezer Kane/Ben Crane came back to life as a vampyre after his father spoke the immortalitas spell. Ebenezer created other vampyren and almost destroyed the magical and human communities. It took the combined might of the Conclave to stop him. During the present day, Ebenezer took on the identity of Ben Crane and decimated Otherworld, the land of the fae, and Aeaea, the shifters' magical island. He stole two of the Crests of the Five, which are physical manifestations of the five mystical elements, for Icarian, the individual behind the chaos. Pierce killed Ben during his attempt to steal the third crest within the crown of the Beast King.

Millicent Carpenter is Drake's elderly aunt Millie. Prior to being murdered and turned into a vampyre, she was a fiercely independent woman who lived life on her terms, but after her transformation, she has been under the control of Ben Crane. Since Ben's death, however, Millie and the rest of the vampyren have disappeared.

Icarian, who appears as a golden ball of light, is the unknown enemy the Blackmoors and the rest of the protector covens have been fighting. Icarian plans to either bring about the Spell Fall, a curse that ends all of magic, by collecting the magical talismans called the Crests of the Five, or to kill one of the Blackmoor brothers in an effort to stop them from triggering the Prophecy of the Three. Icarian's motives and the existence of the ancient divination remain a mystery to everyone except Drake Carpenter.

CHAPTER 1

I DIDN'T want to be here. This place smelled like ripe armpits, and the stench of stale urine only added to the ambiance. It was also extremely loud. Patrons screamed at each other to be heard over the music blaring from something called a jukebox while others assaulted the sticky wooden floor with what they labeled dancing.

It looked more like they were having seizures to me.

But what did I know? I wasn't from this world. I wasn't even human. I was Aiden Teine, and I was born on Otherworld as a fire fairy, a prince and future ruler of all fae. Well, at least until Ben Crane turned me into a vampyre and my father banished me.

I winced. After all these months, the memory still hurt like a stake to the heart.

"Will you lighten up?" Pierce Blackmoor knocked his shoulder into me and flashed a wry grin. He was my boyfriend Thad's older brother, and more often than not, a happy thorn in the side of the warlock I loved. Even though he was gruff and drove Thad crazy, Pierce was a nice guy... once you got past his tendency of acting like a jackass. "You're supposed to be having fun, not sitting here scowling."

I tried to flatten the arch of my upper lip. "I'm not scowling."

"Yeah, well, you're doing a great impersonation, then." He held up two fingers at the bartender, who quickly placed two shots of clear liquid onto the bar. Thad took one and held the other one up to me. "Here. This will help."

I seriously doubted that. One sniff of the contents made my eyes water. "What poison is this?"

"Vodka," he said before downing his drink in one gulp. "It'll loosen you up, and you need it. You've been walking around with a stick up your ass ever since Imbolc."

His foul language offended me. I wasn't used to being spoken to so crassly, but evidently on this plane, and most assuredly around Pierce, inappropriate language was all the rage. Still, he wasn't wrong. I had been on edge lately, and I wasn't entirely sure why.

All I knew was that I couldn't let down my guard. If I did, the monster I kept under lock and key inside me would bust loose. The consequences would not be good for humanity, Thad and my new family, or the rest of the world.

"Drink." Pierce shoved the beverage into my face.

I grimaced at him over the rim of the glass. "Remove that at once."

Pierce arched a cocky eyebrow. "Or what?"

Did he really want me to answer that? Not only was I a being of pure magic capable of harnessing power Pierce couldn't even fathom, I was also a vampyre. I could turn him inside out before he even blinked. Not even his recently grown magical abilities would do much against me.

"Are you really poking a vampyre?" Pierce's shifter boyfriend, Kale, suddenly popped up next to us with a big smile stretched across his tan face. Pierce and I sat straight up on the stools, glancing at the people around us. If anyone heard Kale, he might have unwittingly revealed to humans that vampyren, as well as magic users, lived alongside them. The last thing we needed was the hateful backlash from humans who were terrified of our presence. We had enough to deal with without a sudden onslaught of newly minted witch hunters.

Kale rolled his golden eyes and snatched the glass of alcohol out of Pierce's hand. "Will the two of you unclench?" He downed the drink and grimaced. "No one's paying attention to us. Besides, most of them are drunk anyway."

That was an understatement. Many of the humans inside the bar stumbled about like foals on unsteady legs. To make things worse, they also screeched out lyrics that would drive the musical sylphs mad. If I didn't leave this place at once, I might just release my inner vampyre upon them all.

At least then I'd have some quiet.

"You still need to be careful." Pierce cupped Kale's cheek and rubbed his thumb across his young lover's face. While he might be a brute to the rest of the world, with Kale, Pierce was as gentle as a mewling kitten. "We all do."

Kale answered with a nod and a kiss.

The man on the stool to my left sniffed. "Fucking faggot!"

Tongues of flame licked across my cheeks as the deadly anger within me rose like an advancing wave. Pierce reacted in kind. His massive chest practically doubled in size as he stood and took two steps toward the big tattooed man with a spike sticking through his left nostril.

"What the fuck did you say?" Pierce glared at the miserable excuse for a human being, who stood and stretched to his full height.

Pierce was a big guy—not as big as me, but certainly no one to sniff at. Spike, however, towered over Pierce, his muscles bulging underneath the white tee with yellow pit stains. "You heard me." The man poked Pierce's chest. "Faggot."

I had enough trouble controlling my temper when I was a fire fairy. Now that I was a vampyre, losing my cool proved even deadlier. This was not going to end well.

Before Pierce or I could react, the man's face turned into a grimace of pain as he fell to his knees. Kale had grabbed the man's wrist, wrested it up and behind his shoulder blade, and twisted. Judging from the sweat that instantly broke out across Spike's flesh, his arm was seconds away from being dislocated.

His hollering silenced the bar, and everyone watched the events unfold with humans' customary morbid curiosity. Clearly they were stunned that someone so much smaller than the vile man was capable of overpowering him so quickly, but I wasn't surprised.

Kale was a shifter, and his unique ability to transform into two different avians also resulted in increased speed and strength. He might be small, but he packed quite a punch. I was proud of him.

Kale's actions had a different effect on Pierce, if his parted lips and twinkling blue eyes were any indication. I'd clearly be getting no sleep tonight. Could this evening get any better?

"Are you ready to apologize?" Kale asked as he applied more pressure to the man's arm.

The man yelped. "I'm s-sorry."

"For?" Kale glanced at Pierce, who grinned.

"How about for being a douche?" Pierce answered.

Kale added more pressure and the man howled in reply. "I-I'm sorry... for... being a douche."

"Good." When Kale released Spike, the man slowly rose to his feet. He rubbed his sore arm, glanced at Pierce and me, and snarled. Someone hadn't learned his lesson. When Kale cleared his throat, Spike blanched before he shuffled across the bar and out the door.

The bartender placed three glasses on the bar. "You took care of that jerk without tearing up the place. That's fucking badass."

Pierce snagged Kale and swallowed him in an embrace. "That's my man, the badass."

"Cheers!" the bartender said after filling up the glasses with more of the clear poison. "These are on the house."

Pierce and Kale quickly emptied their free drinks and then eyed the third glass before turning their gazes to me. I motioned for Kale to take my drink, and he did so with a lopsided grin.

"You do realize Thad is going to be upset when he learns what happened." Of course, he had to actually get here first. He'd spent the past few days in Salem finishing up his dissertation, and though I'd wanted to go with him, he convinced me to stay here, considering the recent troubles I'd been having. I hadn't liked it, but he'd been right, like always.

Pierce's snort brought my attention back to him. He draped his big arm around Kale. "I'm not afraid of my little brother."

"Yes, well, you should be." I loved Thad, but when he got upset, it was best to duck. Not even the power of a vampyre fairy could stand against his frosty stare when he wasn't pleased. I'd forgotten to put down the lid on the toilet one morning and he took an unexpected dip. It was a mistake I'd never made again. "You know Thad despises when anyone makes a scene."

"Actually, I abhor it."

Pierce and Kale's eyes grew wide as I slowly panned over my right shoulder.

Thad stood behind me with his arms crossed over his lean, muscular chest. His always-perceptive hazel eyes narrowed into slits as he blew a strand of his strawberry-blond hair from in front of them. Even with the storm brewing across his gaze, I'd never seen a more beautiful sight.

My love was finally home.

THAD, WHO had apparently witnessed the entire spectacle, launched into a lecture of how reckless our actions were. According to him, we couldn't afford to lose our tempers or our control. All it took was one mistake, one unintentional spark of electricity from Pierce's fist or activation of any of our powers, and we would expose magic to the world.

Although potentially exposing magic in a crowded bar was probably riskier than what we'd done, I wasn't about to mention it. I certainly didn't want Thad's fury to swing my way. I liked Kale and Pierce, but that was one bullet I didn't intend to take for anyone.

But even though he was railing at us, I loved him even more right now than I did yesterday. Thad's anger was a facade. He only got this worked up when he was scared. I didn't need my magical fairy senses to tell me that. As the man who shared his bed, I knew Thad better than anyone else. He sought to protect those he loved from harm, which was why he hounded his family so much. He'd already lost his mother, and he had no intention of losing anyone else.

Love was his driving force, and I found it admirable and wickedly hot. If I had my way, Kale and Pierce wouldn't be the only ones keeping everyone else awake tonight.

"I'm glad you're home."

My words cut Thad's rant short. His hard gaze softened and a smile crept across his pursed lips. "Don't try to use your charm on me." He attempted to force his scowl back to his expression, but he was failing miserably. "This could've been a disaster. Have you forgotten that you—"

I pulled Thad into my arms and silenced him with a kiss. The tension immediately left his rigid muscles when our lips touched, and the fear masked as rage almost completely disappeared. It felt good to hold him again, to feel his body pressed against mine. Thad anchored me—a fact my vampyre instincts constantly battled—but he also served as my ballast. Without him, I'd likely fall into the dark ocean that waited to consume me.

That was why I couldn't let him finish his sentence. Only he and I knew the problems I'd been having, and it was a secret I wasn't ready to share.

Pierce groaned. "Will the two of you get a room already?"

Thad pulled out of our kiss but remained in my arms where he belonged. "Only if you'll stop being a jackass."

"Like that'll ever happen," Pierce added with a snort.

Kale shook his head. "Do you two have to fight *every* time you see each other?"

Thad and Pierce looked at each other before turning to Kale. "Yes."

I chuckled because I knew what their response meant. Thad and his brothers' incessant bickering was how they told each other "I love you" without actually saying the words. Warlocks had probably the biggest hearts of all. They just didn't like to show it.

"So did you complete your dissertation?"

Thad glanced up at me, a huge grin spreading across his fair features. "Yes. I submitted it to my advisor and will be defending it in a few weeks."

Kale hollered in congratulations while Pierce ordered celebratory drinks from the bartender. When the beverages arrived, Pierce handed each of us a shot glass before nodding to Thad and me. "Now, drink, and I won't take no for an answer. It's a toast for my brother."

Thad appeared to swallow down his emotions before polishing off the alcohol and wincing. He slammed his glass onto the bar, which earned him a round of applause from Kale and Pierce. When their gazes turned to me, I eyed my drink. If this were ambrosial wine from my father's secret stash, I'd partake in many glasses, but what humans labeled as spirits tasted more like an ogre's bathwater. I held my breath and hastily knocked back the loathsome liquid. When it finally reached my stomach, I feared it would immediately begin a return trip.

"See?" Pierce patted my back roughly with his paw. "It's not so bad."

I cleared my throat and coughed. "Says who?"

"So, anything exciting happen while I was in Salem?" The celebratory mood came crashing down in response to Thad's question. I wasn't surprised he asked it. He preferred study and research to recreation, but even with so many questions left unanswered about Icarian and the Spell Fall, I was amazed he was doing it in a bar. The alcohol had clearly loosened the collar of my conservative warlock. Pierce frowned and ordered more vodka. He was clearly intent on having fun and not talking business.

"No, thank the Gate." Kale took the new beverage Pierce handed him. For such a small guy, he matched Pierce drink for drink. His shifter metabolism had to be responsible. "We've had too much excitement already."

No one could argue with that. We'd been through a lot, and the recent mess with the witch hunters hadn't helped things. Mason, Thad's younger brother, and his boyfriend, Drake, were still dealing with the consequences of learning they were spell bound as enemies, not lovers. The added bombshell that Drake was also a witch hunter by birth hadn't made coping with the fallout any easier. It had been a lot for everyone to digest.

Thad hooked his index finger with mine. The gesture was innocent and sweet, but whenever Thad touched me, my burning flesh longed to get naked and sweaty. "How's Drake coping?"

I had to will my rising passions under control. Although I didn't care, Thad wouldn't be pleased if I ripped off his clothes and took him right here. "He's better." At least that was what he wanted everyone to think. My fairy senses revealed the truth. Something had been worrying him since our last confrontation with Icarian, but he wasn't sharing. It had bothered me at first, especially since secrets had gotten us into enough trouble, but Drake was a big boy. He would tell us when he was ready, so I didn't push or let on that I knew something was up.

"Where'd you drift off to?" Thad's question brought me out of my thoughts and back to his hazel eyes that made me forget how to breathe. Fortunately, a kiss stolen from his lips gave me all the oxygen I needed.

"I'm here with you, as I should always be." I sat on the stool and tugged Thad between my legs. I had to have him close to me. I didn't feel complete unless some part of me was touching some part of him. Thad had claimed that was part of our magical connection, the blood tie that bound us together. Whatever it was, it made me feel like I was flying.

"I couldn't agree more." Thad beamed in my embrace. He pressed another kiss to my lips before turning around in my arms and facing Pierce and Kale. "Any new developments since I've been gone?"

"Will you give it a rest?" Pierce's bark caused Thad to tense and me to bare my teeth. I didn't like it when anyone raised their voice to the man I loved. Pierce either didn't notice or didn't care. Knowing him, it was likely a combination of both. "We've been facing a constant shitstorm for months. Can we just have *one* night where we can hang out and *not* talk shop? That was the entire purpose of getting out tonight, wasn't it?"

Thad lightly patted my knee. It was his way of telling me that Pierce was right, so I exhaled through my easily riled-up temper and relaxed. "Fine. I suppose I can do that."

Pierce cracked a huge smile. He gave Thad another drink, and while he swallowed it with a grimace, my skin crawled.

Someone was watching us.

"Is something wrong?" Thad leaned his head against my chest and glanced up at me. His eyes were big and bright, and a huge grin spread like sunshine across his expression. He was enjoying himself, which he didn't do often. I couldn't ruin that for him, especially since a quick glance around the bar revealed no impending threats other than inebriated humans.

I pressed a kiss to his tasty lips and savored the sweetness. "Nothing at all."

A COUPLE of hours later, we finally left the bar. Even though the strange sensation I'd had earlier had passed, my guard remained up. As Thad had often said, it was better to be safe than sorry. Although most human phrases made little sense to me, that one spoke volumes. Keeping Thad from harm dominated my list of priorities, so I scanned every shadow for a hidden threat.

Right now, though, the only danger was Thad and Pierce. They led the way, their arms draped around each other's shoulders as they tripped down the sidewalk that would take us to our vehicles, which were parked behind the building. If they made it without falling, I'd be surprised.

"I love you, man," Pierce said between hiccups. He lightly punched Thad in the chest as they walked, which caused him to stumble sideways. Fortunately Thad steadied himself against the wall before both of them tumbled to the ground.

They evidently found almost busting their heads open hilarious. They broke out into uncontrollable laughter that made them sound like inebriated gnomes.

"Clearly warlocks cannot hold their liquor."

Kale snorted as he walked steadily by my side. "What was your first clue?"

In the months I'd know him, I'd never seen Thad behave like this. Unless we were naked in bed, he was usually serious and in control. Seeing this side of him made me smile as much as it made me roll my eyes. He was more human than he pretended to be.

"You've learned how to drive, right?"

Kale's question pulled me out of my thoughts and back to the Drunken Duo, who were still in the middle of expressing their undying brotherly love. "Yes, I have." But I wasn't really good at it. According to Thad, I drove worse than Mason, who sped everywhere and swerved all over the road. I took offense to the comparison. Mason was reckless; I drove defensively. The other vehicle operators who drove thirty in a forty-five and took five minutes to make a left-hand turn were the problems.

"Good, because we're the designated drivers tonight."

I sighed. We definitely were, which likely meant I'd be pouring Thad into bed instead of pouring myself all over him. It wasn't how I'd planned on spending his first night back in Havenbridge, but it certainly beat falling asleep without him.

"I take it you've learned as well?" I asked.

Kale wasn't from this world either. As a shifter, he'd been born on Aeaea, a magically shrouded island that kept his people separate, and safe, from the rest of the world. He nodded as he fished the keys of Mr. Blackmoor's Jaguar out of his jeans pocket. "Of course. You can't—"

Choked sobs suddenly caught our attention. I glanced over at Pierce and Thad, who continued weaving toward the cars while Kale trained his ear on the sound.

"It's coming from over there," he said with a nod to the alley between the bar and the building next to it. Kale darted toward the darkened area, and the hairs on the back of my neck stood. What was he doing? After everything we'd been through, running toward an unsecure darkened area wasn't the brightest move. But I had to remind myself that Kale was a shifter and a man of compassion. He couldn't ignore someone in distress any more than I could. His animal instincts would alert him to danger, but as he rounded the building and stood in front of the alley, he showed no signs of caution.

My gut tensed. What if his instincts were off? Someone had been watching us earlier.

"Kale, wait." I took a step toward him before glancing over my shoulder. Thad and Pierce were oblivious, too focused on reaching the vehicles. If I didn't follow Kale, he'd face whatever was waiting in there alone. If I went after him, I'd potentially be leaving Thad defenseless. He had no clue trouble might be brewing, and it wasn't like I could tell him or Pierce. In their current state, they would likely overreact and use their magic. While the street was empty and most of the patrons had left the bar hours ago, that didn't mean a human wasn't watching from a window somewhere.

I had no choice. Thad was in no immediate danger, but I couldn't say the same for Kale. I sprinted toward the alley he had entered.

By the time I'd turned the corner, I found him crouching before a man sitting with his back against the outer wall of the bar and weeping. The shadows kept me from seeing his face, but based on what Kale was saying, I had a good idea who it was.

"Listen, I'm sorry I hurt you, okay? What I did was no better than what you said."

It was Spike, and judging from the number of tears he wasn't holding back, his pride had taken a beating. Could my senses have been the ones that were off? Although Spike had been a jerk, he was obviously no threat.

"I-it hurts so bad," Spike said between heaving sobs.

Kale glanced over at me, and even in the dark, his golden avian eyes reflected regret. Personally, I didn't think Kale had anything to feel sorry about. Spike's behavior had been reprehensible, and if Kale hadn't done something about it, I would have. I most assuredly wouldn't have been as gentle.

"It'll stop hurting soon, right?" he continued. His sobs grew less frequent, as if he was slowly coming out of it. "At least that's what the voice says."

Voice? I stood up straight and scanned the area.

Kale sat on his haunches and stared at Spike. "What voice?"

Spike's human form melted away. His skin turned gray and withered, his hands grew into talons, his mouth filled with razor-sharp teeth, and his prehensile tongue wrapped around Kale's neck. Kale scrambled for air as Spike choked the life out of him. I lunged forward, ready to tear Spike in two, when hisses followed by cries of surprise from Thad and Pierce erupted from behind me.

I whirled around as prehensile tongues shot out from the interior of Thad's car and dragged Pierce and Thad inside. My flesh tingled. I was seconds away from reverting to my vampyren form. It was the only way I could save Thad and my new family. But if I transformed in the open, I ran the risk of exposure.

If I didn't, my loved ones would die.

"Choose your path carefully," a voice hissed from the shadows behind me.

I spun around to find a female vampyre emerging from the shadows in the alley, and I was glad Drake and Mason weren't here. Neither one needed to see Drake's aunt Millie like this. But as surprised as I was to see her, two things about her appearance perplexed me.

Why hadn't Kale or I sensed her, and how was she able to communicate? The vampyren we'd come across—with the exceptions of Ben and myself—could barely speak, much less string thoughts together. We'd been led to believe that only magical creatures who'd been turned could control the overpowering vampyren instincts. That obviously wasn't the case. "What do you want?"

She nodded to the sky. "Come."

She had to be joking. I was no fool. "And if I don't?"

Kale yelped in pain as Spike increased the pressure around Kale's neck.

"I think the answer's rather obvious, don't you?"

My skin burned as the desire to tear her neck from her shoulders rose within me, but I had to fight it off. She held all the cards while I held none. If Thad or anyone else was going to make it out of this alive, I had to follow wherever she led and hope that once we got there, I'd be able to bring everyone back.

I stepped into the darkened alley and shifted into my vampyre form, turning into the monster I hated and did my best to suppress. Letting him out was dangerous, especially since he'd proven difficult to control lately, but whether I'd be able to rein him in when I was done was a problem for later. "Lead the way."

Her withered lips widened into a beaming smile lined with razor-sharp teeth that resembled my own. A second later we took flight, blending with the night sky.

I FOLLOWED Aunt Millie and the rest of the vampyren to the middle of Wyman Woods, a conservation area located on the west side of Havenbridge. At this time of the night, the park was closed to visitors, which meant we could conduct our business without severe threat of exposure and I could kill every last vampyre if I needed to.

The aberration I'd become certainly couldn't wait to dismember something. It whined against the restraints my will imposed upon it.

Before I could unleash it, I needed answers.

"Why am I here?" My voice came out in a low growl.

She rattled her tongue at me before she sucked it back between her pointed teeth. "Why are *any* of us here? We have Ebenezer Kane to thank for that."

She was toying with me, and I didn't appreciate it, especially since I had no idea where Thad and the others were. If anyone hurt them, I'd bathe in their blood. My vampyre hissed in excitement. "That's not what I was asking, and you know it."

Her lips parted in a toothy, deranged smile.

"Intimidating me won't work." I gestured toward her bared fangs, which immediately retreated.

Her eyes widened as her tongue slid over the area where her fangs had been. "Did you just—"

"I'm not here to answer your questions. You're here to answer mine." She gulped and stood taller. "Where have you brought me? Is this… your nest?"

"Would I really bring you to our home? I'm a vampyre, not an idiot. If you knew the location of our nest, you'd exterminate us in our sleep."

That had always been the plan. We had searched for where they hid, and if we found it, we planned to eliminate them without fuss.

"And don't waste your breath lying about that bit of truth. You might be a vampyre, but you're not one of us."

I couldn't have been more thankful about that. I *wasn't* like her or the rest of her undead allies. I could tap into the powers of a fire fairy *and* a vampyre. While Aunt Millie and her brethren might be able to cut down a group of humans or *homo magus*, I could do the same to them. I'd proven that on more than one occasion.

"Then *why* bring me here?"

"You really don't know?" A grin hitched up the corner of her lips as the vampyren around me hissed in amusement. I counted at least a dozen moving in the shadows where they'd likely stashed Thad, Pierce, and Kale, but there were probably more. When we last encountered them, there had only been three. Aunt Millie and her two counterparts had obviously been busy creating an army.

"Did you find humor in my question?"

"Binding your vampyre to your fairy will is admirable and impressive, but it also blinds you."

"To what?"

"To what you're becoming."

The vampyre within me surged forward. Before I knew it, I had wrestled her to the ground. My tongue wrapped her neck, and my claws were poised at her throat. With one slice, her vile blood would spill upon the ground, and then I'd cut down every single vampyre around me until I found the warlock I loved.

The vampyre I'd become pleaded with me to do it, but the fae in me didn't want to prove to her that I was becoming even more fiendish.

The fear reflected in Aunt Millie's cold dead eyes told me that it was too late.

I had become an even greater threat than the one she posed.

I released my grip and backed away. The surrounding vampyren eyed me warily, uncertain if they should fight or flee. Honestly, I wasn't certain either.

Aunt Millie rose off the ground, rubbing her throat but keeping her gaze fixed upon me. If I attacked again, she'd take flight and Thad, Pierce, and Kale would pay the price. "You've sensed it already, haven't you? You can feel the change coming."

I had felt... *different* the past couple of weeks. Strange emotions twisted my insides, making it increasingly difficult to force my vampyre to submit to my fairy will. Its already unpredictable nature had grown even more unstable, as if its fight for dominance had turned into a battle for survival.

But what did any of this mean? If Aunt Millie had answers, it was past time for her to share them and end this charade. I recalled my vampyre, returning to my previous form far easier than I'd anticipated, and the fairy prince I'd been raised as filled my words. "End this game, speak your intent, and return my family to me at once."

"And what about us?"

In response to her question, more vampyren stepped out of the shadows and crept closer to where we stood. There had to be at least thirty more joining the dozen from before, and those were only the ones I could see.

I leveled my gaze at her. "What about you?"

"We're your family too."

I scoffed. "Is that why you've tried to kill me and your nephew on countless occasions? Because you consider us family?"

The anger in her eyes flickered, replaced with what looked like regret. "Do you truly believe I wanted to do that, that *any* of us wanted to do those things? Did you want to kill your warlock after you'd been turned?" She spat at the ground. "Of course you didn't. You were compelled to attack him, to want to slit his throat and drink your fill. I did what I did for the very same reasons *you* did. I was ordered to."

Had Drake been right all along? For months he'd begged us to believe that his aunt, the real Millicent Carpenter, lived somewhere within the monster Ben had turned her into. Everyone believed it was wishful thinking. Maybe it wasn't. Maybe humans *were* capable of controlling themselves, just like I'd been able to.

"But that doesn't explain Spike." I gestured at the new vampyre with the piercing through his nose. "If you truly don't want to kill, why kill him? Why make *him* a vampyre?"

She studied me in silence for a few moments as if she were weighing her options. "For you."

I took a step back, completely caught off guard by her ominous answer and the never-ending waves of fear that radiated off her and the rest of the vampyren. What had them so terrified? What army could they possibly think I'd need, and why would it even be necessary?

Before I had a chance to voice even one of those questions, a gust of wind blew through the forest, sending dirt and debris flying around us and turning my blood into ice. The vampyren glanced around nervously, hissing at the air. Their growing terror roared into panic and overwhelmed my fairy senses.

I held my hand in front of my face, trying to block the onslaught of dust that stung my eyes. "What's going on?"

"I thought we'd have more time, but he knows we're here."

She didn't have to say anything more. It had to be Icarian, the being behind all our problems and the one trying to end magic with the Spell Fall. He clearly didn't want Aunt Millie or any of the vampyren to share whatever news they possessed.

Aunt Millie made a high-pitched squeal. In response, three vampyren emerged from the darkness, carrying Thad, Pierce, and Kale through the gale-force wind before placing them at my feet. Besides being unconscious, they were unharmed. Their clothes weren't drenched in blood, and their throats remained intact. My paralyzed heart suddenly beat again.

She *had* been telling the truth. Without Ben, the vampyren were capable of choosing not to kill, but what did any of what I'd learned tonight mean?

"We didn't come to fight, only to offer our help."

The wind howled. In the distance, limbs creaked and popped, and the trees bent at precarious angles. In a few minutes, their roots would no longer keep them tied to the earth as the storm's fury increased in strength.

"Help with what?" I screamed over the roaring tempest.

In the blink of an eye, she stood before me. "We know what Icarian plans next, and it's a curse that will lay waste to all."

"What is it?" I grabbed her forearms, forcing her darting gaze to mine. "You went through all this trouble to get my attention, so tell me. *Now*."

She tore her arms from my grasp and hovered before me. "I cannot." Her tone softened, turning almost tender. "If I do, there will be nothing I can do to save Drake. Icarian will see to that."

Even though protecting Drake spurred her actions, she was leaving something out. I could sense her apprehension as easily as I could scent blood on the air. "Then why are you here?"

"Because you're the only one who can stop what comes."

"How?"

"Embrace what you are, and the rest shall become clear."

I couldn't do that. If I embraced my vampyre, I could lose more than the fairy I'd always been. I could lose— No, that wasn't even a consideration. There had to be some other, less cryptic solution, but I wasn't going to find it tonight.

Aunt Millie and the rest of the vampyren flew away from the approaching squall, disappearing into the night. I yelled for her to return at once, but the rising winds drowned out my words.

She had answers we needed. I had to follow her, to get her to talk, but one glance at my unconscious family squelched the impulse. If I left, they'd be vulnerable, and Icarian would use that to his advantage.

I wouldn't allow that to happen, so I stood my ground and faced the storm.

CHAPTER 2

FOR SEVERAL minutes the wind howled and battered the night. I stood tense over my family, prepared to sacrifice myself to save them, but the attack never came. Instead, the roaring wind reminded me of a child having a tantrum. Debris and limbs flew all around me, but they never got close enough to be a threat.

Icarian was putting on a show. I'd already seen the extent of his power when he battled Mason during Imbolc. If he wanted to, he could kill us now and end our threat, so why wasn't he striking?

Something told me finding the answer to *that* question would reveal everything.

A moment later, the winds abated. Icarian's departure left behind an echoing silence that was shattered when Pierce woke up. "What the fuck happened?" He sat up on the ground, covered in dirt and leaves. "Where are we?"

"Wyman Woods." I bent down and swept the stirring Thad into my arms. I had almost gone mad with worry when I saw the vampyren carrying his limp body. Only the warmth of his skin could dispel the chill tonight's events had settled across my flesh.

He gave me a reassuring smile and leaned into my touch. "How did we get here?"

"You don't remember?"

He stared off into space, his eyes darting back and forth as he searched his memories. "The last thing I remember was opening the door to the car, and then—"

"Holy shit!" Pierce sprung up from the ground, arcs of blue lightning fanning from his fists as he scanned the forest. "We were ambushed by those undead bastards."

Kale, who'd also returned to consciousness, stood by Pierce and nodded. "That's right. I remember being in the alley with that guy from the bar before he—" He placed his hands around his throat and winced when his fingers brushed the reddened flesh. "He turned into a vampyre and almost killed me."

"I'll fucking kill *him*!" A volt of electricity spiraled off Pierce's fist and struck the earth in a fierce crash.

I motioned for Pierce to power down. "He's gone. They're all gone."

"Did you fight them off?" Thad asked as he rose, checking me for signs that I'd been hurt.

"I didn't have to. They weren't looking for a fight."

"Are you fucking kidding me?" Spittle sprayed from his mouth as Pierce pointed at Kale's neck. "Kale was almost strangled to death."

I glared at Pierce. Though he'd matured over the past few months, he still thought with his fists first. "And if they wanted you dead, you'd be dead. I may be more powerful than most vampyren, but not even I could have saved all of you from an entire horde."

Thad arched a single reddish eyebrow. "Did you say a horde?"

I nodded.

"But I thought there were only three left?" Kale asked from within Pierce's embrace.

"Not anymore. It seems they've been expanding their ranks. I can't tell you how many there were, but I'd estimate over forty."

Pierce cursed. "Three of those fuckers almost killed us a few months ago. How are we supposed to fight against an entire army?"

That was a good question, but according to Aunt Millie, that army was for me to command. How that could possibly be true still confounded me. I needed answers, and I needed them fast.

Thad stood before me. He placed one hand on my cheek and stroked it while he grabbed my hand with the other. His touch quieted the winds of confusion that battered my mind. It reminded me that as long as I had him, I'd be able to weather whatever came my way. "What did they want?"

"To help."

"To *help*?" Pierce ran his hands through his short-cropped black hair. "Why on earth would we need *their* help? They're monsters."

Red dominated my vision, and the calm Thad's touch brought to my world vanished. I whirled and charged toward Pierce. "Is that what you see when you look at me? A monster?"

Pierce's eyes widened in surprise, while Kale stepped between us. "Aiden, stop."

I would *not* stop. Even though Pierce and everybody else said they accepted me, I'd sensed the truth a long time ago. All they would ever see was a monster. That would *never* change.

Pierce gently moved Kale out of the way. "What are you going to do, Aiden? Slit my throat and drink my blood?"

That was precisely what I wanted to do, what every instinct in my body demanded I do.

"Aiden, listen to me." Thad spoke softly as he inserted himself between his brother and me. The warm tones of his voice wrapped around me, repainting my red world with soft blues and greens. "Are you listening to me? Because I have something very important to say."

I tore my stern gaze from Pierce, and when I focused on Thad's handsome, angular face, the anger swelling in my chest ebbed a few feet. How could I maintain my rage in the face of such love and devotion? Everyone else might see a monster, but Thad didn't. He'd only ever seen me.

I took several deep breaths and nodded.

"My brother's an asshole."

A surprised chuckle exploded from my throat.

Pierce glowered at Thad and sneered. "Yeah, well, fuck you."

"It's true." He turned to face Pierce, who refused to meet his gaze. "You say the first idiotic thing that comes to your brain instead of thinking about how your words affect others."

"Why are you busting my chops?" He pointed at me. "Look at what your boyfriend was about to do."

I glanced down, and my breath hitched. My flesh was no longer a creamy white. It had turned pale gray, and talons extended from my hands. When had I changed into a vampyre?

I glanced up at Pierce, who eyed me warily. Kale stood next to him. A tentative smile stretched thin across his tan features.

"I didn't realize... I would never have...." Regret constricted my throat and turned my words into a faint whisper. "I can't believe it happened... again."

"Again?" Kale glanced back and forth between Pierce and Thad. "It happened before?"

Pierce settled his gaze on Thad. "What else are you keeping from us?"

"Not now," Thad said with a dismissive wave.

"Yes, now."

When Thad locked eyes with his brother, Pierce let out a deep breath and backed down. His piercing stare, however, told Thad they'd be discussing this real soon. Thad clearly accepted the unspoken condition with a nod before turning to me.

"Can you change back?"

I wasn't certain. When I consciously altered my form, I could change back and forth at will. That wasn't the case when I unconsciously shifted. The first time that happened, it took me a few hours before I reverted to my fairy form. I'd spent most of the day locked up in our bedroom to keep it secret from the rest of the Blackmoors.

Was this part of the change Aunt Millie had been talking about? Would my fairy side submit to the vampyren within me? The idea terrified me. The fairy I'd been had fallen in love with Thad, and it was that part that tied us together. What would happen to us if I lost that part of myself?

Tears fell from the corners of my eyes, and Thad wrapped his arms around me. He ran his finger through my long, matted hair and pressed a kiss to my chest and my chin before bringing my lips down to his.

"We'll get through this, Aiden, just like we've always done. Together."

I grabbed on to Thad, careful not to unintentionally skewer him with my claws, and held on to my lifeline. His breath became mine as his soft whispers played like a lullaby to my soul. It was the magic of our blood tie, when our bodies dissolved into one. The beast inside me fell asleep, and a second later I returned to the man I truly was.

Thad grinned up at me and brushed his lips against mine. "See? All better."

I leaned my forehead against his and sighed. "What would I do without you?"

"That's one question we'll hopefully never find the answer to."

That suited me just fine.

"Are the two of you done now?" Pierce grumbled behind us. "Because clearly you've got a ton of shit to catch us up on."

Thad held my gaze with his. It was his way of asking me if I was ready to share what I'd been going through. Honestly, I wasn't sure, but as long as I had Thad with me, I would be able to face whatever happened next.

THE HASTENING spell Thad cast on the four of us allowed us to speed down the mostly deserted road back to the Pig's Eye, the bar where our evening came to an abrupt end. Even though Pierce demanded we talk once we got back to the cars, Thad told him it would wait until we got home. Then we would tell everyone.

I was uneasy the entire ride back to Blackmoor Manor, and so was Thad. Silence ate up the air in the car as we drove home. Although he had confidence in me and in us, he worried about his family's reactions to our secret as much as I did.

In truth, it terrified me. They were the only family I had now. If Mr. Blackmoor turned me out, where would I go and what would happen to Thad and me? I had no doubt he loved me, but his bond to his family ran strong. Would losing the Blackmoors mean I'd lose Thad too?

"It'll be fine." Thad, who had sobered up after our vampyren encounter, parked his car in front of the sprawling estate that had become my home, and forced a smile. "Dad will likely be pissed, but he'll get over it."

I hoped he was right, because I couldn't bear another loss. "I suppose we should... how do you say it? Take off the Band-Aid?"

Thad grinned at me as he did whenever I used a human phrase incorrectly. "*Rip* off the Band-Aid, and yes, we should."

We got out of the car and walked up to the porch where Pierce and Kale waited. Pierce's scowl didn't cut a jagged path across his face as it had earlier. While his knitted brows communicated his irritation, he managed to flash me a thin smile. Kale likely had something to do with that. He had an uncanny ability to calm Pierce down and make him see reason.

"I shouldn't have said what I did," Pierce mumbled as Thad and I ascended the steps. Kale nudged him with his elbow, which made Pierce throw him a sideways glance. "Do I have to?"

Kale glared up at him and arched an eyebrow in reply.

Pierce exhaled. Evidently the answer was a firm yes. "I'm... sorry."

That hadn't been easy. Warlocks would rather gouge out their own eyes than apologize. Perhaps I had nothing to worry about after all. "No apologies necessary." I held out my hand, and when Pierce took it, I gave him a hearty pat on his shoulder. "I should not be keeping secrets."

"Damn straight." A roguish grin slanted his lips. "Dad's gonna rip you a new one, you know?"

"Pierce!" Kale chided while Thad smacked his brother across the back of his head.

"What the fuck?" Pierce complained. "It's true."

Thad snorted. "You don't need to be a dick about it."

The Blackmoors cursed more than a pack of trolls. "It's fine." I laced my fingers with Thad's and took a deep breath. "It's time to face the orchestra."

Pierce chuckled, and I screwed up my lips. I'd get these sayings right one of these days.

Thad delivered a peck to my cheek and opened the front door to a series of explosions.

"You're *so* dead!" Mason's voice reverberated through the house, and judging from his tone, he was engaged in deadly combat. Was our foe already here?

We sprinted down the hall toward the closed doors of the study up ahead. Electricity crackled from Pierce's clenched fists before he fired a lightning bolt into the door. It blew off its hinges and exploded inward.

When we charged inside, Mason and Drake stood facing us with mouths gaping. Digitized characters engaged in a gunfight flashed across the television behind them. They weren't in trouble; they were playing a video game.

"What the fuck?" Mason brushed sawdust and wooden shards from his shirt and out of his long black hair.

Pierce glanced around, his scowl twisting into a question mark. "We thought you were being attacked."

"We couldn't sleep, so we were playing *Call of Duty*, you dumbass. You might want to scope things out before you start blowing shit up." He turned to Drake and the irritation that had transformed his eyes into flaming pits of blue flickered. "Are you okay?"

"I'm fine," Drake answered in his usual Southern drawl as he studied us with his perceptive gaze. "But clearly somethin' has happened. What's wrong?"

Before anyone could answer, Mr. Blackmoor's angry voice boomed behind us. "What the hell is going on?" He thudded into the room, covered in his stone armor, clearly ready to pummel into bone dust whatever had attacked his family. When he realized there was no threat, he clicked off his active power and a half-awake man in his pajamas replaced the intimidating stony visage. Mr. Blackmoor surveyed the damage before crossing his arms over his big chest and leveling his icy blue gaze upon us. "Someone better start talking. *Now.*"

Thad spoke up first. "We were attacked tonight."

Mr. Blackmoor's cold stare softened as he rushed to our sides, giving each of us a once-over. He might be one of the most powerful warlocks on the planet, but when his children were in trouble, his fatherly instincts took over. It made my heart swell. "Are you okay? Was anyone—" He stopped when he noticed the red marks on Kale's throat. His jaw clenched. "Who or what did this?"

"Vampyren."

He took a deep breath in response to my answer. "Tell me everything."

I filled him in on the night's events, leaving out the troubles I'd been having maintaining control over my vampyren form. He had enough to process. With Mr. Blackmoor, it was better to give him bad news one bit at a time. He might be a loving father, but he was still a warlock. No matter what emotion he might be feeling, he expressed it as rage.

That was why I was surprised when the furniture didn't suddenly levitate off the floor and crash through the window and out onto the lawn. Instead, he sat back in his chair and scratched his fingernails through his scruff. "And you said there were forty vampyren with Aunt Millie?"

"From what I could determine, yes. But there were likely more."

Worry cast a long shadow across his features. Mr. Blackmoor already fretted for his family's safety after our recent confrontations with Icarian, who had previously aligned himself with a shadow weaver, banshees and, most recently, witch hunters. Adding a cadre of vampyren to the mix only deepened the lines across his forehead, especially since the Blackmoors had been removed as a protector coven.

Any threat we might face now, we faced alone.

"Aiden?" Drake crept up next to me. He gnawed on his lower lip and wrung his hands as his emotions overwhelmed my magical senses. He was relieved to hear his aunt was still alive. He'd been carrying around a mountain of guilt since Icarian made him believe he had put a stake through her heart, but as the waves of relief cleansed that stain upon his soul, worry took its place. "My aunt Millie… was she… is she—"

"She's still in there, Drake." I placed my hands on his shoulders and squeezed. "I think you've been right this whole time."

Tears streamed down Drake's cheeks as he flew into my arms. Sobs racked his body as he abandoned the hopelessness that had threatened to swallow him up since Imbolc.

"Are you sure?" Mason moved behind Drake, sniffling back tears of his own. Although he hadn't known Aunt Millie long, he'd grown extremely fond of her.

"As certain as I can be."

"But how is that possible?" Pierce glanced over at Thad, who shrugged.

I didn't have a ready answer because nothing about tonight made any sense. Seeing Aunt Millie and the rest of the vampyren operating under their own steam shattered everything we'd been led to believe about their kind. All I could do was tell them what I'd witnessed.

"For one, she wasn't lost to the bloodlust. She was in complete control."

"As she and the rest of her undead pals attacked and kidnapped us." Pierce's stern gaze communicated his disbelief.

"She did that to get my attention. She didn't have to warn me that some new evil was coming our way, but she did." I glanced around at the many uncertain stares. "That *has* to count for something, doesn't it?"

"Yes." Drake's answer came out strong and confident as he met the doubtful gazes.

"Although I hate to say this, I have to." Thad paced the length of the study, his hands clasped behind his back. He was in his brainiac mode. "Icarian tricked Drake into believing he was conversing with his aunt a few weeks ago. How do we know he isn't behind this 'revelation'?"

That was logical but also improbable. "Because I could sense her emotions. She was real, not a magical construct."

Kale cleared his voice. "Are you certain your senses are… reliable?"

Mr. Blackmoor switched his gaze from Kale to me. "What does that mean?"

Thad stopped midstride and cleared his throat, forcing everyone's attention to him and off me. I loved him for that. I wasn't ready to open that can of insects just yet. "You said she wanted your help. Did she tell you with what?"

"All she managed to reveal was that she knew what Icarian planned next and that she had been building an army to help me stop it."

Thad stopped pacing and locked eyes with me. "Building an army to help *you*?"

I nodded while Thad searched the wood floor for answers.

"What the fuck does that even mean?" Pierce stood and stomped toward me. "She's been fighting alongside Icarian for months. Why are she and the others turning traitor now?"

I met him halfway. "Honestly, I think you're responsible for that."

Pierce glanced around the room at the shocked expressions before pointing to himself. "Me? How am *I* responsible?"

"When you vanquished Ben on Aeaea, I think you freed the vampyren from his control. If you think about it, we haven't battled them once since that night."

Drake nodded. "That's what Aunt Millie—Icarian—told me a few weeks ago. I know a lot of what he said had been a ruse to get Mason and me to turn on each other, but do you think he was tellin' the truth?"

It certainly appeared so, and when I told Drake that, hope lit up his eyes for a moment before the spark died. What else had Icarian told him that he didn't want to be true?

Thad cleared his throat. It was his signal he was ready to begin piecing everything together. "So let's say Aunt Millie *isn't* Icarian in disguise and that she *is* speaking the truth."

Pierce snorted. "That's a lot of ifs."

Thad ignored his brother's commentary. "How are you and this army she's amassing supposed to stop Icarian?"

"I'm… not certain."

Mr. Blackmoor titled his head to once side. "But you have an idea, don't you?"

I couldn't deny it. Whether Icarian had wanted her to or not, Aunt Millie had offered a clue on finding the answer. It was a solution I didn't want to accept, especially after one gaze into Thad's warm hazel eyes. If what I suspected were true, he'd worry as much as I did. I didn't want that for him, but I also couldn't keep any more secrets from my family. I swallowed hard before nodding.

Thad flew to my side, his eyes wide with concern. "Why are you just telling me this now?"

I traced my finger along his jawline, taking the time to memorize every dip and curve of his handsome features. "Because I didn't want you to worry."

He met my gaze and stood tall. It was his way of telling me he could handle it. "Tell me. What do you think it means?"

"I think she wants me to embrace my vampyre instincts."

Confusion wrinkled his brow. "I don't understand."

"Neither do I," Mr. Blackmoor added. "You *are* a vampyre. What more does she want you to embrace?"

I took a deep breath. Once I spoke the words, there would be no taking them back. "In order to truly embrace being a vampyre, I have to reject my fairy side, the part of me that keeps me anchored, the part of me that—"

"Loves me?" Thad whispered.

When I nodded, the room exploded as everyone voiced their concerns. They knew as well as I did that my fairy side kept me from turning into a monster. If I abandoned that part of myself, it was anyone's guess what would become of me.

"WILL EVERYONE please be quiet?" Mr. Blackmoor railed after several minutes of ear-shattering chaos. The room immediately grew silent. Though everyone was still on edge, they did as Mr. Blackmoor commanded. The only one who hadn't been vocal about his concerns was Thad. He stood a few feet away from me, staring into space. "What possible reason could there be for you to reject the side of you that keeps your inner vampyre under control?"

Thad flinched in response to the question. I longed to go to him, but he wasn't ready. Yet.

"There can't be one." Mason glanced at Thad before turning his concerned gaze to me. I motioned for him to let his brother be, and for once, Mason did as he was asked. "This *has* to be a trick, and Icarian has to be behind it. He thought revealing Drake was a witch hunter would come between us. It sounds like the same ploy to me."

I couldn't argue with his logic. Icarian had hoped revealing that Mason and Drake were spell bound as enemies and not lovers would force them to kill each other as they had in every previous life, but he failed. Their love proved stronger than the hate from their many pasts. "But this wasn't Icarian. This was Aunt Millie—the real Aunt Millie, not the one Icarian created with dream magic."

Drake worried his lower lip. He did that whenever he had something to say but didn't want to say it. "And you're sure it was her? I thought I was talkin' to her, but I wasn't. Icarian was able to fool me and I'm her nephew."

"It was her. I know it."

"Because of your magical senses?" Pierce shot me an even stare that reminded me my magic wasn't exactly credible these days.

If I weren't so worried about Thad right now, I'd show Pierce exactly how reliable my powers could be. "I could sense the desperation and fear radiating off her and the other vampyren. I wouldn't have been able to sense such emotions from a spell. No matter how real it might appear, it *wouldn't* be real."

Mr. Blackmoor cast his gaze between Pierce and me. His arched eyebrow told me he knew we were having a disagreement about some unknown subject, but instead of pursuing it, he let it go. "Fine. Let's just do what Thad suggested earlier and agree that it was Aunt Millie. What could Aiden be 'turning into,' and what curse is she talking about?"

Kale sat up. "Could it be the *immortalitas* spell?"

"No." Pierce shook his head and drew Kale back into his arms. "That spell's been wiped out of every coven's book of spells. That can't be it."

"It could be the Spell Fall." Drake crossed over to Thad, who still stood silently in the middle of the room, and rubbed his back. No matter what inner turmoil Drake might be experiencing, he always thought of others first. I was proud to call him brother. Thad's faraway gaze, though, didn't refocus on the here and now. Thad had transported himself someplace our current predicament didn't exist.

I fought the urge to go to him, to take him in my arms and remind him of what he told me earlier—that we'd get through this together. Thad still wasn't ready. He stepped away from Drake's offer of comfort and turned his back to the room. He had to process everything first, and when he did, he'd come back to me, even if I had to drag him kicking and screaming.

"I don't think so." Mr. Blackmoor's words drew me back to the conversation. "The vampyren have known about the Spell Fall from the very beginning. This has to be something new, something we don't know."

"But something the Conclave probably knows about." Mason's comment was met with a room full of nods.

"Of course they know." Pierce's words crackled. "They've known about every *damn* thing we've faced so far."

"So we should contact them." Mason glanced over at his father, who was the only one capable of communicating with the magical governing body.

"No!" Thad spun around. A snarl curled his upper lip as he bared his teeth at his brother's suggestion. "We *cannot* do that. We have to take care of this on our own, *without* the Conclave."

Mason eyed Thad warily. "Why?"

Instead of replying, he dashed over to me and took my hands in his. My love was back from the land of reason, where he'd clearly found some strength. "I will figure this out. I'll find some way of stopping Icarian's plan *without* you having t—" His emotions choked back the rest of his words.

"Nothing can take me from you, Thad." I stroked his fair cheeks before sliding my fingertips across his trembling lips. "We're blood tied. Nothing is more powerful than that."

He smiled and nodded, but his neck was corded with tension and terror. Thad didn't take much on faith. He was a man of intellect, not emotion. Yes, he loved me—but he understood that love because of our blood tie. If we broke that connection…well, he wouldn't know what to think.

Luckily, as a fire fairy, I'd long since mastered emotional riptides. I had to be the life preserver for Thad as he had been for me these past few months, so I pulled him into my arms and held him to my chest. He needed to hear how my heart beat only for him. He had to feel the warmth his touch ignited across my flesh. He had to know beyond a shadow of a doubt that our connection transcended everything else.

He was mine and I was his. It was as simple and logical as that.

"Do you understand now?"

Thad gazed up at me and nodded. The churning waters receded, and the man I loved once again stood on solid emotional ground. "I do."

"That's great." Mr. Blackmoor's voice yanked us out of our moment and back to his piercing baby blues. "There's something else going on here. What aren't the two of you telling me?"

This time it was my turn to cling on to Thad as a wave of apprehension almost brought me to my knees. I didn't want to tell my surrogate father I had kept something from him. I could bear the anger, but not the disappointment.

Thad placed his hands on my cheeks and forced my gaze to his. "We can do this. Together."

I stole a kiss for strength before turning to Mr. Blackmoor and telling him the truth.

AFTER I finished, Mr. Blackmoor stood in stunned silence for several moments. Mason, however, had no trouble finding his voice. Not that I was surprised. The boy had more opinions than he did common sense. Although right now, I couldn't exactly claim higher ground.

"You haven't been able to control your vampyren form?" Mason gaped at us before turning his wide-eyed expression to his father, who remained mute. "And this has been going on for how long?"

Thad came to my defense. "It's only been a couple of weeks."

"A couple of weeks?" Pierce stood and locked gazes with us. "I thought you were supposed to be a brainiac. Keeping that from us was plain stupid."

I gritted my teeth. "Don't blame Thad. When it happened, he wanted to tell everyone. I'm the one who made him keep it a secret."

Pierce snorted. "Nobody makes Thad do shit he doesn't want to do. We all know that."

Thad scrunched up his lips in reply. Pierce had him there.

"The two of you *chose* to keep this a secret." Pierce could barely contain his rage. Lines of lightning streaked across his body as the storm within him grew. He was reacting the way I expected Mr. Blackmoor to respond. Even though I found the emotion extremely annoying, Pierce was slowly growing into the High Priest he'd eventually have to become, one who protected his family from all threats no matter what or who it was. "You've both seen what happens when we keep secrets from each other. Why would you do that?"

I glanced down at the wooden floors. "I was scared."

"Of what?" Kale placed his hand on Pierce's muscled shoulder, and he immediately relaxed. If I could smile, I'd let Kale know how much I appreciated that, but my heart lodged in my throat when Mr. Blackmoor gave me his back and leaned against the fireplace.

"Of how you'd respond." I swallowed hard as I met the gazes of everyone else in the room. "While I appreciate how this family has embraced me as one of its own, I know you fear that you might wake up and find me crouched on the edge of your bed, waiting to devour you."

Drake crossed over to me, his eyes wet with tears. "We don't think that. Right?" He glanced over his shoulder at Mason, Pierce, and Kale, who glanced away. Thad sniffed in evident judgment.

"Not consciously." I gave him a thin smile. "But subconsciously you do. I'm a fire fairy. I read emotions as easily as you read a book. I can sense the fear and apprehension, and I don't blame you for it. This family has been through a great deal with Ben, Sersie, and Icarian. Your lives have been in danger for months, and vampyren have been a part of those threats. Having one of your enemies sleeping under your roof can be… unnerving."

Mr. Blackmoor's stance grew even more rigid, and I turned away. The anger that rolled off him hurt my heart, and I waited for him to grab me by the collar and throw me out the front door.

"So I didn't tell you because I didn't want to add to your fears, but my actions have likely done the exact opposite. Now you don't just fear me. You can't trust me either."

"That's absurd." Drake wiped away his tears and stood tall. "We've all kept secrets, and we had our own reasons for keepin' them."

"Drake's right." Thad crossed the room and stood behind his father. "We've all made mistakes."

"But we keep making the same ones!" Pierce railed. "When is this family going to learn *not* to keep secrets from each other? We're no better than the Conclave when we do that."

My breath hitched, and so did Drake's. Whatever truth Drake kept in his pocket had to be huge.

"Enough." Mr. Blackmoor's tense voice cut through the room like a banshee's wail. "I'm so angry I could spit rock."

I shouldn't be here anymore. The family didn't trust me, and Mr. Blackmoor couldn't even look at me. I had to leave on my own. If they threw me out, I'd never recover. "I'll go."

Mr. Blackmoor spun around and pointed at me. "Move one inch and I'll knock you upside your head with my fist." He held up his clenched hand, which had turned into solid rock.

That would definitely hurt even me, so I remained where I was as Mr. Blackmoor marched toward me. When he got within striking distance, I flinched, awaiting the blow I deserved. Instead, he wrapped his arms around me and held me tight.

"I should be the one apologizing to you." His words caused the jaws of everyone in the room to practically hit the floor. Mr. Blackmoor had never said he was sorry about anything in all the time that I'd known him.

"What could you possibly have to apologize for?" I pulled out of the embrace and gazed down at a powerful warlock who'd been reduced to tears. "I'm the one who lied."

He grinned up at me and patted my cheek. "Because you were afraid of being rejected. And why wouldn't you be? Your own father banished you. Your people turned their backs on you. Your life has been filled with those you love abandoning you, and I blame myself for making you feel as if you weren't safe, that you couldn't come to me with what was going on."

"I won't let you take this burden from me. These were my actions, not yours."

He nodded. "Yes, they were, but I'm the father here. You are my son."

I couldn't speak, and the world turned fluid.

"And you're right. A part of me did fear you and the power you possess, but you've more than proven that you're capable of controlling yourself. You pose no more danger to this family than anyone else in this house, and I'm sorry for making you feel that way even for an instant." He cupped my face in his hands. "Can you ever forgive me?"

Suddenly I wasn't a big intimidating fire fairy or a monstrous vampyre. I turned into a frightened child clutching the only father he now had. "There's nothing to forgive."

"If you have nothing to forgive, then neither do I or anyone else in this house." He pulled out of the embrace and cast his gaze across the room. "Isn't that right?"

One by one, everyone nodded—even Pierce—and the smile that stretched across my face reached down to my heart.

CHAPTER 3

I SAT at the kitchen table, staring out into the rear lawn of Blackmoor Manor. Even though my heart still swelled with the acceptance the Blackmoors had given me despite my lies, the desire to fling open the back door and fly away filled my soul.

This family was in danger. That was as obvious to me as the gentle sweep of the moonlight across the land. Something was coming, and it was worse than anyone could imagine. I felt it not with my perceptive fairy senses but in the swirling tempest of anger and bile that riled my vampyre.

If I was smart, I'd leave, find Aunt Millie and the rest of my kind, and face this threat with them. At least then, Thad and my new family would be out of harm's way. I had to protect them because they wouldn't protect themselves.

They'd rush headfirst into danger, heedless of the hefty cost it might bring, and they'd do that for me because whether or not I was part monster, I was a part of this coven. For them, family came first, above all else.

It was admirable, and one of the reasons I loved them all.

It didn't make it any less foolish. There was no need for them to put themselves in danger when whatever was coming our way had set its sights on me. This was my problem. Whatever change I faced, whatever I was *becoming*, was for me to deal with. They were my dangers to overcome, and I'd willingly sacrifice myself for my family.

"Are you okay?"

I jumped in my seat. "You startled me."

"I see that." Thad grinned down at me, evidently quite pleased with himself. He was the only person capable of catching me off guard. My fairy and vampyren senses typically alerted me to others' presence, but Thad was different. Around him, the ramparts I erected never rose and the warning bells never sounded. With him, I was always safe, and my defenses were unnecessary. "I thought you came in here for a snack. When you didn't come back, Pierce suggested you'd gone out for a bite."

I rolled my eyes. Naturally Pierce would take my absence as meaning I'd gone hunting for blood. "No, I'm just thinking." I pulled Thad into my lap, and my previous desire to depart receded. I could never leave Thad's side. It would hurt him as much as it would devastate me.

"Let me guess. You were contemplating leaving and fighting this without us?"

Though my mouth opened and closed, no sound issued forth. It always amazed me how well Thad knew me. It was also a little scary.

Thad flicked my nose and chuckled. "You're not as mysterious as you'd like to think, Your Highness."

I was in for it now. Thad only addressed me by my royal title when he was about to point out how stupid I was being. He was the only person alive whom I allowed to get away with pointing out my flaws. When I was still a prince on Otherworld, no one dared even attempt such a thing. Oh how I missed those days.

"I know your first instinct is to protect me."

"Always."

He pressed a kiss to my lips and leaned his forehead against mine. "But going out on your own weakens us. We're stronger together. We've always been. You and I faced down the fae, the vampyren, Ben, and your father on Otherworld, and we did that together."

"I know. I just don't want anything to happen to you. If it did, especially if it was because of me, I don't know what I'd do."

"You wouldn't hurt me."

I met his stern gaze. "How can you say that? I've lost control of my vampyren form a few times now, and according to Aunt Millie, I'm changing into something and no one knows what that is. This new *thing* I'm becoming is even deadlier than a vampyre, judging from how the vampyren reacted to me when I lost my temper. If *they* are afraid of what I might do, you should probably be too." Why couldn't someone as rational as Thad see that?

"Are you done, Your Highness?"

I sighed.

"Good. Yes, you've lost control a few times, but I was never in danger at *any* of those times. In fact, I'm the one who brought you out of your bloodlust. Would you have hurt Pierce back at Wyman Woods? Yes." He tapped his index finger on his chin while a devious grin slanted across his lips. "And I might have even let you. My brother needs a good kick in the ass every now and then."

"How can you joke about that? I could've really hurt him."

He held my face in his hands and delivered kisses to my forehead, nose, and lips. "Because you are *not* a danger to anyone you love, and least of all to me. You forget how strong you are, Aiden. It takes great power to rein in the vampyre within you. I've seen the toll it takes. I've been with you on every hunt, and even when you're feeding on a doe or a fox, even when your vampyre is demanding you let it out and kill everything in your path, I see *you* in there, fighting it, battling your way back to me."

He was right. I did do that. No matter how strong the bloodlust might be, my blood tie to Thad always won out because he was magically my other half. I beat back the monster and returned to the surface because that was where Thad was, and wherever he was, that was where my heart would forever be.

"I love you." I buried my face in his neck, inhaling the cool, crisp scent that reminded me I was home.

"And I love you too." Thad grabbed my hair. "Now stop being stupid." He yanked me out of his neck to drive home his point. It stung a little, but it also turned me on a lot. The deep growl from the back of my throat and the stirring in my groin told him that.

He arched an eyebrow at me. "Really? Now?"

I flashed an impish smile and shrugged. What could I say? Even in the face of danger and unknown threats, Thad had the power to make me forget about everything else and focus only on the power our bodies exerted over each other. "You're really hot."

He rolled his eyes in feigned exasperation but also pressed himself harder against me. If he kept that up, he'd be naked on top of the table in no time. "Will you focus?"

I cleared my throat. "If you insist."

"You heard my father. You're a part of this family, and we'll deal with this together. Do you understand?"

I bowed my head in reverence. "Yes, my liege."

"I like the sound of that." Thad sat back, a grin hitching up the left corner of his mouth. "You may address me that way in perpetuity."

Even though he was joking, it sounded right to me. My heart was Thad's kingdom, and I lived and died by his rule.

THAD AND I rejoined the family in the library, where they had moved to talk strategy. Whenever the earth was about to open up underneath our feet, we retreated to the room that housed the Grimoire and the rest of the Blackmoors' spells.

When we walked in, Mr. Blackmoor and Pierce were thumbing through various books, looking for information on curses Aunt Millie could have been referring to, and holding heated debates over their findings. As always, Thad rushed over to help calm them down.

Mason, who preferred to avoid research of any kind, lay facedown on the sofa, snoring, while Kale read through a leather-bound book with the words *Mystical Creatures* embossed in gold across the royal-blue binding. He'd clearly been given the task of learning what I might be turning into.

Although I appreciated the effort, I doubted he'd find anything useful in there.

Instead of being nose-deep in a book trying to find answers, Drake sat in one of the red leather chairs, facing the cold, dark fireplace. He was in deep thought, and the emotions that rolled off him revealed his turmoil. He held answers to questions no one had yet asked, and it was time to ferret them out.

I sat on the chair to his left. "Penny for your views?"

"What?" He gazed at me out of the corner of his eye before nodding. "Oh. You mean 'penny for your thoughts'?" He chuckled in spite of the scowl that had taken permanent residence on his lips. "I'm gettin' you an idiom dictionary for next Yule."

I had no clue what that meant, so I merely smiled. "So?"

"So *what*?"

"Penny for your thoughts?"

He waved off my words. "What I'm thinkin' about isn't worth what you're offerin'."

The stench of rotting fish—one only my magical senses could detect—filled the air. That only happened when someone lied to my face. "Would you care to try that again?" I held up my hand to prevent any more deception. I didn't find the scent of decaying sea life appealing, and neither did my stomach. "And keep in my mind that I can read your emotions, so I know when you're lying."

Drake's eyes widened. He'd forgotten, but instead of speaking, he pressed his lips into a thin line. He wasn't going to make this easy.

"I know you know something. I've sensed that ever since we saved you from your uncle and his battalion of witch hunters." His darting gaze confirmed my suspicions. "I haven't said anything before because I believed you'd eventually seek someone out."

"Keep thinkin' that and leave me alone," he scowled. Drake rarely reacted in anger to anything. He had a big heart and ready smile in most situations. Now, defiance filled his steady gaze as if he'd embraced the warlock answer for everything—anger.

That meant he was terrified, and it only made me more determined to get him to open up. "I'm afraid I can't. We're facing something extremely dangerous, and if you have answers we need, you have to share them."

"Like you did when you hid your problems with your vampyren form?"

I winced. He wasn't pulling any punches. "Fine." I stood. "If you won't tell me, maybe Mr. Blackmoor will be able to get the information out of you."

Drake flew from the chair and blocked my path. The sudden ruckus caught everyone's attention. Well, except Mason's. He had yet to stop snoring.

"Is everything okay?" Mr. Blackmoor arched an eyebrow at us.

"Yeah." Drake grabbed my hand and led me out of the room. "Aiden and I just felt like thinkin' out loud, but we don't want to disturb you. We're gonna go in the next room."

Mr. Blackmoor accepted the lie with a nod, clearly focused on finding answers. Thad, however, knew something was up. His wide gaze asked if everything was okay. I gave him a smile and a nod before he returned to his reading, and Drake dragged me into the study.

"I can't believe you're a snitch."

I had no clue what that meant, but judging from Drake's even stare, it wasn't good. "What do you know about what's coming? About what's happening to me?"

Drake ran his fingers through his sandy-blond hair and groaned. "I don't know anythin' about that. I swear."

Interesting answer. "Then tell me what you *do* know and what's been bothering you since our last encounter with Icarian. What did he tell you?"

His mouth opened so wide I could've fallen inside. "How'd you know?"

"You changed after we got home from defeating Icarian and his witch hunters. At first I thought you were still dealing with everything you'd learned about your past and your guilt for allowing Gerald Wa to wipe your cousin's memories."

Drake's gaze fell to his shoes. "That's been part of it."

It had been a tough decision, but even though Will Hopkins hadn't been trying to kill us, Flint, Will's father, aimed to wipe us from existence. All knowledge of magic had to be erased from their memories.

"What's the other part?"

"If I tell you, you have to promise not to tell anyone, *not* even Thad."

I crossed my arms over my chest. "I can't promise you that. I tell Thad everything."

"Well, you can't tell him this. I haven't even told Mason. It's too dangerous."

"You're asking me to lie to the man I love."

Drake shook his head. "I'm askin' you to keep somethin' from him that could save his life."

In the blink of an eye, I held Drake by his wrists. "Thad is in danger, and you've kept this a secret."

"It's not just Thad. Mason and Pierce are in danger too."

"What?" Kale stood at the entrance to the room. All color drained from his normally tan face. "What danger?"

Drake pulled his wrists free from my grip and sighed. "Come in and close the door."

WHEN DRAKE finally finished speaking, Kale fell back onto the couch. I understood the reaction. Right now an air sprite could knock me on my royal ass.

"Are you telling me that Icarian is trying to bring about the end of magic because he's afraid of Pierce, Mason, and Thad?"

"That's what he told me." Drake's previously tense shoulders and scowling face relaxed. Even though he hadn't wanted to share what he knew, doing so lightened the weight he'd been carting around all these weeks. "He's afraid the growth of their powers signifies the start of the Prophecy of the Three he mentioned. Have either of you heard about that before?"

Kale shook his head, still unable to communicate. I mirrored his gesture. "How can he be so sure Thad or his brothers have anything to do with this prophecy?"

Drake sat back on one of the armchairs and sighed. "The growth of their powers. He claims they've tapped into abilities once thought impossible and accessed others that were extremely rare."

"Like becoming a shadow weaver," I said.

Drake nodded. Mason was the only warlock in over five hundred years to possess the ability to command the darkness.

"What about Thad and Pierce?" Kale whispered. "How do they fit in?"

Drake rose and crossed over to Kale. He held on to the young shifter's hand, trying to give him the comfort he clearly needed. Although Kale's smile expressed his appreciation, Drake's gesture didn't work. Fear for the man Kale loved twisted his features as much as it wrenched my gut.

"Icarian said Pierce's abilities evolved into somethin' never before experienced. It should have stopped with harnessin' lightnin'. Instead, he's able to turn his body into energy and see auras."

Thad and I had discussed Pierce's power growth shortly after Yule. In all the books Thad had read, he found no other documentation of a warlock with Pierce's enhanced abilities. He'd attributed it to Pierce's magic evolving in response to the threat he faced. It made sense at the time, but now I wasn't so certain.

"As for Thad." Drake settled his hooded eyes on me. "He tapped into fae magic on Otherworld."

I nodded. That should not have been possible. Magic had defined rules. Warlocks could only harness black magic, and fairy magic could only be mastered by the fae. At least until Thad. He and his brothers *had* unknowingly broken many dictates governing magic. If there was one thing I knew about the Gate, it was this: the mystical energy that flowed from it demanded order.

"So the Spell Fall is supposed to do what? Restore balance?"

When Drake nodded, Kale stood, a golden blaze roaring in his eyes. "That doesn't make sense. The Spell Fall shuts the Gate and closes off magic. How can doing *that* restore the balance when it seems to throw the entire world *off*-balance?"

"Because Icarian believes endin' magic is one of the only ways to stop the men we love from corruptin' it."

My body grew hot, and the vampyre within hissed in satisfaction. It wanted me to embrace the magma flow that coursed through my body. If I did, it could wrest the reins of control from my hands and take over. That wasn't happening today. I swallowed down the scorching flames and took several deep breaths. "Thad isn't evil, and neither are Pierce or Mason. It's ridiculous to even fathom that they might be heralds of this prophecy."

Kale nodded. "I agree. This sounds like a ploy. For all we know, Icarian has his own agenda and is using this 'prophecy' to further his own plans."

Drake chewed on his bottom lip. He clearly didn't agree.

"What is it?" I crossed over to Drake and Kale. "What else don't we know?"

"There's more?" Kale ran his fingers through his thick locks.

Drake met our gazes before darting his away. "It just that… well, look how powerful Mason got when he battled Icarian. He filled the entire sky with shadows that he used to beat someone capable of overpowerin' everyone includin' the High Priests."

That had been an impressive show of magic, but it also had a logical explanation. "He did that for you." Mason's love for Drake had to be responsible for his power surge. If it had been Thad about to be killed by Icarian, I'd tap into every ounce of strength I had just the way Mason did.

A smile lit briefly across his lips. "I know that, but it points to a pattern, doesn't it?"

"What do you mean?" Kale asked.

Drake stood and paced. "Pierce, Thad, and Mason are warlocks, and warlocks are ruled by their emotions, right?" When we nodded, he continued. "And each time we've been in danger, whether it's the witch hunters who kidnapped me or Ben and Sersie who tried to kill the both of you, they've done whatever they had to do to save us. Their love for *us* gave them the power they needed. What if it's their love that causes them to tap into magic beyond their control? What if that power begins to control them?"

Although I hated the way that sounded, it certainly was a possibility. Harnessing powerful magic beyond his control had driven Bartram Kane mad. His grief and love for his son made him cast the *immortalitas* spell that turned Ben into a vampyre and almost led to the destruction of the human and magical communities.

But I refused to believe the same would happen to Thad or his brothers. While Thad could be cold and aloof, his heart was pure. It was one of the reasons I fell in love with him. "That's why we must tell them."

Kale nodded in agreement while Drake's blue eyes widened.

I wasn't going to allow Drake's fear to rule my actions. I turned and headed for the door. "If they know about the prophecy, we can all work together to prevent it."

Drake flew in front of me, barring my path. "You can't."

I appreciated his conviction, but his immunity to magic wouldn't prevent me from lifting him and moving him out of my way. "I won't keep this from Thad. I have to tell him."

"That's what Icarian wants you to do. It's why I haven't said a word to anyone."

Kale's hand on my shoulder stopped me from brushing Drake aside. "What do you mean?"

"The Spell Fall has always been Icarian's Plan B."

I crossed my arms over my chest and huffed. "And what's Plan A?"

"Killin' either Mason, Pierce, or Thad."

It took me several moments of controlled breathing to get my anger under control. The vampyre I struggled to restrain almost burst free. In my current state, that would not have been helpful.

Although I loved Drake, I was furious at him for keeping this a secret, and my vampyre would have zeroed in on him and made him pay. Fortunately, I managed to shove the foul demon back into its prison before Drake became my next meal.

"You should have told us." I forced the words through my gritted teeth. "We could have been looking for a solution this entire time."

"Aiden's right." Kale abandoned his passive dovelike nature for the eagle within. If he shifted now, his screech would likely shatter glass. "You've placed every one of us, including Pierce, Thad, *and* Mason, in terrible danger. Why in the world did you keep this to yourself?"

To Drake's credit, he didn't back down. He stood tall and faced our anger head-on. "Do you not remember how the protector covens and the Conclave reacted after Mason kicked Icarian's ass?"

I did. Everyone had been wary. The Edwells accused the Blackmoors of being unstable, and our nemesis on the Conclave, the one Pierce referred to as the Warlock Hag, had been ready to wipe them from existence. If that wasn't bad enough, Drake had revealed that someone besides Icarian was after the Crests of the Five, the talismans needed to bring about the Spell Fall. That person had stolen the Air Crest from the shifters, and no one had any clue why.

"It was a tense situation."

Drake snorted. "Yeah. I would've added only more fuel to their hate-fire."

"So why not tell *us*, then?" Kale wasn't going to let Drake off the hook that easy.

"I was afraid of what Mason, Thad, or Pierce might do."

Kale's pinched eyebrows revealed his confusion, but Drake's answer made complete sense. He knew what Icarian feared and what his plans were, but he also knew the Blackmoor brothers. Like Drake said, their love and their need to protect their family and us guided their actions. If they believed one of their deaths would bring an end to all the chaos we'd suffered, only one solution would make sense to them.

"One of them would sacrifice himself for everyone else."

Kale's breath hitched as realization dawned across his expression. "Pierce would die to save his brothers."

Drake nodded. "I know. Mason would too."

"And so would Thad."

Drake grabbed our hands and squeezed them tight. "That's why we can't tell them."

"Tell us what?" Thad stood at the open door of the study with Pierce and Mason standing on either side.

Drake spun around, his eyes wide, while Kale sputtered. They might as well have been caught with their hands in the cake pan. Thad studied them for a few moments before turning his scrutiny to me. "Aiden? What are you three keeping from us?"

I should tell him everything. It was the right thing to do, especially since I'd already kept an important secret from everyone else. But the muscles in my throat constricted, preventing the truth from coming out.

"We've been racking our brains for answers." I forced a smile to my lips, thanking the Gate that none of the Blackmoors possessed empathic powers.

Thad's eyes grew wide. "And?"

"And we've come up with nothing." I winced as my lie wiped the hope from his gaze. Although it irritated me to deceive the man I loved, I had to do it. If I didn't, either Thad or his brothers would act rashly. Until I found another solution, Drake's secret was safe. Kale nodded in agreement while Drake let out the breath he'd been holding.

Pierce frowned. "That's what you didn't want to tell us?"

Why did he have to pick this moment to be so inquisitive? Typically a simple answer appeased his cursory curiosity. "We're also tired and want to go to bed, but we didn't want to interrupt you."

"Thank God." Mason stomped across the study and grabbed Drake's hand. "I'm beat. We'll figure this out tomorrow."

"When?" Thad's scowl prevented Mason from dragging Drake out of the room. "Tomorrow's Ostara. When will we have the time to find answers *and* celebrate the Sabbat? We need to find out what's happening to Aiden now."

Although I loved Thad's dedication, it had been a long day, and we needed rest. "And we will." I took his hand and led him toward the stairs everyone else had already begun to ascend. "We always do."

Thad loudly sighed before allowing me to take him upstairs to our bed. Hopefully, holding him in my arms would chase away the icy chill that spread across my soul.

CHAPTER 4

I COULDN'T fall asleep. No matter how hard I tried, its numbing embrace proved elusive, so I quietly got out of bed and gazed out at the night sky, searching for answers amid the twinkling stars but finding none.

I'd never felt so helpless, not even after I'd been turned into a vampyre. Even though I'd been terrified and hopelessly lost, Thad had stayed by my side, helping me learn how to cope with the anger, fear, and guilt that consumed me. His love and patience centered me. They gave me hope. But this situation, this damn prophecy and whatever was going on with me, threatened all that. It hovered over us like a fiery missile, waiting to obliterate everything.

I wasn't going to allow that to happen.

The only way to prevent it was to learn about this Prophecy of the Three, but where was I going to find that information?

The light clicked on behind me. "Can't sleep?" Thad's soothing voice cut through my troubled soul, making my body ache for his comfort.

"No."

He pulled back the covers and patted the mattress. "Come here."

I couldn't move. If I went to him now, he'd know I was keeping something from him, and though it cut me to the bone, I had no other choice but to be strong and bear this weight alone. "I'll be fine. You get some rest."

Of course, Thad didn't listen. He got off the bed and came to me instead.

The moonlight shining through the open window glinted like silver along his naked flesh. It made him even more beautiful than he already was, and I swallowed hard as he approached.

Instead of assaulting me with questions, he hooked his hands around my neck, leaning his long, lean body against mine. He brushed his lips across my chest and then my lips. As always, he knew exactly what I needed. "I've missed you."

I had missed him too. We'd been apart for days, and instead of enjoying a proper reunion, we had been pulled into yet another nightmare.

I placed my hands on his slender hips and nodded, unable to speak around the emotions clogging my throat.

"I know you're scared, but you don't have to be." He ran his hands down my back, along my sides, and up to my chest. "I'm here with you. I'll protect you."

I grumbled. "I'm supposed to protect you."

"No." He lifted up on his toes so he could rest his forehead against my chin. "We protect each other. That's the way this works, Your Highness."

"You do realize I know what it means when you call me that?"

A devious smile curled across his lips. "Then don't give me reason to call you Your Highness, Your Highness."

"Yes, my liege."

"Good." He grabbed my hand. "Now you need to come back to bed."

The slight rouge to his cheeks told me exactly what he was planning, and more than anything I wanted to feel his flesh upon mine, to taste his skin, to chart fiery trails across his neck and chest, and to lounge in the musky parts of him that reminded me of heaven.

When we made love, when we were truly one, it reminded me that nothing could ever come between us, and right now I needed that assurance. But how could I do that when I was keeping a secret from him?

I loved and respected Thad too much to allow him to share his body, heart, and soul when I was keeping part of mine from him. Until I could be honest with him, I wouldn't tarnish our intimacy.

"I can't."

He nodded as if he'd been expecting that answer. "Is it because of what you're keeping from me?"

"What…. When did…. I mean, how did—"

He pressed his finger to my lips to stop me from making even more of a fool of myself. "You, Drake, and Kale are terrible liars."

"Your brothers…?"

"Are idiots and don't suspect a thing."

"But you…?"

"Knew you were lying from the start."

"And you're not…?"

A grin spread wide across Thad's lips. He was clearly enjoying my inability to complete a thought. "Mad? No. I'm not thrilled, but I'm not mad."

I took a deep breath before attempting to speak again. I planned on actually finishing a thought this time. "Why didn't you say anything if you knew?"

Thad climbed slowly back into bed, making sure he arched his back so his ass was on display. He cast a wicked glance over his shoulder and wiggled those glorious muscled mounds at me. He knew exactly what he was doing, and my groan told him I was enjoying every minute of the show.

"Tell me. Please." My words came out in a low husk, but a stronger desire than having my question answered set a scorching path across my skin.

He slipped beneath the sheets. I had the sudden urge to yank them free, but I knew the score. Thad was in control, and I didn't care. I'd been under his spell from the first moment I laid eyes on him.

He patted the mattress, and I quickly slid under the covers next to him, awaiting my next command.

"I didn't say anything because your attempt at deception was rather pathetic."

I couldn't deny that. Kale and Drake hadn't done a good job at schooling their features, and I was unaccustomed to lying. The fae were typically blunt and honest. It made no sense to do anything different among a species that could read each other's emotions. "But why aren't you mad?"

He arched an eyebrow. "Do you want me to be?"

"No. Of course not. I just don't understand why you're not upset."

He slid his body on top of mine, and the weight of his warm, naked flesh sent a surge of fire straight to my groin. "Let me ask you a question first."

I nodded while tracing my palms down the curve of his back before resting them on his butt.

"Do you accept that you're a member of this family?"

"I do." The Blackmoors had shown me more love and understanding than my own kind. It was one of the many reasons I felt awful about not divulging what Drake had told me. "And I'm proud of that."

"As you should be." He kissed the tip of my nose before licking a trail down my cheek and around my chin. His breath seared my sensitive skin. "Members of this family do two things. When they make a promise to one another, they don't break it. If they have to lie, they do so to protect those they love the most."

I pressed my lips to Thad's, inhaling the sweet words he spoke into my soul. "I do love you. More than anything else."

"I know, and that's why I know that whatever secret you have, you're keeping it for a good reason."

"But what about what Pierce said earlier? He said we needed to stop keeping secrets, that they would destroy us if we didn't and that they made us no better than the Conclave."

Thad rolled his eyes. "I love my brother, but you can't listen to him when he's being righteous. If the shoe was on the other foot, if he had to withhold information to keep anyone in this family safe, he'd do it without a second thought."

That was true. He'd done it before. Chances were he'd do it again.

"But that's not even the real reason I'm not mad."

"Then why?"

He rested his forehead upon mine. "I trust you, Aiden. I know you're a good man, and I know that when the time is right, you'll tell me what I need to know."

All my fears and frustrations leaked out of the corners of my eyes, and Thad was there to kiss them away. His faith in me settled my soul. We'd survive whatever waited for us around the bend of this raging river, because no matter what, Thad believed in me and in us, and it was past time for me to get that through my thick royal skull.

No super magical being or prophecy could stand against that kind of power, so I embraced Thad's love and devotion. I held on to it as tightly as my hands clasped his thin waist before I rolled him over and pressed myself on top.

"What are you doing?" The deep, warm coppery pools of his eyes made my heart stop, and his smile started it back up again.

"I need you." My words came out as a desperate plea as I lowered my mouth to his. I nibbled on one delicious pink lip before reluctantly letting it slip free. "It's been too long."

"Yes, it has." Thad surfed his hands toward my ass and grabbed a handful.

A growl rose in my throat as I lapped feathery circles around his neck and earlobe, which always drove Thad crazy. He moaned softly, squeezing my butt in one hand while the other scratched along my back.

The graze of his fingernails combined with my burning need spurred me on. I nibbled on his neck, kissing a path down his chest to his nipples. I swabbed my tongue across the pebbled flesh, teasing the nub with my tongue and my panting breath.

Thad arched into the contact, his squirming body communicating his need. I rolled the puckered skin between my teeth, giving him the pain and pleasure he craved. He grabbed my shoulders, forcing me off his chest and back onto his lips.

He dove his tongue into my mouth, drinking in our kisses while I slid my hands between our bodies, taking his length in my grasp. Thad pressed harder into our kiss as he pumped himself into my hand. I ran my fingertips along the moist slit, coating my fingers before bringing them to our mouths so we could savor the sweetness together.

Panting, Thad pulled away, his eyes wide and his pupils shot. "I love when you do that."

If he liked that, he was going to love this.

I delivered one final kiss to his lips before crawling down the length of his pale body. I stopped at his chest and his stomach, licking across his flesh while Thad ran his fingers through my hair. His soft cries inflamed my passion, encouraging me toward my destination.

After darting my tongue in his belly button and swabbing along the sparse reddish nest on his groin, I held his throbbing shaft in my hand. Thad threw his head back against the pillow as I flicked my tongue along his length before circling it around the tip. I lapped up the milky pearl before trailing a path down the other side.

"Holy shit, Aiden." Thad rarely cursed, and I loved being the one who made him drop his naturally cool, collected self and turned him into a wild beast.

"Feel good?" Before Thad could even answer, I slid the head of his cock into my mouth and wrapped my tongue around it.

Thad groaned, balling up the sheets in his hand and yanking. "Oh God yes!"

I swallowed him down to the base, using my throat muscles to increase the pressure and his pleasure while I tickled the underside of the weeping crown with my tongue. When I bobbed up and down, using my hand and my mouth in concert, Thad's breathing grew ragged.

"Please don't stop." The faraway look in his eyes told me he was getting close, but I wasn't ready to bring him over the edge yet.

I pulled him from my wet warmth and grinned up at him.

"What the hell?" He forced the words out in breathy rasps.

"Soon." I pressed a kiss to his inner thigh before running my tongue along his sac. Thad's legs trembled as I lifted them and placed them on my shoulders. I leered up at him. "Is that okay?"

He nodded vigorously, so I nipped at the swell of flesh between his ass and balls. The lapping circles of my tongue caused a string of curse words to fly from Thad's lips as he writhed under me. I gently pushed his knees back, exposing the entrance that I sought, the place where Thad and I physically joined, and I delivered soft kisses along the musky, puckered flesh. The heady scent drove me wild as I slid my tongue along the rim, snaking circles before pressing inside.

"Aiden, please.... I need...."

I knew what he needed because I needed it as well. My body yearned to be physically joined with Thad. Even though he and I were magically bound together, we weren't connected across past lives or soul mates. We had never been destined for one another. Our bond was special and even more unique. We had been mystically tethered ever since our first meeting. My body became his and his body became mine. It was how we knew each other so well, and it was the essence of the blood tie that connected us.

It gave us power, and when we made love, when our bodies physically became one, it made me feel like I could snatch the sun from the sky.

"Please, Aiden...." Thad's breath caught as I lapped my way from his center over his balls and along his throbbing hardness before traveling back down again. I repeated the pattern several times before Thad grabbed my head and forced my gaze to his. "Just do it. Please...."

He was right. It was past time.

"Feed on me."

I sat back on my haunches and gaped at him. "What?"

Thad sat up, running his fingers across my chin and along my cheeks. He pressed his lips to mine, and his tongue came alive in my mouth. "Feed on me," he muttered when he pulled back from the kiss.

I leaned back. "There's no way I'm—"

"You've done it before." His mouth found mine again, and every panting breath filled my chest with his need and his desire. "I like it, and you like it."

Of course I did. It brought our blood tie to a whole new level, but the idea was crazy. I gently extracted myself from his insistent lips and sat back on the bed. "That was when I wasn't having trouble with my vampyren form."

Thad scooted toward me, wrapping his arms around my neck and his legs around my waist. I had to prop myself up on my arms to support us. "You have more control than you think you do. You need to see that you're not a slave to the vampyre. It's a slave to you, and there's no better way to prove that than for you to feed on me."

He'd lost his mind. "I could kill you."

My comment brought a silly lopsided grin to his face. "That's what you said the first time you fed from me, and you didn't." He licked at my neck before biting down. I grabbed his ass as pain and pleasure roared through my body, inciting my vampyre to surge forward.

"Thad—"

"Remember." His whisper sent his hot breath fanning across my flesh, and the beast inside me continued to creep out of his prison. "I'm your liege, and I command it."

"Fine." My cock hardened, and I shoved him back onto the mattress. The vampyre was coming out whether I wanted him to or not, so I wrapped the chains I used to keep it under control around its neck and pulled. "Turn your head to the side."

Thad waved his index finger at me. "Not there." He opened his legs wide. "Here."

I moaned at the sight of Thad splayed before me, and I let the vampyre out enough to lengthen the fangs I used to pierce my love's flesh. I fell between his legs, but before I began, I darted my gaze to his. "Are you sure?"

Thad gnawed on his lower lip and nodded.

I extended his leg, exposing the area where the femoral artery pulsed. My vampyren eyes could see the crimson liquid coursing underneath the skin, and a second later, my teeth pierced his flesh. Thad cried out, clutching my shoulders as the coppery liquid filled my mouth.

I drank it hungrily, and the monster within me roared in triumph. It begged me to continue to feed, to savor every drop to the last, but I shoved the beast away. I was the fae prince, and it was the beast. It answered to me.

I pulled away, panting. The red haze of bloodlust had vanished, but the fire of passion roared even stronger.

Thad grinned at me. "See. I knew you could do it."

He was right as always, but now it was time to do something else. The vampyre had fed, but now it was time to satiate the fae prince. I flipped Thad onto his stomach.

He moaned as he pushed out his butt. "Yes. Take me," he uttered before burying his face in the pillow.

I lowered myself on him, the curves of our bodies aligning perfectly as I delivered a kiss between his shoulder blades and the back of his neck. "I love you so much."

He rose on his elbows and craned his head back, teasing me with a wicked swipe of his tongue over my lips. "I know, and I love you just as much." He thrust back against me and grinned. "Now take me and take me hard."

My low, hoarse growl caused him to shiver. I reached into the nightstand and clicked open the bottle of lube while Thad urged me to hurry. I slathered a generous coating along my aching shaft and grabbed my throbbing cock. With one hand holding my body over Thad, I slid along his crevice.

Thad ground against me, rubbing my length along his cleft before reaching back. I gasped as he closed his hand over me before placing me at his center and pushing back.

The heat in Thad's eyes as he gazed over his shoulder spread across my cock as I slipped into his clasping warmth. I held my breath as I slid deeper and deeper, delighting in how Thad's muscles opened and clenched at the same time until I was buried firmly inside.

I fell onto Thad, holding him tight in my arms as I began a slow, tortuous piston in and out of his flesh. "You feel so good."

"I've missed this... so much."

And so had I. I craved Thad's touch, and I'd been miserable these past few days without him. Now that he was in my arms and I was inside him, I vowed never to be apart from him again. No matter what, we would be together. I'd do whatever I had to do to make it happen.

Icarian could try to come between us, but he would fail.

My thrusts became stronger, more powerful, as the passion our bodies created worked to its crescendo. Thad moaned with each sweaty collision, and the bed frame rattled. He clutched at my thighs and chewed his lower lip as I pounded into him harder and faster, pumping in rhythm to his backward thrusts.

"I'm almost there."

"Me too." Thad shoved his hand between the mattress and his body. He timed his jerky movements with each shuddering thrust until he reared his head back and let out a cry.

The muscles around my cock spasmed, bringing me over the edge. I slammed my sweat-slick body against him as his fluttering muscles ripped the orgasm from me in long, velvety strokes.

Spent, I collapsed on top of Thad, lacing my hands with his and nuzzling my face into his neck. "That was…." I couldn't find the words.

"Tell me about it. We needed that."

"Yes." If I could have said more, I would have told him how strong I was because of him, how much I appreciated his trust and his love. Because of him, I had faith in myself again. I used my kiss and my embrace to speak what my heart longed to say. Thad curled up against me, and I snuggled into his loving arms, overwhelmed by the emotions that cleansed my battered soul.

"IT'S TIME to get up, my love."

Thad pressed a kiss to my lips. I instinctively wrapped my arms around his neck, pulling him on top of the sheets and me. I shut my eyes tight and shook my head like a petulant child. "No. Let's spend the day naked in bed."

That sounded immensely better than dealing with the ogre-sized tasks that lay before me. Why spend time searching for answers to ominous questions when we could live out our lives in each other's embrace?

To put it in Pierce's eloquent terms, Icarian and his plans could suck it.

"That would certainly be fun." He combed his fingers through my hair and let out a huge sigh. That never boded well for me. "But it's Ostara. We have a Sabbat to prepare for."

I groaned and rolled over, pinning Thad beneath me. Ostara was my favorite high holiday. The ritual commemorated the spring equinox and the return of life from winter's long slumber. The fae typically celebrated the occasion with a weeklong feast and hours of dancing. I'd settle for five more minutes alone and naked with Thad, but when my hand traveled down to grope bare flesh, I grabbed fabric instead.

My eyes fluttered open. "You're dressed?"

"As I said, Your Highness, we have a Sabbat to get ready for."

I set my big fingers to unbuttoning his shirt. "Let your brothers get the altar ready for once."

Thad chuffed. "Yeah, right. They're probably still in bed, hoping I'll take care of everything."

That was Pierce and Mason's MO, but I wasn't giving up so easily. "Isn't it time for Pierce to learn how to do this on his own?" I unfastened one button on his shirt and quickly worked on the next. "He is the next High Priest, after all."

Thad interrupted my industrious fingers by placing his hands over mine. "Yes, but I need to be there for Dad. This Sabbat is going to be rough for him."

I'd forgotten about that. This was the first time in four generations that the Blackmoors would be performing a ceremony without the other protector covens. The Conclave had seen to that when they stripped the family of their special status in the magical community. Just thinking about it infuriated me. I didn't even want to imagine the foul mood Mr. Blackmoor would be in today.

I rolled off Thad and exhaled. "I suppose you're right."

He held his chin up high as he sat up and hauled his legs over the side of the mattress. "Of course I am." He grinned over his shoulder at me. "Your Highness."

I lunged at him, but before I could wrestle him back onto the mattress, Thad dashed off the bed and toward the open closet, giggling like a schoolboy. It was music to my ears. "I'll make you pay for that later."

"I certainly hope so." Thad wiggled his hips before he disappeared into the closet to pick out my clothes for the day.

I hated wearing them. They were bothersome and completely unnecessary. On Otherworld, the fae rarely, if ever, felt the need to cover their bodies, but humans and the *homo magus* lived in shame of their nakedness. Although it made no sense to me, I went along with their prudish customs and even attempted to liven up the boring garments Thad had purchased for me.

That had been an epic failure.

According to my fae sensibilities, all colors went together, but apparently I'd been mistaken. If flowers could pull off purple and red, why couldn't I?

Thad emerged from the closet with tan pants and a forest green shirt. I liked the deep green, but I would have paired it with orange. Tulips did.

When Thad discovered I had yet to move, he arched one reddish eyebrow at me, which was my cue to get going. I threw the covers aside, exposing my nakedness. "Are you sure you want me to put on all those clothes?"

His eyes lingered on my groin before he shook away the haze of lust that made him bite his lower lip. "You know I prefer you naked, but I think my brothers would likely protest."

I sighed. It was worth a try at least. I got out of bed, and instead of taking the clothes from Thad's outstretched hand, I headed for the bathroom. After I relieved my tiny fae bladder and washed up, I came back out to find Thad sitting on the edge of the bed, staring at the wall. The light that had turned his hazel eyes golden a few moments ago had vanished.

"What's wrong?"

He smoothed out the green fabric of the shirt he'd strewn over his lap. "I've just been thinking."

He didn't need to say anything else. Although he said he understood why I kept a secret from him, it bothered him more than he let on. "And?"

"Whatever you, Kale, and Drake are hiding must be pretty big if you're not sharing it with me."

It was, so I nodded in reply.

"Does it have something to do with Icarian?"

I nodded again.

"I suspected Drake had been keeping something from us since Imbolc."

I wasn't surprised Thad had guessed the reason for Drake's strange temperament. He had uncanny, almost magical insight. It was as if he could read emotions like I could.

"It's not just about you, is it? We're in all danger again, aren't we?" He didn't need me to respond to know the answer. Anything connected to Icarian threatened all of magic and most specifically this family.

Although I didn't want to, I had to ask, and if Thad gave me the answer I didn't want to hear, I'd do as he wished. "Do you want me to tell you?"

He took my hand in his and held it tight. "No." He leveled his gaze to mine. "You made the decision you did for a reason. I respect that."

How had I gotten so lucky to have this man fall in love with me? "Then why did you look so sad a few moments ago?"

Thad blinked, bringing his emotions back under control. "I'm just… worried. Something is coming our way, and I don't know what I should be doing to protect those I love." He leaned his head on my shoulder. "I'd do anything to keep everyone safe."

I did know that, which was precisely why we couldn't tell Thad or his brothers about the prophecy until we had more information. "Then let me tell you this." I kissed the top of his head before leaning into him. "Not knowing what I know actually keeps you and your family safer."

"So you believe the information Icarian gave Drake might be a lie or at least a twisted version of the truth?"

It was certainly what I hoped. I couldn't even imagine Thad or his brothers turning into magical beings that threatened all of creation. "Yes."

"And you have a plan?"

I didn't, but I would have one soon. "We're... working on that."

"Good." Thad ran his fingers across my lips and smiled. "I know you have my back."

I held his hand to my mouth and kissed it. "Always."

"Well, then." He stood and gazed down at me. The man I loved gave way to the warlock I had better obey. "Now get dressed. There's a lot to get accomplished, so don't make me crack the whip."

I was tempting fate, but I couldn't help myself. "That actually sounds hot."

His icy stare brought me to my feet.

"Yes, my liege. Right away."

A second later, Thad was out the bedroom door, yelling for his brothers to get the hell up. Curse words echoed down the hall, followed by slamming doors and feet stomping across the floor.

It already sounded like every other Sabbat I'd celebrated with the Blackmoors, and if this one followed suit, I had to be ready for anything.

CHAPTER 5

I STOOD in the middle of the rear lawn of Blackmoor Manor, marveling at how the heavens had changed. The cold gray winter skies had abandoned their gloom. Streaks of pastel pinks and blues painted their way across the canvas, and the sun shot its warm arrows across the land, waking the earth from its months-long slumber.

I bathed in the light, spreading my arms wide. I inhaled the sweet scent of honeysuckle and freshly sheared grass, filling my lungs and my soul with the scent of rebirth.

It was what my sighing soul needed if I was going to survive the growing chaos behind me.

"You're doing it wrong!" Mason screamed from inside the house.

"Shut your stupid hole." That was Pierce's eloquent reply. They had been arguing over how to decorate the altar in celebration of Ostara for the past half hour. Unfortunately for everyone within earshot, Thad had taken my advice and set his brothers to task while he oversaw Drake and Kale, who worked cooperatively, in the kitchen.

The same couldn't be said for Pierce and Mason. They'd been at each other's throats all morning. They argued about whether the altar should be placed outside or in the library. The disagreement prior to that had to deal with who looked at whom the wrong way.

"The white candle goes on the left, *not* the right."

"It goes on the right, dumbass." Pierce snorted. "Right is east."

I turned toward the sun and tuned out their endless arguing. Although I loved them, I had entertained the idea of ripping out their tongues just to gain a few moments of blissful silence. That was when I realized I needed to abandon the pandemonium for the serenity nature provided.

They'd awoken the vampyre, and he needed to go back to sleep.

Closing my eyes, I banished their scuffle from my thoughts. I focused instead on the sunlight kissing my fair flesh, and the beads of sweat bursting from my skin. When I became one with nature, my fairy senses kicked in, and the world around me glowed in a latticework of threaded energy connecting me to the sky, the earth, and everything in between.

I was one with nature again, and I was at peace. The vampyre had been silenced.

"Aiden Teine." The sharp tone of the Sabbat taskmaster sliced through my serenity, but instead of making the monster inside me hiss, it made my fae heart sing.

I opened my eyes. Thad stood before me, looking me up and down. His puckered lips and flinty gaze clearly communicated how displeased he was with my chosen apparel. "You know we have a lot to get done, right? I remember asking you to decorate the dining room, and you know what I found when I went in there?" He placed his hands on his hips and tapped his right foot on the ground. "The gemstones for the celebration feast were *still* in the box."

I couldn't help the smile that spread wide across my face. Even when he was in a high state of pissy, he was the most beautiful sight I'd ever seen. "I know. I'm sorry about that." I nodded toward the house, where Pierce and Mason still argued over candle placement. "But I needed to take a break before I broke one of *them*."

"Tell me about it. They're driving me crazy!" Thad ran his fingers through his strawberry-blond hair. His ruffled locks reminded me how he looked last night after I ravaged him, and it made me want to sweep him up in my arms and have another go. "I swear if they don't stop soon, I won't be responsible for what happens next."

I took that as my cue. I wrapped my arms around his waist and pressed him against me.

"Aiden!" He darted his gaze to the open back door before settling his wide hazel eyes on me. "Someone might see us."

Even though I knew what had him so concerned, I played dumb. "And? Considering your brothers have boyfriends, I think they know that two men in love sometimes embrace."

His tense muscles immediately relaxed, but the snarl on his lips refused to retreat. Accepting the challenge, I pressed my lips to his, forcing them to part and accept my tongue into his mouth.

Thad moaned into the kiss, his hands clutching at my arms and bare back. His body vibrated with a different kind of tension now, and it was one I was adept at relieving.

"Okay, you made your point." He pulled out of the kiss but not out of my embrace, which was probably a good idea, considering the hardness pressed between us. His lips spread into a beaming smile as he shook his head at me. "I shouldn't get so worked up." He glanced down and waggled his eyebrows. "Or get you worked up either."

I nipped the tip of his nose. "I like getting worked up with you."

The apples of his cheeks flushed as they always did when I came on to him, which was pretty much all the time. Thad knew what he was getting into, though, when he fell in love with a fire fairy. We were passionate creatures, and when I was around Thad, I basically turned into a walking erection.

"Yes, I know. But perhaps we shouldn't be getting worked up out here."

I liked where this was going. "So should we go upstairs, then?"

Thad gazed up at the sky, clearly looking for his patience. "We have to get everything ready, and you—" He grabbed my naked butt and squeezed. "Need to put on the clothes I picked out for you earlier."

"Have I told you I hate wearing clothes?"

His lips turned into a slant. Apparently I had. Why was Havenbridge so different from Otherworld?

"Don't start." Thad pointed his index finger at me as if he knew what I was thinking. "You're not on Otherworld anymore."

I frowned. It was a lucky guess.

"You need to be dressed before Dad gets back. I told him we'd have everything set up for the ritual, remember?"

I did. Mr. Blackmoor had been in an even fouler mood than I had suspected. He charged through the house like a rampaging rhino, yelling at anyone who had the misfortune of crossing his path.

No one took it personally, though. He was furious at the Conclave for stripping him of his family's honor, a point he made clear every time he raised his voice, but what could be done? The most powerful warlocks, witches, and wizards alive made up the Conclave. Whether we agreed with them or not, there was nothing any of us could do.

So instead of dealing with his grumpy father, Thad had sent him to town to buy some things for the ritual while Thad took charge of getting the house ready. Judging from the raised voices still emanating from the house's interior, things were moving along at a snail's pace.

Thad smacked his forehead into my muscled chest and sighed. "I swear I'm going to kill my brothers before the day is done."

"I'll help."

He grinned up at me before pressing his lips to mine.

"Oh hell no!" Pierce's voice boomed behind us.

We faced the house and were greeted with Pierce stomping across the lawn toward where we stood, Mason at his side, pretending to upchuck.

"Go. Away," Thad grumbled at them through gritted teeth.

Pierce scowled at Thad. "The last thing I expect to see when I look out the back door is my brother in the arms of a big naked fairy."

Thad lost it and railed at Pierce for calling me names. What was Thad so angry about? I was six four, weighed over two hundred pounds, and wasn't wearing clothes. I *was* a big naked fairy. But once again human colloquialisms evaded me. All that was important, though, was ending this fight as quickly as possible.

I stepped out of Thad's arms and faced Pierce and Mason.

Pierce held up his hands to block the view. "Aw, man. That's just not right."

"Will you put that thing away?" Mason shut his eyes and spun around. "You're going to poke someone's eye out."

I took two steps forward. "I just might unless you go inside and do what Thad has asked you to do."

Without another word, Pierce and Mason headed toward the house while Thad shook his head at me.

"What? They shut up and got back to work, didn't they?"

"Yes, they did." He arched a reddish eyebrow at me. "I wonder how Dad will react when he comes home and sees you like this."

A second later I sprinted for the back door.

THIRTY MINUTES later, dressed in more clothing than I found comfortable, I gathered with everyone else outside on the rear lawn, where Thad had positioned the altar. A pale green cloth draped over its surface with green and purple fabric layered on top, symbolizing the spring flowers blooming across the land. On the right side of the altar stood a white candle and a basket of eggs. Both items represented the approaching light, while the black candle and a lunar pendant on the left signified the retreating darkness.

Dressed in brown pants and a red button-down, Mr. Blackmoor approached the altar. His bearded grim face from this morning had softened, and the storm of fury that roared across his blue eyes had passed. The ticked-off warlock had given way to the reverent High Priest.

He scanned the surroundings, making sure his family had formed the required circle around him and the altar. Thad stood to my right. His high chin and focused gaze told me he was ready. Mason, who fidgeted on my left, was an entirely different story. He kept whispering to Drake and trying to get his boyfriend's attention, but the glassy, faraway look in Drake's eyes indicated his thoughts still lingered on Icarian's prophecy.

Although I'd wanted to speak to him and Kale before the ritual, it had been impossible to find a moment alone. When this was over, though, I planned to strategize with them even if I had to abduct them.

"Shut up." Pierce elbowed Mason in the ribs, which earned him a snarl.

Before Mr. Blackmoor had a chance to bark in complaint, Kale placed himself between Pierce and Mason, bringing their quarrel to an end. He shushed Pierce before handing him the black sheet he'd need for the ceremony.

Mr. Blackmoor smiled at Kale in evident appreciation before raising his hands, which signaled the beginning of the ritual. We grew silent. He nodded to the north, west, and south before saluting east, where the sun rose and the season of rebirth Ostara celebrated began.

"Today is the spring equinox, a time of equal parts light and dark." He walked the inner perimeter of the circle, creating a symbolic ring within the one our bodies created. "Spring has arrived, and it is a time of rebirth. The planting season will soon commence, and life will form once more within the earth. As the earth welcomes new life and new beginnings, so can we be reborn in light and love."

Mr. Blackmoor stopped before Pierce, who had draped the black sheet over his head. It symbolized the shroud of death that came for us all, and even though it was a part of the ritual, my blood grew cold. "Do you, Pierce, wish to experience the rebirth of spring, and step out of the darkness and into the light?"

Pierce stepped into the circle and approached the altar. "I do."

Mr. Blackmoor placed his hands on Pierce's head. "With the blessings of the earth, and the life within the soil, you are reborn." After removing the sheet from Pierce, he spread his arms wide. "You have stepped once more into the light, and you are welcomed by all."

Our applause brought an end to Pierce's rebirth, and as he rejoined our circle, Mr. Blackmoor handed the black sheet to Thad.

The ceremony continued until everyone had been symbolically reborn but me, and as I stood there with the ceremonial shroud in my hand, I felt foolish. I'd already been reborn as a monster.

"Aiden?" Mr. Blackmoor stood by the altar, awaiting my entrance into the circle of life.

I nodded before covering myself with the fabric and closing my eyes. The low timbre of Mr. Blackmoor's words filled the darkness, but halfway through the ceremony, he started to mumble. His garbled words turned into whispers before disappearing completely.

"Are you still there?" I asked from beneath the sheet. When I didn't receive an answer, I pulled the fabric free. A dense fog had swallowed up the land, preventing me from seeing more than a few inches in either direction. "Thad?" I stepped to my right, expecting to bump into him, but he wasn't there.

My heart rose in my throat. I moved to my left, looking for Mason and Drake, but they were gone too. "Is anyone there?" My voice echoed around me, twisting my words into a mocking plea that rolled through the mist.

A low growl rumbled in my throat. Someone was playing games with me, and only one being could be responsible.

Icarian.

Plumes of flame exploded from my clenched fists as I harnessed my fae abilities. If he wanted a fight, I'd be glad to give him one. "I know you're there, Icarian. What do you want and where's Thad?"

"Your warlock is safe." A female voice drifted around me. "But I am not Icarian."

Why did she sound so familiar? "Who are you?"

"Who I am is unimportant. What matters is what is to come."

I arched an eyebrow at the swirling mist. First Aunt Millie brought me a warning, and now a disembodied voice. Why did everyone but me know what was going on? Someone had better start giving me straight answers soon or they wouldn't have to worry about a prophecy. They'd have to contend with one ticked-off vampyre. "And what's coming?"

"Death." Her response made my flesh crawl. "In more forms than even I can foresee."

She spoke as if she had the prophetic powers of the ancient Greek oracles, but their kind had been extinct for more than a millennium, and their ability to glimpse into the future had vanished along with them. Was this yet another sign of the imbalance in magic Icarian had mentioned?

"Death doesn't frighten me. I have already conquered it."

"Yes, Aiden Teine, you have." So she knew me. Now I had to figure out how. "But death comes in many forms. Its shape is as fluid as the mist around you." In response, the fog danced and swirled as if an unseen hand stirred it before it reformed into the shape of a transparent woman, comprised only of water vapor, standing a few feet in front of me. If I'd seen her before, I couldn't tell. Her features constantly shifted. Whoever she was, she was intent on keeping her identity a secret, but she couldn't hide from me.

"What does that that mean?" I opened up my magical senses and sent them out into the mist, searching for her emotions, which were like fingerprints to my kind. While everyone experienced the same emotional spectrum, each feeling resonated uniquely within each individual. When Mr. Blackmoor was angry, the emotion built slowly like an impending volcanic eruption. For Pierce, it crashed like thunder. For Mason, it stalked forward like a lion, and for Thad, it swept downhill like an avalanche. If I'd encountered her before, I'd be able to figure out when and where by her emotional signature.

"Are you listening to me?"

A hand struck my face, hard. The blow brought me out of my thoughts and a scowl to my lips. The monster inside me hissed. She was playing a dangerous game. While oracles might possess powerful abilities that allowed them to peek into the future, they were nothing compared to the fury of an unleashed vampyre.

The mist woman's eyes of vapor narrowed. "My time here is limited, and instead of listening to the warning I bring, you busy yourself with learning my identity?"

I wasn't surprised she had figured it out. She *was* an oracle. I crossed my arms over my chest. "What have you come here to tell me?"

"I haven't come here to tell you anything. I've come here to show you."

The mist around me exploded in a blinding light, and when it faded, darkness stretched farther than I could see. Bizarre guttural noises echoed in the void, and they had a strange effect on me. They repulsed me and made my flesh crawl, but the eerie song also called to me as if it were inviting me to join the dirge.

I had no intention of adding my voice to the chorus. If I did, my gut told me I'd never see Thad again.

I clutched my hands to my ears, trying to drown out the onslaught that continued to batter my body and soul.

A bright crimson dot suddenly hung in the sea of black. The spot grew thick before it cut a scarlet path down the gloom. The beast within me rattled its cage, longing to be set free and claim the red for its own.

I had to pull back on the reins, straining to keep the vampyren instinct from taking control, but it was growing too strong.

My muscles bulged, and sweat poured from my flesh. Still, the tether frayed, and when it finally broke, I'd lose everything. If I was going to win, I needed more strength, so I tapped into the wellspring that gave me the power I needed to maintain control.

I closed my eyes, forcing memories of Thad to float up from my subconscious. His thin pink lips parted into a mischievous grin as they did before bed every night. His cool, crisp scent hovered on the air around me, and when he told me he loved me, the music those words created in my soul silenced the screaming storm of whispers that threatened to rip me apart.

I panted in the darkness, trying to regain my strength in preparation for the next wave, but it never came. Instead, the woman made of mist reappeared.

"What was that?"

"You know better than I."

I didn't know what the whispering voices portended, but I recognized the drop of blood.

"What does it mean?"

"It's an omen, a glimpse of the future unfolding before us."

A pit of foreboding despair opened in my stomach, threatening to consume me. "Why show this to me?"

The mist around her grew thinner. "I'm... uncertain. The future is like a river, forever changing. I merely go where the currents take me, and they brought me to you." Her form stretched and broke apart until only a disembodied head remained. "The blood drop is your future. Whether it falls or not is up to you."

The ground violently shook before cracking open under my feet. I hovered for a few moments, trying desperately to summon my fairy wings and take flight, but they refused to form.

I fell into the pit and tumbled into the void.

I HIT the ground hard.

"Aiden?" Thad's voice almost brought a smile to my lips, but the pain exploding throughout my body turned it into a grimace. What the hell had happened?

I opened my eyes, and Thad hovered over me, his angular, handsome face beaming down at me in a mixture of relief and worry. Beyond him, the spring sky, instead of the mist-shrouded land I'd left, once again filled the heavens. I was back from wherever the hell I'd been taken to.

"Are you okay?"

Although it hurt to do so, I cupped Thad's cheek in my hand. I was pleased to see him, even though the mist woman had told me he'd been safe. I had believed her, trusted her, and I wasn't entirely sure why. "I'm better. Now."

"Good." Mr. Blackmoor crouched on the other side of me before patting my shoulder in relief. The wide smile on his lips reflected in the rich blue pools of his eyes.

"What the fuck happened?" Pierce grumbled to my left. He had his hands on his hips and gazed down at me as if I'd just walked into a glass door. If he wasn't careful, he'd find himself flying headfirst through a window. "One minute you're standing there in a trance, and the next you fall back on your ass."

I furrowed my brows. "I was here the whole time?"

Pierce glanced sideways at Kale, whose friendly tan face grinned down at me.

"Yes." Kale kneeled beside me. "You had us worried."

I sat up, and the world spun around me. Thad grabbed me and, as always, provided me the support I needed. I took a deep breath, centering myself. "I'll be fine."

"Can you tell us what happened?" Drake stood behind Thad, wringing his hands while Mason rubbed his shoulders. He obviously worried that whatever just happened to me had something to do with the prophecy. I suspected he might be right.

It couldn't be coincidence that a seer appeared the day after we'd been discussing Icarian's ominous prediction.

"I think I just met an oracle."

Mr. Blackmoor stepped forward. "An oracle? But they've—"

"Been extinct for hundreds of years." I rose with Thad's helping hand. "I know."

"So we've got oracles roaming around now?" Pierce glanced at Mr. Blackmoor, who didn't respond. He was too busy scanning the air before him, searching for an answer to some puzzle he'd yet to share. "What's next?"

That was a good question. Too many magical players crowded the stage, and the sudden appearance of an oracle wasn't a good sign. Their presence in the past typically meant disaster hid around the corner.

Did that make Icarian right?

"Are you sure it was an oracle?" Though Thad spoke to me, he studied his father, obviously trying to figure out what was going on with him. I wondered the same thing. A river of hope rushed off Mr. Blackmoor and slammed into a dam made of gut-wrenching anguish. What was going on?

"I'm not sure, but she could see the future, and it brought her to me."

Thad snapped his attention back to me. "To you? Why?"

I didn't want to say the words, especially considering the way everyone gaped at me. Aunt Millie's warning had unsettled everyone last night. Adding an oracle to the mix threatened to push everyone over the edge.

"Aiden." Thad's voice forced my gaze to his. "Why did the oracle come to you?"

I took a deep breath. "To share a vision that I think was… a warning."

My words stole the breath from everyone around me except Mr. Blackmoor. His wrinkled expression softened as if that made sense to him, but why?

"Another warning?" A storm brewed in Pierce's eyes. The news clearly terrified him. "What does that mean?"

I had no real answer to his question other than what my gut told me, but before I could answer, the ground beneath us lurched.

Drake fell forward, colliding with me. Everyone else held their arms out to their sides to maintain their balance.

"What was that?" Thad glanced around, his eyes wide as I pulled him into my protective embrace.

The earth moved again. The pounding within the soil grew stronger, more powerful, like a thundering heartbeat. The trees lining the perimeter of the manor shook as if the wind rustled through their limbs, but the air was suddenly still and heavy. The vibrations underneath our feet gave way to a high-pitched grind before the soil violently shook once again, sending us all to the ground.

Car alarms blared in angry response from the front driveway. The glass on some of the first-floor windows of the house shattered, and the walls creaked and groaned from the stress as the grinding grew louder, more turbulent, with each passing second.

"What's going on?" Pierce attempted to stand, but the roiling earth forced him to his knees.

Kale leaped into the air and shifted into an eagle to escape the shaking ground that leveled the world around us. He circled above, no doubt trying to discern the cause of the tremor, but I didn't need Kale's avian eyes to tell me what was going on.

A tsunami of fear crashed upon me, overwhelming my fairy senses. Panicked screams only I could hear drowned out the violent thrashing as a few trees in the forest came crashing down.

"It's an earthquake!" Drake screamed.

He was wrong. This wasn't a natural disaster.

This was a soul quake, and whatever caused it had just struck downtown Havenbridge.

CHAPTER 6

THAD BARRELED down the main road, clutching the steering wheel of his car so tightly his knuckles turned white. He hadn't said much since shortly after the earth ceased moving and I told everyone that I feared Havenbridge had been attacked.

On Mr. Blackmoor's orders, we all headed for the automobiles parked out front and sped away from Blackmoor Manor and toward town.

"How are you doin'?" Drake asked from the back seat. I met his gaze through the rearview mirror, and I was pleased to see the return of the strong and confident young man I'd come to know.

"I can breathe again, so that's a start." The previous onslaught of emotions had almost drowned me, but when the quakes subsided, so had the never-ending waves of terror. It had been awful. It was as if I had suddenly been psychically linked with every human in town and experienced all their emotions at once. That had never happened to me before. While the emotions of others sometimes flowed over me without warning, I'd never been exposed to so many people at once or from so far a distance.

Were my powers growing? Was I becoming whatever Aunt Millie had warned me about? If I were somehow now able to emotionally link with crowds of people across vast distances, just what the hell was I becoming?

I had no clue. All I did know was that it had taken every ounce of willpower I had to shield myself from the barrage, and even though I still had no idea what we were heading into, we had to get there as quickly as possible.

"It's bad, isn't it?" Thad's shoulders were tight and his voice was barely a whisper.

As the resident family brainiac, he knew the answer better than I did. The land only reacted that harshly when a truly devastating spell had been cast, one that bent the rules of nature and magic and twisted them into something too perverted to exist.

I placed my hand on his thigh and squeezed. "We'll figure it out. We always do."

"Is it the Spell Fall?"

"It can't be." Thad held up his hand in response to Mason's question, and frost formed along his fingers. "If magic was gone, I wouldn't be able to do this."

"So what is it?" Mason sat forward in his seat and stuck his head between us. "Do we even know what we're heading into?"

"Do you even need to ask?" An irritated scowl crawled across Drake's upper lip. "It's Icarian. He's up to somethin' again, and it's time we put a stop to him."

Thad glanced at me briefly, his pinched expression asking me if this was the secret I'd been keeping from him. Since I wasn't certain, I placed my hand on his thigh and squeezed in response.

"We're almost there." Thad decreased his speed a hair before sliding into the turn that would take us to town. The forest to our left disappeared as the road opened up, allowing us to see straight into the heart of the town.

"Holy shit!" Mason took the words right out of my mouth.

Billowing clouds of smoke spread over Havenbridge, blocking out the sun and casting an ominous shadow across the land. Choked by the soot and swirling cinders, the azure spring sky lost its claim over the heavens as an orange-red haze took its place.

Havenbridge was on fire.

"What happened?" Drake asked in a whispered gasp.

Thad focused on the road, his gaze hard. "That's what we're going to find out."

He floored the accelerator, and moments later he brought the car to a skidding halt outside a temporary barricade set up by one of the town's deputies four blocks from downtown. The officer waved us off, pointing the way we had come. He was evidently trying to keep people out of the chaos while Havenbridge's fire and police departments handled the situation.

They weren't prepared for whatever waited inside the chaotic haze, but we were.

The four of us got out of the car as the screeching tires behind us heralded the arrival of the rest of the family.

"Get back in your cars." The dark-haired officer, whose silver nameplate identified him as Dailey, did his best to sound as authoritative as possible, but it was hard to take him seriously. His chin quivered, and he had likely only started shaving a few years ago.

Mr. Blackmoor and the others stampeded to our side. "Have you learned what happened yet?"

"Earthquake." Dailey's reply came out more as a question than an answer. He obviously hadn't been inside the hazard zone where the flashing lights of police cars and ambulances zoomed down the streets. Countless cries for help echoed in the distance. It set my nerves on edge, but there was something else, something beyond the emotional spectrum I typically experienced. Being this close to the epicenter, I sensed another power at work. It pulsed around me, beckoning like a long-forgotten memory.

I erected an emotional blockade to keep it at bay and prevent the town's pain and suffering from turning me inside out. Even though the torment still cut deep, I had to get in there.

A fire fairy never allowed innocents to suffer.

"Let us through."

Officer Dailey shook his head at me and blocked my path. When I growled down at him, he took a step back.

"We don't have time for this." Mr. Blackmoor gestured, and the officer crumbled to the street, fast asleep.

Everyone gaped at him, our open mouths questioning his actions. If anyone had seen him casting a spell, Mr. Blackmoor could have broken one of the Conclave's cardinal rules. He waved our concerns away as Pierce picked up Dailey and placed him in his patrol car. "Everyone's too preoccupied with whatever the hell has happened to notice us. Right now we have to get in there, figure out what's going on, and help as many people as we can."

He was right. Havenbridge had been openly attacked. We couldn't afford to play by the usual rules.

Mason and Drake shoved the barricade aside, but before we could sprint into the chaos, Mr. Blackmoor's upturned hand froze us in our place. "Get in there and help whoever you can, but don't use your active powers. That will only draw attention to you and create even more chaos. Be careful and be smart." He met each of our gazes, and after we nodded in reply, we ran straight into the heart of the madness.

BLACK PLUMES of smoke choked the streets, making it difficult to see more than a few feet. It also made it difficult to breathe. Thad held his hand to his mouth, coughing, as we surveyed the burning building in front of us. It had once been First Havenbridge Bank, but the facade had crumbled to the ground, spilling red brick onto the street like blood, and immense heat rolled from the fire raging inside.

"Is anyone in there?"

I opened my magical senses briefly. The swirling hysteria of the frightened and injured slammed into me like the scream of a banshee, and if that wasn't bad enough, whatever magic I had sensed earlier returned with a vengeance. It stabbed my spirit in a hail of needles, as if it was searching for a way to pierce my soul. I gritted my teeth against the pain, focusing on the job at hand, and sent swirling bands of energy into the building to search for signs of life. They found nothing. Either everyone had gotten out of the building before disaster struck or they'd all been killed.

I shut off my magical senses and the stabbing pain immediately stopped. "No."

Thad realized what my answer likely meant and laced his fingers with mine. Light fae thrived on life. It fed our powers and our soul. To be surrounded by so much death haunted me and drained my light while calling to the darkness growing inside and humming around me. Thad's touch kept it all at bay.

"Over here!" Mason called from across the street.

Thad and I dashed to where he and Drake were digging through the rubble that had once been Starbucks, a place near and dear to their hearts.

"A friend of ours from school got a job here," Drake said as he hauled away debris. "He might still be inside."

My fairy senses detected several faint heartbeats, and my soul rejoiced. "People are alive in there." I scrambled over several twisted tons of metal and brick toward where the emotional signatures registered the strongest, and started heaving wreckage over my shoulder.

Thad, Mason, and Drake did what they could, clearing the smaller piles of rubble, but without access to their powers, they weren't much use. Being a vampyre fae gave me extraordinary strength that any passerby would attribute to my muscles, massive size, and adrenaline.

"Is anyone there?" a voice under the pile screamed.

Mason crawled up to the chunks of building keeping us from those trapped inside and cupped his hands around his mouth. "Yes! We're almost there."

Uncontrollable sobbing echoed underneath us as the combined despair of those trapped inside gave way to a rush of hope. It spurred me to work faster. Sweat poured off me in tiny rivers, but I refused to let the physical exhaustion slow me down. These people's lives depended on me.

A low rumble preceded the earth lurching once again. The sobbing turned into panicked screams as whatever had previously throttled the town returned with a vengeance. The remains of the bank across the street groaned before tipping forward.

A rainstorm of bricks fell around us. Mason lunged toward Drake, covering him with his body, while Thad glanced up at the building falling our way.

"Thad?"

"Don't worry. I've got this." He stood behind me and motioned at the falling structure. "*Protegat nos.*"

The crumbling building slammed into the invisible wall of energy he had summoned. The debris slid off Thad's magic and crashed all around us. It was a riskier move than the one Mr. Blackmoor had pulled on Officer Dailey, but if he hadn't, everyone but me would be dead.

A cloud of smoke and dust exploded around the felled building and worked its way into our lungs. I hacked and wheezed as I removed the remains of the Starbucks, paying no mind to my bleeding fingers. I had to get these people out of here before another quake rattled the ground.

With a final roar, I lifted a large chunk of concrete from where it had fallen, pushing the limits of my supernatural strength, to find a boy no older than Mason and Drake, caked in dirt, ash, and blood. I heaved the debris to the side and reached for the scared young man. When he took my hand, I pulled him free. Thad guided him off the unsteady pile of shifting debris as I yanked three more terrified people from where they'd been trapped.

While Drake and Mason attended to the survivors, I bent over, resting my hands on my knees as sweat fell off me like rain. Every muscle in my body burned with fire hotter than the blazing infernos around us. Soot and smoke lodged in my wheezing lungs, and I had trouble catching my breath.

"I'm here." Thad stood next to me, resting his hands on my back. "*Sana.*"

His healing spell sent a refreshing breeze through my body, clearing my clogged lungs and repairing the damage I'd done to my muscles. Although this was a quick fix designed to get me through the worst of injuries that only rest and blood would fully heal, I wasn't stopping. Thad's nod told me he understood. He couldn't be more perfect for me.

"What now?"

I glanced around, uncertain where to go next. Mason and Drake were leading the people I'd rescued back to our cars, but so many others needed us. Their emotional pleas for help buzzed around me like a swarm of mosquitoes.

I had no idea where to start.

THAD AND I rescued several more people from burning structures, which proved a lot easier than the Starbucks collapse. I entered and exited the blazing buildings without so much as a singe. Earthly fire had no power over a fire fairy, but to keep up the ruse of humanity, Thad escorted me into a shadowed alcove and uttered a spell that hosed me down before I charged into each building.

Seeing their savior sopping wet prevented most people from questioning how I survived the flames to get to them, especially once I used my fae magic to put them to sleep while I carried them to safety.

Shortly after our third fire rescue, Thad and I stumbled upon Mr. Blackmoor, who was supporting a crumbling wall with his back, preventing it from crashing down on an unconscious mother and her wailing child. Unseen by the little boy, Mr. Blackmoor had transformed his back into rock, which allowed him to bear the weight, but his trembling legs showed he was moments away from falling over.

I rushed to his side while Thad darted to the child and swept him in his arms, blocking his view of his mother and us over his howls of protest. I placed my shoulder against the wall, and with one heave, Mr. Blackmoor and I sent the wall falling backward.

Wiping the sweat from his brow, Mr. Blackmoor gave me a nod of appreciation. "Thank you, son."

The term of endearment brought tears to my eyes. "I'd say anytime." I squeezed his shoulder and gave him a smile that told him how much I appreciated his regard. "But let's not do that again."

His eager nod told me he agreed.

"We need to take this child and his mother to the paramedics," Thad said, still cradling the boy.

Mr. Blackmoor nodded. "I'll do it. You two keep going and keep your eyes peeled. Whatever caused this is likely still here."

As he took off with mother and son, I swept my gaze past the raging fires and thick gray smoke. Our enemy was here somewhere, and it was watching.

"We should go that way." Thad nodded toward Havenbridge Square, which was one block away.

We sprinted toward the town center, where lights from the many parked ambulances and police cars flashed murky shades of blue and red across the smoke-thick air. Although it was difficult to see through the choked atmosphere, people lay sprawled across the quadrangle, bleeding and seriously wounded.

Paramedics surged in all directions, carrying the wounded on stretchers toward the vehicles waiting to take them to the hospital a few miles away. Police officers administered first aid to those in need while Pierce and Kale helped victims out of the destroyed structures lining the square.

"Who needs us the most?" Thad asked.

Everyone, from what I could see, but I had to abandon my earthly senses for the paranormal in order to detect where we'd do the most good. I closed my eyes, shutting out the human world, and opened my eyes to the magical.

Bands of mystical energy filled the area, connecting all life to each other. Several cords had been severed, their magical light fading away as the person once connected to the thread abandoned this world for the one beyond the Gate. As I scoured the threads, searching for the one that glowed the weakest but hadn't yet been snuffed out, a strange scraping sound caught my attention.

I turned to my right and froze.

A man limped away from where we stood, dragging a frayed, dark cord behind him. Unlike the others darting around the square, his string of energy connected him to no one and nothing else. He had been snipped free from the bonds of humanity, yet continued to stand upright and walk.

That shouldn't be possible. Magical tethers linked even the vampyren to those around them. Their mystical cords were grayed out and sullied, but they maintained a tenable tie to life around them.

Whatever power had severed this man from the rest of creation was likely responsible for the soul quake that ravaged Havenbridge.

"This way." I nodded toward the disheveled man, who disappeared around a building before I sprinted after him.

Thad hollered for me to wait, but I didn't. Something about the stumbling man pulled me toward him. I had to reach him. Now.

I turned the corner, expecting to see him staggering ahead, but the churning clouds of smoke from the raging fires choked the street, making it impossible to see more than a few feet.

"What's going on?" Thad huffed behind me. Lines of black ash streaked across his face, and worry hooded his eyes. I'd give anything to erase those troubling emotions, to hold him in my arms and tell him everything would be okay, but I couldn't. Not when every internal alarm within me blared.

At the end of this street waited a nightmare like none we'd experienced before.

"I'm not certain. I saw… something."

Thad surveyed the smoke-shrouded street before turning to me. "What did you see?"

"A man."

"Was he hurt?"

I didn't know how to answer that. Based on what I'd seen, he shouldn't be walking. "I'm not certain of that either."

"Then let's find him." Thad started forward, but I pulled him back. "What?"

Fear crouched on my chest, and I fought the desire to tell him to run, to find his family and take them home. They'd be safe there, but not for long.

"Aiden?"

"Something's not right" was all I could answer as I peered into the coalescing clouds of smoke.

"Of course not. Havenbridge is burning to the ground and we don't even know why. What could Icarian possibly gain by doing this?"

The smoke parted down the middle of the street as if someone had drawn back a curtain. The man stumbled along at the end of the road, still dragging the severed cord behind. "There he is!"

Thad took off. He didn't see what my fae senses revealed. The bands of mystical energy were invisible to Thad. All he saw was a man in need.

"Thad, wait!"

"He's hurt," Thad called over his shoulder as he ran. "We have to get to him before something else happens."

I grumbled in reply and shot off after him. Even though Thad only had a few seconds' head start, the billowing clouds of smoke closed, hiding him from my view. "Thad!" My heart raced in my ears when I didn't get a response. I screamed his name again at the top of my lungs.

If he didn't answer soon, I'd activate my fairy powers and use my flapping fiery wings to blow the smoke from the street. I didn't care if I exposed magic. At least I'd be able to see the man I loved and the danger he charged into.

"No!" Thad's strangled cry replaced the fear in my heart with rage. He was in trouble, and I pumped my legs faster, determined to tear apart whoever or whatever made him scream like that.

The smoke suddenly lifted, and Thad knelt before a huge crack in the ground, sobbing. What was going on, and where had the huge hole come from? My need for answers quickly surrendered to my need to stop. If I didn't, I'd sprint right over the edge.

I put on the brakes, skidding to a halt a few inches from the precipice of a gaping sinkhole. Whatever had once been here was gone, swallowed up into the earthen pit that descended at least twenty feet.

I dropped to my knees behind Thad, checking him for wounds. "What happened? Are you hurt?"

Instead of replying, he threw himself into my arms, burying his face in my chest. His tears soaked my shirt with each shuddering sob. I kissed his head, running my fingers through his hair and down his back, doing everything in my power to calm him down long enough for him to tell me what was wrong.

"It can't be gone. *She* can't be gone."

"*Who* can't be gone?" I surveyed the edge of the hole and peered over the rim, searching for the man I'd been chasing or the woman Thad was referring to. All I could see at the bottom was destroyed earth and cracked stone. If either of them had fallen over the edge, their suffering had ended below.

I pulled out of the embrace, forcing Thad's bleary eyes to mine. "Thad, what happened? What used to be here?"

He nodded his tearstained face toward a sign on my right that read *Waterside Cemetery*.

I didn't understand, and my arched eyebrows clearly communicated that.

Thad choked down his grief long enough to answer. "My mother... was buried here."

CHAPTER 7

A HUGE rainstorm broke over Havenbridge, putting out most of the fires, and the winds that accompanied the downpour lifted the smoke and carried it away. What remained was complete and utter destruction.

Most of Havenbridge lay in ruins. Buildings that once stood proud had collapsed while others were charred, smoking husks. Debris littered streets that had either cracked open or jutted outward like broken bones. The wounded staggered in shock or searched the many emergency vehicles for missing friends and family.

Their collective emotions crashed upon me in grief-stricken waves that threatened to pull me under, and the pain Thad and his family suffered almost did me in. They huddled together under the gazebo that had somehow survived the quake in the middle of Havenbridge Square. Their features twisted in pain after learning that Mrs. Blackmoor's final resting place had been destroyed.

"I'm going to find Icarian and I'm going to kill him." Pierce's nostrils flared as he paced. If he wasn't careful, lightning would fly from his clenched fists and expose magic to the already terrified citizens of Havenbridge.

Kale rushed to his side, and though fury still tracked across Pierce's steely gaze, Kale's gentle touch caused Pierce to release a portion of his anger and embrace the comfort Kale offered.

"Why would he do this?" Mason leaned against one of the wooden railings and slid all the way to the wooden floor. His customary brashness had vanished in favor of defeat. The blow had knocked all the fight from his body. Drake responded by sitting beside his boyfriend and wrapping his arms around him. Mason leaned into him, his voice dropping to a barely audible whisper. "What could he possibly gain from attacking us this way?"

"I don't know. It doesn't make sense." Drake nuzzled his cheek against Mason's before bouncing his gaze to Kale and me.

He was right. It didn't make sense. Kale's nod told me he agreed. Based on what Drake revealed to us, Icarian's plan was to stop the prophecy by either causing the deaths of one of the men we loved or bringing about the Spell Fall. Destroying a gravesite or even Havenbridge didn't fit into that plan, and Icarian only made moves that furthered his motives.

Something else was going on. The answer was out there, drifting around me on invis̶̶ ̶̶winds.

"It's obvious." ̶̶̶̶̶stood off to the side. The torment he'd experienced earlier when I found ̶̶ ̶̶t the destroyed graveyard had been replaced with an icy calm. When̶̶ ̶̶he faced a situation that cut too deeply, he shut off his emotions, ̶̶̶̶̶ing to the cool logic that allowed him to maintain focus. Although his brothers had loved their mother deeply, Thad had been the one who was the closest to her. Losing her had devastated him. Losing the site where he often visited her had eviscerated him.

I moved behind him but didn't make contact. He didn't want comfort right now, but that didn't mean I couldn't let him feel the weight of my presence. I was here when he was ready. He glanced over his shoulder and pressed his lips into a thin smile before continuing. "He's trying to weaken us."

His conclusion made sense. The Blackmoors had been responsible for thwarting Icarian's plans for months. If he wanted them out of his way, if he wanted them focused on something other than him and his plans, attacking the memory of their mother was the best way to distract them.

But no matter how logical Thad's reasoning might be, he was wrong.

Icarian could have killed us in the woods last night, but he didn't. In fact, he'd had plenty of opportunities to do so over the past few months, but he had never actually harmed us. He used others like Ben, Sersie, and the witch hunters to do that. If Icarian couldn't hurt us, then there was no way he'd devastate an entire town. Whatever happened in Havenbridge hadn't been intentional. It had to be the result of the curse Aunt Millie warned me about. It likely had ramifications Icarian had not foreseen.

"Weaken us?" Pierce's howl dragged me out of my thoughts. He punched one of the gazebo's wooden beams, and blood immediately burst from his cracked skin. Kale took off his shirt and wrapped it around Pierce's wound. "He hasn't weakened shit. He's only fueled my desire to wipe my ass with him."

"And we will." Mr. Blackmoor faced away from us. He stared at the destruction around him, his shoulders tense and his back stiff. "He messed with the wrong warlocks."

Even though I knew the response my words would bring, I had to speak my mind. "I don't believe what happened was intentional."

"How can you say that?" Pierce barreled toward me like a cyclone, but Kale dissipated the winds of fury with a single tug on his arm. Pierce blew the air out of his lungs and took several deep breaths. "Everything Icarian has done to bring about the Spell Fall ha██ █n designed to either hurt or kill us."

Mason sprung to his feet. "Pierce is rig██ █his is psychological warfare, just like the crap he tried to pull on Dr█████d me."

I shook my head. "What happened here was m█e ██an psychological warfare. It's utter devastation, and that's not w█at Icarian does. He manipulates people like pieces on a chessboard. He doesn't upset the entire board." Their reluctant nods revealed they couldn't refute my point. "Besides, this is different. I can feel it."

"What does *that* mean?" Thad's question brought my gaze to the worry crouching at the corners of his eyes.

My answer wouldn't help his anxiety. "I can't explain it, but I sense a type of mystical energy I've never experienced before." When I inhaled, I could smell it. It reminded me of a musty building that had been boarded up for centuries. "And whatever it is, it's old."

Thad arched one reddish eyebrow. "Old?"

"I know that doesn't make sense, but that's the only way I can describe it."

Pierce glanced around, scanning our surroundings with a long sweeping gaze. He only did that when he had activated his ability to see the auras of energy that magic and every living creature generated. "I don't see anything."

I wasn't surprised. Whatever this was, it was meant only for me.

"But it's there, and it has to be related somehow to the oracle's warning and Aunt Millie's message."

Thad nodded. "I agree."

"So what do we do?"

In response to Kale's question, Mr. Blackmoor turned to us, his eyes aflame with blue fire. "We get answers from the Conclave."

Thad sniffed. "How? They no longer answer your summons, and even if they did, we're not a protector coven anymore."

"Oh, I'll get answers." A devious grin slid across Mr. Blackmoor's lips. I'd seen him furious before, but his anger typically erupted like a long-dormant volcano. Right now, a murderous calm had settled across his gaze. He'd never been more terrifying. "Even if I have to reach into their throats and pull it out myself."

TWENTY MINUTES later, we pulled up in front of a modest cottage with white clapboard shutters and a big wraparound porch. The small statuettes that reminded me of the gnomes from Otherworld hadn't toppled over. They hid amid the bushes, which had not lost a single leaf. On the left, perfectly intact blooms of purple, pink, and yellow dotted the small well-kept garden, where a fountain gently gurgled water instead of lying shattered upon its side.

The idyllic scene reminded me of a place of tranquility, completely untouched by the devastation that had rocked Havenbridge.

How had the Proctors' house survived the heaving earth without suffering any damage? Thad arched an eyebrow at it as we emerged from his vehicle.

While most of the major damage had been restricted to the middle of town, every other structure we had driven past sported shattered windows, at the very least. But the Proctors' unscathed home revealed the witches had cast a spell that protected their house. If they'd had time to do that, that meant they, and probably the other protector covens, must have known the quake was coming—information they hadn't shared.

"Those fucking bastards." Mason stood beside Thad and me, his eyes narrowing to slits.

Drake rounded the car and shook his head. "They knew?"

"It sure seems that way." Thad let out a long sigh. "Dad's going to go ballistic."

As if on cue, Mr. Blackmoor pulled up behind us. He sat behind the steering wheel, staring at the intact cottage, for several moments. His fingers gripped the column so tightly his knuckles turned white. A storm brewed inside his heaving chest.

Pierce, who sat next to him in the car, tried to calm him down, but since we stood a few feet away from where they had parked, I couldn't hear anything he said.

Judging from Mr. Blackmoor's piercing gaze, neither could he. The anger that had previously howled inside him grew to hurricane strength, and his eyes tracked a path of destruction straight through the Proctors' front door.

If we didn't calm the raging winds that fed his temper, we'd find ourselves in the middle of an all-out magical war with our former allies instead of getting the answers we desperately needed.

Mr. Blackmoor exploded out of his car.

"Dad!" Pierce practically leaped out of the Jaguar and crossed toward his father. One glance into the eyes of Mr. Blackmoor's hurricane glued Pierce's feet to the pavement.

Thad rushed past his father and stood before the porch steps. The rest of us gathered on either side of him, ready to do what we could to prevent disaster. But against the fury and grief that powered Mr. Blackmoor, we'd be little more than whispers. "Dad, stop. You need t—"

"Move." Mr. Blackmoor's one-word command made Thad swallow hard.

"I can't."

Mr. Blackmoor took one step forward and Thad took one step back. "I said *move*."

"No. You can't go charging in there like this."

Mr. Blackmoor held up two fingers and swiped the air to the left. Unseen hands moved Thad aside as Mr. Blackmoor ascended the steps amid our pleas to stop. He gestured toward the Proctors' front door. It flew off its hinges and crashed like thunder into the internal wall on the other side.

Cries of concern exploded from inside as Mr. Blackmoor crossed the threshold while everyone else stampeded after him.

I rushed to Thad, who stared at the open front door as shouting quickly followed Mr. Blackmoor's entrance.

"Are you okay?"

"I'm fine." He grabbed my hands and tugged me up the porch steps. "We need to get in there. Now."

By the time we reached the living room, the shouting had descended to cursing and the clicking on of active powers. Mr. Blackmoor stood before the protector covens, covered in his earthen armor, obviously ready to beat answers out of everyone in the room. Lightning arced off Pierce's fists, and shadows curled around Mason, ready to do his bidding. Prepared to defend their boyfriends, Kale and Drake stood on either side. At the first mumbling of a spell, Kale would shift into an eagle and attack, while Drake would do what he did best and cancel out as much magic as possible.

The Proctors, Stonewalls, and Edwells were equally prepared. A dome of magical energy surrounded them. That was the work of Edith

Stonewall, the oldest of her siblings. Both of her parents met our gazes, prepared to take control of our minds or thrust us into inescapable illusions, while Edith's twin, Elliot, stood in front of Kate and Keaton, his younger twin siblings.

"What the hell do you think you're doing?" Fire licked around Mr. Proctor's clenched fists while Mrs. Proctor took her place by his side. Her narrowed eyes revealed she'd be unleashing the fury of nature on us if she didn't hear a suitable answer to her husband's question.

Instead of responding, Mr. Blackmoor took a step forward.

The Proctor children—Adam, Charlotte, and Miranda—joined their parents. Adam's outstretched hands communicated he was ready to unleash a gale-force wind. Charlotte, who typically used her water-based powers to heal, took on an uncharacteristically confrontational stance. I'd never seen her use her abilities offensively before. If she did, I expected to suddenly find myself on the wrong end of a tidal wave. Light blue energy surrounded Miranda's fists as she prepared to either warp us out of her house or send a heavy object crashing on top of our heads.

"They're doing what they always do, Charles." A mocking grin slashed its way across Mr. Edwell's lips in response to Mr. Proctor's question. "Prove how unfit they are to have ever been a protector coven."

A collective growl rumbled in the throats of Mr. Blackmoor and his sons. There had never been much love lost between the two families, but the animosity between them had only grown after the Conclave decided to name the Edwells as the new protector coven for the Order of the Black. While their dislike of each other had never come to blows, it appeared today might be the day.

Mr. Edwell cracked his fat knuckles and wiggled his fingers in evident delight. He clearly couldn't wait to use his ability to manipulate pain to bring us to our knees, while Mrs. Edwell licked her lips in anticipation of spitting her venomous power at us. Their daughter, Charity, took a deep breath as she readied her lungs to unleash a sonic blast.

Someone had to do something before more chaos descended upon us all, and that someone was me.

"Stop!" I darted into the middle of the standoff. While this wasn't a safe place for most, as a vampyre fae, I would survive the titanic clash of power. I was already dead, after all. Plus, I had the added bonus of being able to eventually shake off most spells thrown at me, a fact everyone knew.

"Stop?" Mr. Proctor's voice was low and measured. "Your family bursts into my house and you have the audacity to tell *us* to stop?"

"Don't get all high and mighty, Charles." Mr. Blackmoor's voice sounded like gravel being ground up in a blender. "*Your* family"—he motioned with a rocky fist at the line of power before him—"knew what was coming to Havenbridge, and you didn't warn us or even attempt to stop it."

Mr. Stonewall shook his head. "As always, Oliver, you draw conclusions without possessing any of the facts."

"What more facts do we need?" Pierce growled. "Your house is untouched while Havenbridge is in ruins."

Mr. Stonewall sniffed as if he didn't believe a word Pierce said.

"Pierce is right." Kale looked down his nose at the protector covens. "You should be ashamed of yourselves. You're protector covens. You're supposed to *protect* this town and all of magic. Instead, you hide behind a spell that keeps you safe."

Charity snuffed. "Shut your hole, shifter." Kale screeched in response as his golden eyes blazed. He was seconds away from transforming into an eagle and gouging her eyes out. "You don't know a damn thing about what we've been doing."

"And what *have* you been doing?" Mason spat out his words in disgust. "Standing here and talking like you usually do instead of doing something, like *we* were doing."

"That's enough!" The room grew quiet at the regal timbre of my voice. Although I was no longer officially a prince, I hadn't forgotten how to command a room. "Fighting each other will get us nowhere."

"We're not the ones who started it."

I growled down at Mr. Edwell's squat form, and his beady eyes widened. The man was all bark and no bite. How could someone so cowardly be allowed in the protector covens? "We didn't come here to fight. We came here for answers."

"Perhaps your coven has forgotten," Mrs. Stonewall said. As typical of her wizard kind, her tone was calm and chilled with logic. "You are no longer a protector coven, therefore no longer privy to the sensitive magical information we possess."

"You're right." My words caused Thad and my family to gasp while everyone else nodded in appreciation of my quick acquiescence. Clearly they had forgotten a prince *never* submitted. He wheedled. "From what I see, you have everything under control."

"Are you fucking kidding me?" The vein on Pierce's forehead throbbed as if it were alive.

"No, I'm not." I turned to face the openmouthed disbelief of my family, a bit disappointed that they obviously questioned my motives. Fortunately Thad didn't look like he doubted my sanity or my loyalty. The corners of his mouth hitched up in an approving grin. "Think about it. They cast a spell of protection in order to deal with the threat that almost destroyed Havenbridge."

Mr. Stonewall sniffed. "It was a mild rumble. Nothing more. Stop assailing us with your hyperbole."

Mr. Blackmoor found his answer as interesting as I did. He crossed his rocky arms over his stone chest and his posture relaxed for the first time. "I wouldn't call crumbling buildings and dozens of dead people *mild*."

"What?" Adam grabbed the remote control from the table and switched on the television. A local reporter stood amid the rubble in town as she reported on the unusual seismic activity that had hit Havenbridge earlier that day.

Every single member of the protector covens stared at the screen. They *hadn't* known the quake was coming, but they had erected a protective shield around the house for a reason.

The scowl on Mr. Blackmoor's face gave way to a smile as he resumed his flesh-and-blood form and nodded for me to continue.

"You didn't know?"

Charlotte placed her hand on her slender throat and shook her head at my question. "We had no idea it was that bad. We were—"

Mr. Proctor cleared his throat. "Involved with another matter."

I nodded, pretending I understood. "Right. You were dealing with the horde of vampyren you no doubt discovered in town."

Mr. Stonewall glanced at his wife, who held her breath. "What are you talking about?"

"Oh. You didn't know about that, either?" Everyone now watched as I strolled toward the center of the room. "So you must have been dealing with the oracle, then. What did she tell you? Because what she revealed to me didn't make a lot of sense."

"You're playing games with us, fairy." Mrs. Edwell ambled her lanky frame directly in my path. "Oracles are extin—"

I looked past her scowling face. "That's why I was surprised when she pulled me out of our Ostara ritual to give me her warning. Did she share a premonition with you as well?"

Mrs. Proctor suddenly stood at my side, and her eyes, which had previously been scorched, had softened and rounded. The fear that rolled off her reminded me of how she reacted to the troubles we faced during Imbolc. For the briefest of moments, her blind loyalty to the Conclave had faltered, and the worry she had buried since then suddenly resurfaced.

"What did she see?" She glanced at Adam, Charlotte, and Miranda and swallowed the lump that appeared to have formed in her throat. Like Mr. Blackmoor, she desired to protect her children, and that overrode everything else. "Oracles portend disaster. Is it linked to what the Conclave sent us to investigate, to what we—"

"Camille!" Mr. Proctor's harsh tone tore his wife's attention from me to him. "We are under explicit orders *not* to share any more information with the Blackmoor coven."

Thad arched an eyebrow at the comment while Mr. Blackmoor's scowl marched back onto his lips. The news riled my royal temper as well. After everything we'd done, we were intentionally being left out of the loop.

"Don't talk to me like I'm one of our children, Charles." Mrs. Proctor met her husband's firm gaze with her own. "That decision was ridiculous, and you know it!"

Mrs. Stonewall hurried to Mrs. Proctor in an obvious attempt at corralling her friend. "Perhaps now's not the time for this discussion."

"Oh, stop it, Rachel." She moved away from them and crossed the room to stand closer to the Blackmoors than the rest of the protector covens. The gesture didn't go unnoticed. Her children switched their gazes between their parents while the Stonewalls observed her with matching arched eyebrows. As for the Edwells, if they had been any more shocked, they would have soiled themselves. "I'm sick of you and Charles trying to get me to fall in line at the expense of my children's safety."

Mrs. Stonewall placed her hands on her thin hips. "What does that mean?"

"It means that no one, including you, is being logical."

Mrs. Stonewall jerked her head back as if she'd been slapped, and in a way, she had been. Accusing a wizard of not thinking rationally was worse than forcing a warlock to apologize. It went against their natures.

"The Blackmoors might be juvenile and irritating…." Her comment caused Pierce and Mason to mumble under their breaths. Fortunately, a sideways glance from their father quickly quieted them down. We were on the verge of making some important headway, and we couldn't stop this particular trolley before it left the station. "…but they have been the only ones capable of stopping Icarian. To exclude them and to replace them with"—she motioned to the Edwells—"an inferior coven places the lives of my family in jeopardy."

"Who are you calling inferior, you stupid witch?" Mr. Edwell lunged at Mrs. Proctor, but Mr. Blackmoor barred his path, standing in his stone armor before the sniveling weasel.

"Take one more step and you'll be pulling your teeth out of the back of your throat."

Scarlet energy hummed around Mr. Edwell's trembling fists. "I've had all I'm going to take from you, Oliver. Perhaps some pain will force a little respect out of you."

Mr. Blackmoor reared back his fist. "Bring it."

"The two of you will stop this at once."

Nine robed figures—three in black, three in gray, and three in white—blinked into view. They stood in a tense circle around the two warring warlocks. Now that the Conclave was here, we could finally get some answers.

CHAPTER 8

SHORTLY AFTER the Conclave's arrival, Pierce, Thad, and Mason escorted Mr. Blackmoor to the far corner of the Proctors' living room and away from Mr. Edwell. While I wouldn't have objected to witnessing Mr. Blackmoor squash his rival like a tomato, any violence enacted against another *homo magus* resulted in hefty consequences.

Based on how the Conclave had treated the Blackmoors since Imbolc, they likely would have struck him down without a second thought. That wouldn't provide us with the answers we needed about the soul quake, Aunt Millie's warning, the oracle's prediction, or, more importantly, the Prophecy of the Three.

While I agreed with Drake that we couldn't tell the Blackmoors about the prophecy for their own safety, I had promised Thad I'd come up with a plan. Since the Conclave was here, I intended to take full advantage of the opportunity by approaching Gerald Wa, our only ally on the Conclave, and asking him what he knew.

"Come here." Drake grabbed my forearm and pulled me toward the hallway, but not before collecting Kale on the way. After depositing us in the far corner of the small entryway, Drake glanced over his shoulder and scanned the living room. Whatever he planned to tell us appeared to be for our ears only.

Kale shifted his gaze to me before arching an eyebrow at Drake. "What's going on?"

"You can't tell *them*"—he nodded to where the Conclave stood conversing with the protector covens—"what I told you."

I crossed my arms over my chest and glanced down at Drake. "Why not?"

"You just can't."

That wasn't good enough. Thad trusted me to find answers and come up with a plan. The best way to do both was to seek advice from one of the most powerful wizards on the planet. "But I *can*."

Drake gripped my arm, his eyes wide and pleading. "You don't understand."

"No. *You* don't understand." I loved Drake like a brother. I even appreciated his dedication to the family. But he was young and immature. He and Mason often worked independently, and that had placed them in harm's way several times before. He didn't comprehend the importance of seeking the counsel of others. That was a lesson I'd learned over the past hundred years of my life. "Thad knows we're keeping a secret from him—"

"You told him?" Drake's lips flattened into a straight line.

"I didn't have to. He figured out we were lying to him last night. He trusts me to deal with whatever information we possess, and I intend to do just that."

Kale nodded. "I agree with Aiden. I may not like the Conclave, but Gerald has always been good to us. He'll tell us what we need to know. Besides, bringing him into our confidence could help repair the Blackmoors' relationship with the Conclave."

"You'll place them in even more danger if you do." Drake spoke the words with such foreboding certainty, he reminded me of the oracle in the mist.

"What does that mean?" I asked.

Drake worried his lower lip. What more information was he keeping a secret? "I can't say."

"Can't or won't?"

"Can't. The walls here have ears."

The information horrified me. I'd heard of covens casting surveillance spells in their abodes to detect threats, but to conjure body parts onto the interiors of their dwellings seemed a bit much. A quick sweep of the blue walls with white trim, however, revealed no such monstrosities. "I see no evidence of that."

Drake threw up his hands while Kale suppressed a laugh. "He means we might be overheard."

"Oh." I really, *really* hated human phrases.

"I know it's askin' a lot." Drake grabbed our hands and held them tight. "But I'm askin' you to trust me. What we know *has* to stay between the three of us for now."

Kale nodded quickly and then they both glanced at me, waiting for me to agree.

I didn't want to. Experience told me we were operating beyond the scope of our capabilities. We needed someone with vaster knowledge of magic than we possessed, someone with access to mystical tomes that stretched back to the first of our kind, and Gerald fit that bill. However, the pull of experience proved incapable of withstanding the pair of pathetic puppy dog eyes that gazed up at me. I suddenly missed being an only child and getting my way.

I blew the air from my lungs. "Fine."

Kale nodded as if he expected no other answer, while Drake let out the breath he'd been holding.

"But when we get home, you better tell us everything."

"I will." Drake crossed his heart, which apparently symbolized a sacred promise, based upon Kale's appreciative smile. If that was the case, it was a vow I'd make certain Drake kept.

WHEN WE finally rejoined the others still gathered in the living room, the hushed discussion between the Conclave and the protector covens had just come to an end. An uncomfortable silence gobbled up the air in the room as all eyes turned to the Blackmoors.

Most people would tremble under the weight of such powerful gazes, but my family stood tall with their chins high. I couldn't have been prouder, so Drake, Kale, and I added our support by joining at their sides.

Thad smiled up at me as I slid my hand in his, and he leaned his weight against me. It communicated all I needed to know. No matter what happened next, we'd face it as a family.

A voice emanated from one of the hooded figures in white. "We understand your coven possesses information of great import." The fact that it wasn't Gerald speaking to us surprised me. Usually Gerald lowered his cowl and served as our liaison. Was he choosing not to speak to us, or had the majority silenced him? Either way, the change in protocol didn't bode well for us.

Mr. Blackmoor nodded and stepped forward. "We do."

"Then speak it."

"I will once *you* provide *us* with some answers."

"You dare bargain with *us*," one of the members in black said. The strange metallic tone of the voice made me growl. It was the warlock on the Conclave who hated the Blackmoors, the one who made it her mission to cause this family grief, and the one Pierce dubbed the Warlock Hag. No one in the family understood why she magically altered her voice or what she had to gain by concealing her identity inside the oversize robe and hood that hid her from view.

Whatever the reason for the secret, she carefully guarded it.

"I apologize for the confusion." The words rolled off Mr. Blackmoor's tongue too easily. When a warlock was truly sorry, the words stuck in his throat and refused to budge. "I'm not trying to bargain. I'm simply explaining how this conversation will go."

All nine members of the Conclave stiffened in response, while the protector covens gaped at Mr. Blackmoor. Apparently no one could believe how he was addressing magical beings capable of ripping him to shreds with only a thought, and that disbelief was shared by his sons.

A sheen of sweat glistened off Pierce's upper lip while Mason, who typically enjoyed riling up a hornets' nest, shifted his weight from one foot to the other.

"Dad," Thad whispered.

"My family and I promise to tell you everything we know," Mr. Blackmoor continued, "if you tell us everything you know about what's going on."

"Oliver." One of the figures in gray lowered his hood and stepped out of the line. It was Gerald. His voice was calm yet firm, and I was pleased to see him resume his role. "This is not the way to go about things, and you know it."

"True, but with all due respect, my family is no longer a protector coven." He shot his gaze to the Warlock Hag. "We don't answer to you anymore."

"I will no longer tolerate such insolence." The Warlock Hag zipped through the air until she hovered in front of Mr. Blackmoor. "Tell us what you know or I will rip it from your mind."

"Ladies first."

"Enough." Gerald stepped between them. Judging by the way the Warlock Hag shook in rage, he had just saved Mr. Blackmoor's life. "We must stop fighting each other. We're on the same side."

"Are we?" The Warlock Hag drifted back a few feet.

Gerald locked gazes with her, and silence filled the room. They were clearly having one of the private magical conversations only the Conclave could hear. After a few seconds, the Warlock Hag slowly floated back to her place in line and Gerald returned his kind gray eyes to Mr. Blackmoor.

"Something is clearly troubling you. While you could never be described as warm and fuzzy, your edges are sharper than usual." He rested one hand on Mr. Blackmoor's shoulder and gave it a squeeze. "Tell me. What has happened?"

The grief that had been dammed behind Mr. Blackmoor's anger crashed through the barrier. When he spoke, his words were thick with emotion. "The earthquake that destroyed my town also wiped my wife's grave from the face of the earth."

A river of sympathy suddenly flowed through the room. The sad frowns and slow nods revealed that everyone now realized the source of Mr. Blackmoor's anger. Even the Warlock Hag no longer bristled. Her tense shoulders not only relaxed, they drooped.

Her posture confused me. If I could read the emotions of the Conclave, I'd discover what that was about, but not even my enhanced senses could pierce the magical barriers of someone as powerful as she was.

"I'm sorry." Gerald's wrinkled eyes narrowed and he glanced away. "I had no idea Priscilla's resting place had been disturbed."

Mr. Blackmoor sniffed back his emotions. "Thank you, but I don't want apologies. I want to know *why*."

"We aren't… certain." The Warlock Hag's words caused almost every jaw in the room to drop. It was the first time she had ever given an honest answer to any of our questions, and her tone was sympathetic instead of acerbic, a fact not even her voice distortion could hide. Perhaps miracles could happen.

Gerald appeared just as shocked as the rest of us. He gaped at her in silence for a few moments before slowly panning back to Mr. Blackmoor. "My colleague is correct. We detected an energy surge in Havenbridge like none we'd ever sensed before and asked the protector covens to discern its location."

"What did you find?" Thad asked.

"More than we expected." Mrs. Proctor spoke up first, something Mr. Proctor's wrinkled expression revealed he didn't appreciate. She ignored her husband and once again closed the distance between us. "We discovered a massive cloud of mystical energy hovering over Havenbridge. It thwarted all attempts at deciphering what type of magic it consisted of."

Could *that* have been the power I sensed earlier, the one that smelled old?

"How is that possible?" Pierce asked. "That almost makes it sound as if the magic was alive."

No one had an answer for that, not even the Conclave.

"Since we couldn't determine what it was made of or its purpose," Mrs. Proctor continued, "we realized we had to dispel it."

Her scrunched lips told me it had not been easy. "And what happened?"

"It fought back," Mrs. Stonewall answered.

"That doesn't make sense. Magic isn't sentient."

Mr. Stonewall agreed with my assessment. "No. It's a force of nature. It can only be siphoned and bent to the will of the user. But this energy was unlike any we'd encountered before. It was like it was searching for something or someone."

"But you were able to dispel it?" Mr. Blackmoor asked.

Mrs. Proctor nodded. "It took our combined powers to dissipate it and protect ourselves from the resulting backlash. When it was over, we dropped the protection spell a few moments before Oliver barged in."

That explained why the Proctors' house hadn't been devastated, but it brought up another question. "What or who created the magical cloud?"

Pierce sniffed. "Icarian. Who else?"

The nodding heads in the room agreed with him, but I wasn't so certain. All I could think about was Aunt Millie's warning about how I was changing into something that would be able to stop the curse Icarian released.

Could that magical cloud of energy have been looking for me?

"Aiden, do you not agree?"

Gerald's question brought my gaze to his. "I don't."

"Why not?" Mr. Stonewall asked. "It *is* a logical conclusion."

Only because they didn't have all the facts, and it was time to bring them up to speed, so I filled them in on my run-ins with Aunt Millie and the oracle in the mist.

When I was done, silence descended upon the room until Gerald broke it. "And Millie didn't tell you *what* she thought you were turning into?" When I shook my head, he nodded absently at me and his hands trembled. Why had the information unnerved him so much?

"I don't understand." Mr. Stonewall studied me as if I were a subject he suddenly wished to experiment on. "What does this have to do with why you don't believe Icarian created the magical cloud we encountered?"

"Because you said it felt like the energy was searching for something. I think it was looking for me, and if whatever I'm becoming might stop Icarian's plans, then there's no way he would have created it."

Mr. Stonewall reluctantly nodded.

"I have a question." All eyes were suddenly on Drake. "If the protector covens dissipated the magic that was part of Aiden's transformation, does that mean he's *not* goin' to turn into some other magical creature?"

The question brought a flicker of hope to Thad's hazel eyes as I pulled him into my arms. The thought of me turning into a monster that might sever our blood tie terrified the both of us, but if we didn't have to face that nightmare thanks to the protector covens, I'd give each one of them, including the despicable Edwells, a big sloppy kiss on the lips.

"That depends." The Warlock Hag's response snowed on my parade.

I cut my gaze to her. "On what?"

"If you are truly changing into something else, something only vampyren can sense and something that brought the oracle and her vision to you, then what you are meant to be is already fated to occur."

Thad balled his fists into the fabric of my shirt. "Which means what exactly?"

"Which means the energy will reform, and it will find Aiden when his metamorphosis is at hand."

"I refuse to accept that." I held Thad tightly against me, using my touch to calm the riptide of fear that swirled within the both of us. "There has to be some way to fight this."

Gerald placed his hand on my shoulder and patted it. It was meant to be reassuring, but I found nothing comforting in the bizarre expression that darkened his features. "If it is fated, it cannot be changed."

Anger bubbled like magma inside of me, and a sharp pain pierced my skull. A second later I fell to my knees, clutching my head.

"Aiden?" Thad crouched before me, his eyes wide and his voice shrill. "What's wrong?"

I couldn't answer. All I could do was grit my teeth as a thousand razors sliced through me. I fell forward in agony, clawing at the floor as a fire ignited in my brain and quickly traveled across my skin. I half expected to find my flesh melting from my bones, but no flames sprouted from my body.

The world around me spun, and I collapsed on my side. Thad reached for me, trying to get me to answer him, but I couldn't speak. My tongue had swollen to at least five times its usual size and filled my mouth, blocking my airway.

I opened my mouth to draw in breath, but black bile spewed forth instead. Thad sat back in horror and his face twisted before he lunged forward again. He shook my shoulders, screaming words I couldn't hear at me while other shadowy figures gathered, asking questions I couldn't understand. The sound of my bones breaking inside my body drowned out everything else.

What was happening to me?

Only what is meant to be.

Was the oracle back? I didn't have time to find an answer. My body convulsed and twisted as if some unseen hand was reforming me into something new. When my spine shattered, every color but red drained from my vision until all I could see was darkness.

I HAD no idea how long I'd been out, but when I awoke, a dense fog once again rolled around me. I no longer stood in the Proctor living room. I had somehow been transported to a cemetery, where broken gray tombstones jutted from the ground like cracked, misshapen teeth.

When I sat up, my body screamed. Every part of me ached, even my tongue and my fingernails. What was going on, and where were Thad and everyone else?

"Thad?" My words echoed off the gravestones on either side of me, which twisted my voice into a taunting plea, as if something knew Thad was gone forever. "Oracle, are *you* there?"

When I didn't get a response, I scowled at the air around me. She might not be responsible for this after all. The last time she brought me to her, she came with a purpose, to deliver a warning.

This felt different, more ominous, and my gut told me the longer I stayed here, the harder it would be to get back to Thad.

I rose off the ground, and the world spun. I leaned against one of the tombstones to maintain my balance. When my surroundings stopped whirling and I found my legs, I stood straight and attempted to pierce the white veil that cloaked most of the cemetery from my view.

Although I couldn't see far, I detected no crouched hidden figures, but I wasn't alone. Something waited out there. It had attacked me, and I had to figure out who it was and what it wanted. I closed my eyes and opened my magical senses, expecting to find the same latticework of energy that connected all life the way I had in Havenbridge.

Instead, I saw nothing. The thrumming multicolored threads had vanished.

How was that possible? I should have found the cord connecting me to Thad and the others, to a bird flying overhead, to the insects crawling through the earth, or even to flowers in bloom. Everything but me was gone. It was as if the earth had opened up and devoured everything crawling on its surface.

I concentrated harder, forcing my senses to their limits. I willed the searching ripples farther away from me until something blipped on my magical radar. My eyes fluttered open. Someone or some*thing* of great power was here, watching me. It was close, and its unseen eyes bored through me, searching for something.

But what was it looking for?

I didn't have an answer, and I didn't really care. All that mattered was finding Thad. Everything else could fly through the Gate.

I howled in fury, and my fiery fae wings sprouted from my back in a blazing explosion of heat. The fog hissed as the fire singed the air, dissipating the swirling mist around me. I stretched my wings to their full span, forcing the veil to retreat even farther, and I boldly took two steps forward.

The fog matched my movement, withdrawing from my heat and my light. As I suspected, not even a supernatural shroud meant to either contain me or keep me from Thad could withstand the fire of the fae. My fire was not only capable of killing most vampyren, but it could forge a path out of here and straight to the man I loved.

Whatever awaited me in the swirling shroud had better beware.

With every step I took, the white curtain pulled back. The dry brown lawn where I stood gave way to blackened earth. I held my breath as I sat on my haunches, reaching my uncertain fingertips toward the scarred ground. When I made contact, I didn't scratch my way across hard, charred dirt as I'd been expecting. The ground gave way. It was spongy and moist, and when I withdrew my fingers, a thick, reddish-black liquid coated them.

It was blood. It soaked the earth. But why? I looked up in search of answers only to find the swirling mist had vanished, revealing a landscape that made me shiver and my wings of fire disappear in a puff of smoke.

Corpses in various states of decomposition spotted the area around me, and the rancid stench that burned my nasal passages told me these people had been dead for some time. That was why my magical senses couldn't detect life. There wasn't any left.

What had happened, and who was responsible?

But more importantly, was Thad safe?

My heart thundered in my chest, and as my fear rose, so did my anger. The vampyre within surged. Its instincts swelled like a tsunami, rushing forward to devastate everything before me. If I let the urge take control, it would do just that.

I couldn't let the vampyre overpower the fairy, so I took several deep breaths until I sent the rising monster howling back into my depths.

Eat. Kill.

The words exploded from all directions at once. I spun around, trying to detect where they originated, but only more reddened earth littered with corpses stretched out before me.

"Who's there?" My words came out in a low, throaty growl. Whatever waited to devour me would not find an easy morsel to digest.

Eat. Kill. Eat. Kill. The angry words repeated on a never-ending cycle as if they were formed by a fractured mind only capable of death and destruction.

"Where are you?"

The ground trembled underneath my feet, as if my enemy lived not upon the earth but within it. If that was where it hid, I would yank it from the dirt and force it to tell me what it had done with Thad.

Fire surrounded my clenched fists as I pummeled the ground in a roar of fury. The punch sent peals of thunder into the distance. Sprays of blood exploded from where my fist hit the moist ground, but I didn't stop. I struck the earth again and again until I was covered in the blackish-red liquid and the earth cracked.

The fissure I created grew, cutting a jagged path across the surface and splitting the ground in two. It reminded me of the sinkhole in Havenbridge that had swallowed the cemetery where Mrs. Blackmoor had been interred. I inched toward the edge and gazed down into the blackened depths. My breath hitched.

Scores of decomposing bodies crawled up the sides of the hole like ants emerging from a disturbed mound.

Eat. Kill. Eat. Kill. Eatkilleatkilleatkill. Their angry, murderous thoughts whipped around me like a psychotic tempest. Their voices grew louder, threatening to overwhelm my magical senses. I covered my ears and stepped away from the crevice, placing distance between the voices and me before my eardrums burst.

Another jolt shook the ground, widening the crack into an open mouth that advanced in my direction as the storm of words continued to roar. My gut told me that if I fell into the earthen jaws, I'd never return and I'd never see Thad again.

That wasn't going to happen.

Keeping my gaze on the expanding maw, I shuffled backward until the backs of my legs struck something hard and cold. I fell onto the bloody earth as the earth exploded around me. Corpses spat out of the ground, flying into the air before landing with moist thuds.

I watched in horror as the bloated, rotting bodies dug their dead fingers into the earth and dragged themselves toward me.

Eat. Kill.

The crack in the earth widened, advancing in my direction. I tried to rise, but my arm was stuck and no amount of effort freed me. A quick glance over my shoulder revealed why. A rotted hand had pierced the ground and held me fast.

The image repulsed me, but being restrained ticked off both my vampyre and the fae prince. "Release me at once." Surprisingly the hand did as I asked.

I sprang to my feet and was scanning the ground for more sprouting limbs, when another explosion ripped through the soil behind me. The force sent me face-first into the wet earth. I immediately flipped over, fire trailing from my clenched fists, but the flames of my power and anger snuffed out in response to the object that hovered above me.

It was a tombstone, and the words written across its polished surface read *Here lies Aiden Teine, the fire fairy who killed us all.*

CHAPTER 9

I SAT up, gasping for breath. The bloody wasteland covered in corpses had vanished, and the tombstone no longer hovered in the air.

"Aiden?" Thad sat beside me, his face blanched in fear. He immediately drew me into a viselike embrace that briefly cut off my oxygen, and I returned the favor. As far as I was concerned, I was never letting him go again. At least until I stopped trembling.

Whatever place I'd been whisked off to this time terrified me, and fear wasn't an emotion I was accustomed to. The power I wielded as a vampyre and a fae typically gave me an advantage. However, all the magic in the world couldn't bring life back to a barren wasteland.

"It's okay." The warmth of Thad's words spread across my chilled flesh. "You're safe."

Was I? Was anyone? Based on that dream, vision, or whatever the hell it was, I was the reason everyone was going to die. If I was going to prevent that awful future, I had to figure out what it all meant and do *whatever* it took to keep Thad and everyone safe.

A quick glance over Thad's shoulder at the concerned faces of my family, the protector covens, and Gerald told me they were just as eager to get to the bottom of this as I was.

"What happened?" Mr. Blackmoor asked.

"Not now." Thad's tone cut sharp as he shifted and gazed up at those gathered around us. "Aiden needs to rest."

"No." The Warlock Hag's tone was firm. "We must know what transpired. Right. *Now.*"

Thad tensed, ready to argue, but even though I loved how fiercely he protected me, she was right. Based on the wrenching in my gut, time was not on our side, so I soothed his temper with a gentle caress of my cheek against his.

"Are you sure?" He held my face in his hands and forced my attention to his honeyed gaze. His determined expression told me if I didn't want to talk, he'd flash-freeze everyone in the room and take me home.

I loved him more with each passing second, a message I delivered with a slow kiss. "Yes."

He didn't like my answer, if his scrunched lips were any indication, but his nod communicated he wouldn't push the point.

Even though I wasn't certain what happened or what that damn tombstone floating in the air meant, I did know one thing.

"I saw the dead. They're angry, and they're coming."

"You what?" Gerald grasped my shoulders and, with little effort, yanked me to my feet and out of Thad's grasp. His uncharacteristically violent reaction reminded me of the Warlock Hag than the gentle mentor we'd come to know. What surprised me more was the strength of his grip. It felt like a giant was crushing me. Gerald might appear elderly and frail, a part he played to the hilt, but the old wizard possessed even more power than he let on. "Did you say you saw the dead? And they spoke to you?"

I tried to answer, but I only managed to wince in pain. If he didn't release me, my bones were going break.

"Gerald, stop." Thad appeared at my side. His eyebrows furrowed as he switched his gaze from Gerald's death grip to his wide gray eyes. "Let Aiden go."

Gerald's panicked gaze immediately hooded in regret. "I apologize." He released me and stepped away. "I meant you no harm."

I rubbed my aching shoulder caps while Thad hovered protectively by my side. "I'll be fine."

"Now answer Gerald's questions." The Warlock Hag's tone communicated she'd do far worse than Gerald if I disobeyed. "Did you see and hear the dead?"

I had a hunch the answer they all wanted was no. "Yes."

Gerald spun around and faced the Conclave, and silence descended once again as they entered their private communication mode.

"Stop that!" Mrs. Proctor marched across her living room and stood before Gerald, whose stunned expression reflected the mood in the room. "Stop keeping us in the dark. *What* do you know?"

It was the Warlock Hag who glided forward. "There's only one magical being capable of communicating with the dead."

"A necromancer." Thad grew pale, and a hush descended upon the room as everyone's gaze settled upon me.

It took a while for that information to sink in. Necromancy hadn't existed for millennia, and it was an ability associated with black magic.

Only warlocks tapped into that power, but that particular mystical art had been culled from magic by the earliest version of the Conclave. Like blood magic, death magic proved too unstable. Not only did it drain the life force of the Gate, but it allowed shades, the spirits of the dead, to enter our world, where they created havoc.

To save magic and prevent future spectral invaders from tormenting the living, the Conclave had gathered all necromancers and bound their powers, wiping death magic from existence.

"This defies logic." Mr. Stonewall's usually cool demeanor faded as frustration punctuated his words. "Necromancy is a warlock ability. A fire fairy cannot access black magic."

He was right. I shouldn't be able to talk to the dead. I was a fire fae. Life and light powered my abilities.

"But he's not just a fire fairy," Mrs. Stonewall replied. "He's also a vampyre."

Death had become a part of my mystical cache. When I died and was reborn, I bypassed the natural cycle of life. I became *un*natural, an immortal, indestructible monster. But that still didn't explain how I could harness black magic. I might be a perversion of nature, born from a curse that should never have existed, but accessing magic beyond my realm was as impossible as—

I shifted my eyes to Thad, remembering how he had once siphoned fairy magic in Otherworld. *That* should have been impossible as well, but he had done what no other *homo magus* had been able to do. What made us different? Was our blood tie responsible for granting us access to each other's magic? His parted lips told me he was wondering the same thing.

And if that was the case, if my powers were growing into something that shouldn't be, did that mean Thad's powers would continue to grow too, just like Icarian had warned Drake?

"Are you saying Aiden is turning into a necromancer?" If Mason scratched his head any harder, he'd start bleeding.

Gerald, who'd been struck mute since my initial response, suddenly found his words. "I-it appears so."

Thad rushed over to me and flew into my arms. I clutched him to me, providing as much comfort to him as he gave to me. If what everyone was saying was true, the delicate balance of magic *had* been upset and chaos in more forms than I could imagine waited to devour us whole, just like the corpses in the vision.

I had to do something to stop it, and it was likely the one thing I *didn't* want to do.

"How is this even possible?" The tendons on both sides of Mr. Blackmoor's neck stood out. Fear wrapped its cold, dead hand around him, and as always, he responded with anger.

Gerald could no longer find his words, so the Warlock Hag took up the slack. "That is what we need to discover. Only a spell of disastrous proportions could bring about such a transformation."

"Like the soul quake that hit Havenbridge?" I asked.

"Soul quake?" The Warlock Hag flinched, and the other members of the Conclave glanced at each other. Gerald was the only exception. He clutched his chest as if he were about to have a heart attack. "*Why* would you think that?"

"Because I felt it. I was psychically connected to every human in town when it hit, and their anguish became mine. What happened in Havenbridge also rattled the very essence of the spirit element."

The Warlock Hag tensed. "And *now* we have our answer. A soul quake has only happened once in all of recorded magical history. Someone has recited the *immortalitas* spell—again."

IT TOOK several moments for everyone to process the implications. The *immortalitas* spell had been responsible for unleashing the vampyren curse upon humans and the *homo magus*. If it hadn't been for the Conclave at the time, none of us would be alive today. It had taken their combined powers and the loss of many powerful witches, wizards, and warlocks to undo the damage Bartram Kane caused by attempting to resurrect his son.

If the *immortalitas* spell had been cast, a new curse had been unleashed, just like Aunt Millie had tried to warn me. My heart sank as I realized what that most likely meant.

"I don't understand how this is possible." Mr. Blackmoor directed his swell of anger at the Conclave. "I thought you told us the incantation had been erased from every book of spells in existence."

The Warlock Hag stiffened. "It was. The Conclave of that time saw to it personally."

Evidently that hadn't been the case. A copy of the spell remained somewhere, and Icarian had found it. "Clearly they missed one."

"Clearly," Gerald added with a nod.

The room erupted in terrified, angry voices. The Stonewalls demanded answers, the Proctors threw out ideas for protection, and my family insisted they lead the charge to destroy Icarian once and for all. As for the Edwells, they sneaked into a corner, where they likely piddled on the floor.

I turned away from the chaos and my world instantly reduced to the single glorious image of Thad resting in my protective embrace. I pressed a kiss to the top of his head, inhaling the sweet scent of papaya from his shampoo as my breaking heart took snapshots of this moment to capture for eternity.

I'd forever remember the way his strawberry-blond hair resembled fire against my fair skin, how he snuggled deep into my chest, searching for warmth and comfort. I'd always recall how he chewed on his lower lip when he was in deep thought or when he was trying hard not to be afraid, like he was right now. I could never forget how his eyes reminded me of a springtime sunset. Just as the sun spread peace and serenity across the land when it kissed the horizon, gazing deep into Thad's golden orbs calmed my spirit. It filled me with hope that a newer, brighter day would eventually rise for the man who'd always carry my heart.

When Thad caught me staring, his thin pink lips parted in a grin that blazoned onto my soul.

"I'll figure this out." His steady gaze expressed his determination. He'd find a way to stop my transformation into a necromancer. I had no doubt he'd comb every magical book in the Blackmoor library searching for answers that weren't there or wouldn't be found in time.

I traced my fingertips across his perfect pink lips, committing every velvety curve to memory. I didn't have the heart to tell him my metamorphosis was not only inevitable but had already begun.

"Are the two of you even listening?" Pierce's bark drew us back into the pandemonium of the Proctors' living room.

Thad cut his gaze to his brother. "What?"

The Warlock Hag floated before us. "Does the fate of magic mean so little to the two of you, or are you simply incapable of controlling your hormones?"

The air around Thad chilled. That only happened when he'd reached the limits of his patience and was about to go full-on blizzard. I didn't blame him. We had enough to deal with already. The Warlock Hag's continued snark wasn't helping matters, and neither would Thad, if he unleashed his building fury. I placed an arm around his waist to rein in his temper. Fortunately the contact caused the falling temperatures to stabilize.

The Warlock Hag locked her shadowed gaze on Thad and tilted her head to one side. "Were you just about t—"

"No, he wasn't." My blurted response earned me her undivided attention. I needed her to focus on me and not on the fact that Thad had been seconds away from attacking. "He's just on edge. I think we all are, considering the circumstances."

"Perhaps." Her flat tone communicated she wasn't convinced.

Mr. Blackmoor cleared his throat, his shoulders tense. He obviously realized his son had almost lost control. "Can we get back to business?"

"Oliver's right." Gerald sat back in a chair, but even though his words indicated he wanted to move back to the previous topic, his steely gaze lingered on Thad. Why did I feel as if he was trying to see straight into Thad's soul? "We can't waste our time pondering *how* Icarian found the *immortalitas* spell."

"I disagree."

Gerald glanced at me and sat up straight. "Why is that, Your Highness?"

He hadn't used my royal title in months. Why was he addressing me as such now? "If we know how or where Icarian found the spell, we might be able to track him down."

Thad nodded. "Aiden's right. Finding Icarian gets us one step closer to stopping him."

"And how have attempts at locating Icarian fared thus far?" He laced his fingers in his lap and returned our even stares.

He already knew the answer. Our efforts had gotten us nowhere. But that only meant there was information we didn't possess. Perhaps Icarian wasn't even his real name. That would explain why scrying spells couldn't locate him.

"Precisely." Gerald smoothed out his gray robes. "Which is why we must focus our efforts on learning what new threat he has unleashed instead. If we don't know what it is, we won't be able to stop it."

"Isn't it obvious?" Mason's confident tone surprised everyone in the room. While he was arrogant about many subjects, when it came to magic, he deferred to others, mostly because he spent as little time as possible learning his craft. "He's creating an army."

That made sense. For months Icarian had been using others to do his dirty work. He sent Ben and Sersie to steal the crests, and when that failed, he made a truce with the witch hunters. Now that his allies had been permanently taken care of, he needed new soldiers to do his bidding.

"I think Mason's right." Thad's arched eyebrow and smile indicated he was impressed *and* surprised by his brother's conclusion. Mason responded by flipping him off.

"But what kind of army did he create?" Drake darted his gaze from Thad to Gerald. "More vampyren?"

"I don't think so." Mason couldn't have been more pleased to astound us once again, if his impish grin was any indication. "If the oracle is sending Aiden these visions, then she's already told us what we're facing: zombies."

He uttered the word as if it were no big deal, as if he were talking about fictional monsters from the video games he played or the television shows he watched. The stoic gazes that filled the room and hushed the Conclave forced Mason's grin to march off his expression.

The crawling corpses I'd seen in the bloodied cemetery had been dead *and* moving. If Mason was right, that meant the human and magical communities faced a threat even greater than the vampyren.

"Is Mason right?" I asked.

After several more moments of quiet, Gerald reluctantly nodded.

"Then we must find them." Mr. Blackmoor's fist turned to stone. "If Icarian unleashes his army of undead, countless lives will be lost."

And they would turn the world into a big, bloody graveyard.

"It's even worse than that." A dark cloud of dread floated across Gerald's expression.

"How is that even possible?"

The Warlock Hag responded to my question. "If Icarian unleashes his army, he also runs the risk of once again revealing the existence of magic to humanity." The situation grew more dismal by the moment, and it only reinforced the decision I'd already made. "But we have been provided a solution."

"What is it?" Thad asked.

When she waved a robed hand at me, I wasn't surprised. "Aiden must embrace his transformation and become a necromancer. Then he can command the dead."

She was right. That had to be what Aunt Millie's warning had meant and what the marking on the tombstone had been referring to. If I remained a fire fairy, everyone would die. If I embraced what I was, I'd be able to stop Icarian's new army. Unfortunately, doing so came with a hefty price.

"No." Flames licked the apples of Thad's cheeks. "In order to do that, he has to abandon his fairy and fully embrace death magic. I won't allow it."

Before the Warlock Hag or the Conclave could react, I held up my hand and met her gaze. Instead of using words, I unleashed the emotions in my heart in her direction, and her nod communicated she understood.

Thad glanced back and forth between us. "What did you tell her?"

Instead of answering his question, I drew Thad into my arms and pressed kisses to his furrowed brow and curled lips. He refused to surrender to my touch. Just like the Warlock Hag, he knew what I was saying without me having to speak the words.

He wrapped his arms around my neck and clasped them tight, glaring at the Conclave, who had gathered in wait behind us. "I won't let you do this." Although his tone was firm, his chin trembled.

"I know." I didn't want to lose Thad either, and if I embraced death magic, that meant abandoning my connection to the light of the fae and to the blood tie that bound us together. But this was bigger than us. All of magic was on the line, and whether Thad knew it or not, so were his life and the lives of his brothers. While I would never let Thad sacrifice himself, I'd gladly offer myself up in return, no matter how badly it hurt.

Before I did that, though, I had something to do first.

I stepped out of Thad's embrace and crossed over to Drake, who furrowed his brow.

"Aiden, what's—"

I punched him in the face, sending him sprawling to the floor, unconscious.

"What the fuck?" Mason fell to his boyfriend's side, the shadows already coiling about him in response to Mason's power.

I turned to the Warlock Hag and nodded.

Mason's powers shut off, and the rest of my family found themselves incapable of movement. If I hadn't taken out Drake and his magical immunity, he would have activated his ability and shielded my family from the Warlock Hag's spell, making it impossible for her to prevent the people I loved from stopping me from doing what had to be done.

Mr. Blackmoor shook his head as realization dawned. "Aiden, no."

"Don't be a dumbass," Pierce grumbled as he tried to force himself forward.

Kale mirrored his actions. He even attempted a shift, but he remained human. "There has to be another way."

I couldn't have asked for a better family. "If only there was."

"Don't do this to me. Please." Tears streamed down Thad's cheeks.

"I'm doing this *for* you." I ran my fingertips across his fair flesh, skirting over the lips that had breathed new life into my soul. I loved Thad so much, more than I thought possible for a fire fairy whose past relationships rarely outlasted a season. Now I'd give anything for just one more day, even one more moment in his loving embrace.

I glanced over at the wet faces of the Blackmoors, which included a no-longer-scowling Mason. He *finally* realized what I was doing. "And for my family."

Their weeping eyes pleaded with me to reconsider, promising we'd find another way, but I couldn't take the chance. Too much was at risk.

I placed one final kiss upon Thad's trembling lips, and the world halted, as if the Gate was allowing me to draw out a moment that would have to last me a lifetime. I ran my fingers through Thad's hair before cupping his face and gazing deeply into the eyes of the man who had become a part of me, the man who taught a fairy the meaning of true love, and the man I too briefly had as my own. "I love you, Thad. Please don't forget that."

He shook his head, trying to force back his tears and failing miserably. "I could never forget you. I love you enough for the both of us." He sucked back his sobs and stood tall. "Just you wait and see."

Although it took every ounce of willpower not to scoop Thad in my arms and fly away, I turned around and approached the Conclave. "I'm ready."

I glanced over my shoulder, blowing a kiss to Thad before the Conclave's magic spirited me away from the warlock I loved and might never see again.

CHAPTER 10

I COULDN'T believe my eyes. Below me, a lush green island rested upon a blanket of clouds that stretched beyond the horizon. The patch of land hovered amid the vastness of outer space. Countless stars winked in greeting, and meteors streaked by in a flash of amber before heading past Earth, which had replaced the sun in a sky that was no longer blue. It had been painted over with the radiant hues of the cosmos.

Was this where the Conclave lived? What Pierce referred to as their Fortress of Secritude?

Before I could ask the Conclave, who floated silently on my left, we sped forward, zooming toward the island at a velocity that would have torn me apart had I not been under the Conclave's power.

A sprawling ivory palace came into view as we drew closer. Its glistening walls rose from the land, unapologetic in their grandeur. They boldly defied those who gazed upon them to violate their sanctity, for if an intruder dared to breach the perimeter, the power that maintained the sanctum's lofty perch would decimate them.

Around the castle stood majestic trees with crowns more regal than those of the ancient forest in the Arbor on Otherworld. They surrounded the castle and stood sentry across the land, ready to defend the citadel. Their armored trunks reached out protectively in an expanse of green that enhanced the fortress's beauty while threatening to snatch the heads off trespassers with their mighty limbs.

"Is this where you live?"

Gerald nodded. "Welcome to the Veil."

A second later I no longer descended toward the island but stood in the middle of a circular room. Due to the sudden change in perspective and movement, I had to stretch my arms out to my sides to keep from falling over.

When I was certain I wouldn't fall headfirst onto the blue marble that covered the floor, I noticed the nine stone columns that rested at regular intervals along the perimeter. They didn't connect to the domed ceiling overhead. Instead, they rose to only half the height of the room and ended in square slabs.

Each member of the Conclave stood at the top of one of the columns and gazed down at me from their perch. Why did I suddenly feel as if I were on trial?

"Is there something wrong?"

"We're curious," said one of the white-robed figures in front of me. "How is it possible for a fairy, even a vampyre fae, to be imbued with necromancy?"

They definitely believed I was guilty of something. "How would I know? I'm just as rattled about this as you are."

"Really?" This time a figure in gray behind me spoke. "Why do we sense you possess more knowledge on this subject than you care to give voice to?"

I did my best not to betray my emotions. If the Conclave believed I was hiding information from them, magical law allowed them to reach into my mind and take it. If I had still been a prince and hadn't been banished, my father would bring the might of the fae down upon their heads for such a violation.

But I was no longer a fae prince. I'd been adopted into the Blackmoor coven, which meant I was subject to the laws of the Conclave.

I couldn't let them peer into my mind. If they did, they'd learn about the Prophecy of the Three. I'd promised Drake I wouldn't tell Gerald or any member of the Conclave what Icarian had told him, and even though I still didn't know why, I had to trust he had a good reason.

"I think it has something to do with my connection to Thad, what he calls our blood tie."

"Explain." The metallic tone of the voice on my right told me it was the Warlock Hag's turn to talk.

"I'm not certain I can."

Gerald lowered his hood and smiled down at me. "Please try."

I nodded, thankful for at least one friendly face. "When Thad and I met, I felt connected to him almost instantly. I could practically feel his heart beating in *my* chest, and it was like we were one person. It was as if... I'd come home. I knew he'd do anything for me and that I'd do anything for him, that together we could overcome any obstacle. When Ben killed me and turned me into a vampyre, it was that physical bond I had with Thad that kept me from turning into a monster, and then it was feeding on him, his actual blood, that kept me strong and sane and... me."

"So you believe your love for Thad Blackmoor has somehow given you access to black magic the same way he once tapped into the magic of the fae?"

I nodded in response to the black-robed figure on my left.

"That concerns us." The Warlock Hag's tinny voice returned my attention to her. "The Blackmoors have displayed incredible growth in power recently, and now the men they are involved with are experiencing evolutions in their own abilities. We are currently faced with a human who possesses immunity to magic and a shifter who can turn into two different avians. The delicate balance of magic has been upset, and we must find out why."

Icarian had a theory, the Prophecy of the Three, and his solutions were either the Spell Fall or the death of one of the Blackmoor brothers. Would the Conclave arrive at the same conclusions? That had to be why Drake didn't want me to tell the Conclave what he knew. It wasn't a chance I was willing to take either, so I had to get them off this path and back to the reason I was here.

"I understand, but what does any of this have to do with me?"

"You are yet another example of the imbalance that has run rampant for too long," said one of the wizards in front of me. "And we will not allow this pattern to continue."

That sounded like a threat, and neither the fairy nor the vampyre in me appreciated it. "What do you mean?"

"It means this." The Warlock Hag drifted away from her pedestal and hovered before me. "We will allow you to complete your transformation into a necromancer. We will allow you access to our magical library to help you learn the craft so you can take control of Icarian's undead army, combat him, and bring an end to the threat of the Spell Fall for good."

I tensed, waiting for the *but* I knew was coming.

"However, necromancy cannot be allowed. It was eradicated for a reason, and when this is over—"

"You'll eradicate me?"

The Conclave, including a glum Gerald, nodded in unison.

What could I say? I had no choice. Either I agreed to what amounted to a death penalty for saving their collective behinds, or Thad and everyone I loved would be wiped out by a plague of zombies.

"Just let me do what I have to do to save Thad. When it's done, you can do what you need to do to me."

The Warlock Hag nodded in acceptance to my terms. "Then proceed."

"What does that mean?"

"If the energy we detected was truly the power of a necromancer searching for its host, as you posited, then you must open yourself up to the energy to begin the transformation."

"And if it's not?"

She hovered back a few feet as if she was trying to distance herself from what was about to happen. "There's only one way to find out."

Her answer wasn't very comforting, but I didn't see as if I had any choice. Either I did what I didn't want to do or Thad and everyone else I loved would suffer. I closed my eyes, centering myself, and the vampyre inside me hissed in anticipation. It obviously longed for me to let down my defenses and open myself up to a power that would make the energy that fed it even stronger than it already was.

I lowered the walls of restraint brick by brick, and the anger and hate that fueled the monster inside bubbled up from within me like a long-contained fire. My body shook as my fairy refused to surrender, fighting back with all its natural power.

That was when I felt it.

A power even older than I was swirled around me on darkened currents. Its musty smell invaded my lungs as it wrapped around me like a python. It longed to enter me, to claim its first vessel in centuries, and though I knew it had to be done, a tinge of fear rippled through me.

I couldn't let it consume me. I had to remember what and who I was doing this for, and as long as I could do that, I hoped to always be the man I was at this moment, the one who planned on loving Thad for eternity.

I opened my arms and sent the barrier keeping it out falling to the ground.

Pain more terrible than any I'd previously experienced slammed into me, and I fell to my knees, screaming. Black fire spread across my skin, which bubbled like tar before melting and falling off in thick wet globs.

I held one hand in front of my face, staring at my skeletal fingers, and the vampyre within me hissed in anger. It leaped out before I had a chance to reel it back in. It quickly learned that was a mistake.

My prehensile tongue, which rattled in anger at the Conclave, dislodged and tumbled out of my mouth. My talons melted off my fingertips, and I fell backward onto the floor when another jolt of agony ripped through me.

What was happening to me?

"Your vampyre is dying." The Warlock Hag answered my thought. "Soon your fae will follow."

I flipped onto my stomach and scratched exposed bone and fingernails on the marbled floor as the fire spread across my frame. More of my flesh melted and fell away as I crawled forward in a vain attempt to escape the pain.

My fairy wings sprouted from my back, flapping furiously in an attempt to whisk me to a safe haven, but there was nowhere to go. I hovered a few feet off the floor until the fire that ravaged my body reached the wings I'd had since birth.

The black flames spread across their span, snuffing out their light and their power and sending me crashing to the floor. A quick glance over my melting shoulder revealed the blazing red wings that once carried me through the sky had been replaced with a brand-new set of bony dragon wings.

I crawled across the floor, tears of mourning streaming down my cheeks as everything I had been before this moment ceased to be. When the ebony fire worked its way up my chest toward my face, I cried out in anguish. I glanced up at the Conclave, unable to speak as the fire licked across my face. I extended one skeletal hand to them, praying for help or at the very least a spell to ease my pain.

They didn't move. They stood by in silence as the fire consumed me.

I collapsed on the floor, unable to move or speak as the waters of unconsciousness washed over me. Before I slipped underneath their merciful depths, the last image I saw wasn't the Conclave or the nightmarish flames that ravaged my body.

It was Thad, and the words he last spoke to me resounded in my soul.

I love you enough for the both of us. Just you wait and see.

MY EYES fluttered open. Instead of staring up at the domed ceiling or the Conclave standing upon their perches, I found myself lying on a bed in a room I couldn't remember seeing before.

The room had been constructed with enormous rectangular slabs of smooth stone that glowed with soft golden tones thanks to the candle sconces attached to the walls. A wooden side table sat flush with the wall to the right of the bed. A white pitcher and a crystal vase filled with lavender starflowers sat on top. A lantern that hadn't been switched on rested on the small bedstand to my left, along with another arrangement of starflowers. There were no windows and no other decorations except for the oriental rug that sprawled toward the heavy wooden door across the room.

Was I still in the Veil? And more importantly, how long had I been asleep?

When I tried to sit up to begin a search for answers, my body complained loudly. Every inch of flesh burned as if I were still covered in black fire. A quick glance at my hands revealed that not only were the flames gone, but my fair skin once again covered my bones. Thank the Gate for small favors. I'd already lived the past few months of my life as one monstrosity. I had no intention of living out my final days as a walking, breathing skeleton.

I wiggled my fingers, and I was pleased to see they worked. I wasn't as fond of how the slight movement produced an ache that cut deeper than bone.

It sliced into my soul, but did I even have one of those anymore? The Warlock Hag had said my vampyre and fae were dying. If that was true, was I now a necromancer? Other than the type of magic they practiced or the fact that they had been wiped from the face of the planet, I possessed precious little knowledge about the mystical creature fate had deemed me to be.

"I see you're finally awake."

I startled in response to the familiar voice suddenly speaking in my room, but no matter where I settled my gaze, I couldn't see the man who spoke. "Gerald?"

He blinked into existence at the foot of my bed, wearing his gray robes and a kind smile. "It's good to see you conscious again."

"How long have I been out?"

"About two weeks."

His answer took all breath from my lungs, and even though my body screamed at me, I sat up in bed. "Two weeks?"

"Give or take a few hours," he answered with a teasing grin.

I didn't see the humor. I didn't care that I'd lost fourteen days of my life or that my body had needed that long to recover from whatever the hell had happened to me. All I could think about was the torment Thad had endured while I'd been playing Sleeping Beauty.

Knowing him, he'd spent the entire time fretting about me, wondering if I was okay or if I was even still alive. He probably hadn't slept much either. He'd have been too busy searching through the

Blackmoor library, trying to locate a spell that would either find me or bring me back to him.

My heart broke when I thought about his frantic search for answers and how hopeless he likely felt for not having made any progress. For Thad, those two weeks might as well have been an eternity.

"What about Thad? Is he okay?"

Gerald arched one silver eyebrow at me. "Thad?"

He asked the question as if he had no clue whom I was talking about. "Yes. Thad Blackmoor, the sexy-as-hell warlock I'm in love with. Remember him?"

Gerald scratched his temple as if the name didn't ring any bells.

"He has hazel eyes and strawberry-blond hair and will freeze the balls off anyone who pisses him off."

I was surprised I'd just used the word *balls* in front of Gerald, but I wasn't entirely sure why. My brain felt fuzzy all of a sudden.

"Do you remember how you met Thad?"

What kind of question was that? Of course I remembered when we first met. He was— No, I first saw him when—

The memory was there. I could feel it rattling around in my brain, and when I closed my eyes and concentrated, I recalled every curve and dip of his handsome face. I could smell the crisp scent of pine that followed him wherever he went, and his voice still reminded me of the sylphs singing in the wind, but when I tried to grasp the memory of when I first laid eyes on him, the event slipped through my fingers like sand. "What's happening to my memory?"

Gerald sat on the bed next to me and patted my arm. "I'm actually surprised you remember anything at all, including me."

"What do you mean?"

"Your transformation into a necromancer was rather... violent."

That was an understatement. Unfortunately, I could still recall every tortuous moment I'd experienced. "Is that why I'm having trouble remembering how Thad and I first met?"

"No. The fact that you remember him at all is... fascinating. When the power of a necromancer descended upon you, the process should have wiped clean everything you were before this moment, including any memories of Thad."

"I can't recall everything." In fact, right now I couldn't bring forth any memories beyond the past few days we spent together in Havenbridge. "But I *do* remember him."

I couldn't help the smile that spread wide across my lips. While I had understood that embracing the power of a necromancer might sever my tie to Thad, the fact that it hadn't made my heart sing. It gave me hope that perhaps when all this was over, we might find some way to still be together—once we figured out how to stop the Conclave from murdering me in cold blood.

"I'm pleased to hear that."

"Really?"

"Of course." He practically twittered like a child the night before Yule. "I'm extremely fond of Thaddeus, and his happiness means the world to me."

His answer made my smile extend even wider. Gerald *was* on my side, and I could potentially count on his friendship to help Thad and I reunite once this mess was over.

"I just hope it lasts."

I clasped his hands in mine. "What do you mean?"

His previously glowing face darkened. "You admitted there were some gaps in your memory. Can I assume you recall recent events more easily than those that happened further in the past? Like how you and Thad first met?"

Although I didn't want to, I nodded.

He removed his hands from mine and placed his on top. "That means your most recent memories remain intact, but those too may soon disappear once you begin your training."

"But I don't want them to."

"I don't want them to either." He glanced around as if he were scanning for unseen eyes or ears. When he was satisfied no one was eavesdropping, he leaned closer and lowered his voice to barely above a whisper. "Cling to those memories as hard as you can, Aiden. No matter what *any*one else tells you."

I didn't need to be told twice, but his advice raised a question. "Why?"

"I… can't say, but you must heed my words. If you don't, it may jeopardize everything."

I wasn't certain what he was referring to, but I had to trust him. Gerald hadn't led us down the wrong path before. When I nodded, he flashed me a smile before standing and gathering his robes about him.

"Before you go, can I ask you one more question?"

"Of course."

"Do you know how Thad's been doing these past two weeks?"

He grinned down at me as if I were a child. "It's been two weeks for *us*. It's only been a few hours for Thad."

"I don't understand."

"The Veil exists in a magical pocket outside of standard time and space that the Conclave can manipulate. We can slow down time here to extend our life spans or we can speed it up so the hours and days pass by much more slowly on Earth than they do here. We often do that to detect magical disturbances long before they become a threat or to give a neophyte necromancer the time he needs to learn his craft and defeat our enemy."

I leaned back against the headboard and smiled. Even though I'd been separated from Thad for two weeks, he'd only been without me for a few hours. With any luck, we'd be together again sooner than he realized.

"What happens now?"

Gerald paused at the door before opening it. "For now, you rest. Your training starts tomorrow, and something tells me you're going to need all of your strength."

Before I could ask him what he meant, Gerald closed the door behind him, but instead of falling asleep, I focused on the memories of Thad I still retained. I played them in my mind on a continual loop, determined not to let them disappear.

CHAPTER 11

GERALD HAD been wrong. Not even sleeping for two weeks had given me enough strength to keep up with the furious pace the Warlock Hag set as my tutor on the finer arts of necromancy.

Who had I pissed off to get the one person who hated my family and me as much as she did? Whatever it was, the score had been settled in spades.

For the past three days, I'd been held prisoner in the Conclave's magical library. Granted, it was a gorgeous space. Rows of towering wooden bookshelves surrounded the expansive room, hugging the walls up a spiraling staircase made of dark wood, which, according to the Warlock Hag, ascended more than three miles. It was impressive, but the ample arches and marble flooring didn't make this any less of a prison, and my warden refused to give me one moment of rest.

Whenever I finished one book on necromancy, she had another ready to go, and she hovered behind me, making sure I read at her desired pace. If I went too slow, she berated me. If I got tired, I'd suddenly find myself floating in the air and spinning in circles until I was wide-awake.

She was pure joy.

"You're not concentrating."

Who was she kidding? I was concentrating so hard sweat soaked clean through the ridiculous red acolyte robe she forced me to wear. Who would *ever* choose to dress in this much fabric?

Apparently the Conclave were just as skittish about nudity as most everyone else, a fact she made apparent when I arrived at our first session in the buff. It wasn't my fault my clothes had been destroyed in the black flames that melted my flesh.

"I. *Am*. Concentrating."

She glided over to me, and though she still hid her identity behind her hood, the waves of displeasure radiated off her.

She smacked my lower back. "Stand up straight." She then kicked my right foot. "And widen your stance. You're trying to summon energy from the astral plane, not waiting for a quarterback to throw you the ball."

What was a quarterback? "I know precisely what I'm trying to do."

"Then *do* it."

Like it was that easy. I'd been standing there for over an hour, attempting to siphon ectoplasm, or the energy of the dead, from the other side, and all I had to show for my trouble was a pissed-off Hag and sweat dripping into my crack.

If Thad were here, he'd be so hot for me. He loved it when I got good and sweaty.

"Do you not realize how important this is?"

Of course I did. Based on what I'd read, extraplanar energy was a powerful weapon necromancers used against their enemies. It was volatile and quite explosive when it came into contact with living matter, which meant it would likely do a number even on Icarian. He might be a super powerful magical being, but he was still comprised of matter, just like the rest of us.

If I could harness it, I'd be able to hurt him. Bad.

"Focus!"

My entire body shook with effort. "I *am* focusing!"

"No. You are not."

I stepped out of the pose and whirled around to face her. "How do you expect me to concentrate with you yelling at me?"

"Yet you expect to be able to do so in the heat of battle against Icarian and his army of undead?"

"They'll be *my* army, and I'll use *them* to fight *him*."

She cackled. "You can't summon the required energy to fight him, much less manipulate the magic, and you expect to overpower his will and seize command of his forces?" She floated so close to me I could feel her hot breath fanning across my cheeks. Based on her nasty demeanor, I expected her to reek of rotten meat, not orange blossoms. "You think too highly of yourself, *Your Highness*."

I gritted my teeth. Her tone reminded me of Thad, and only he was allowed to use my royal title as a playful attempt at calling me stupid. "Don't call me that."

"Does that offend you?" She levitated in a circle around me. The gesture was clearly meant to intimidate me. All she was succeeding in doing was riling my temper, and most of the threats I'd faced in the past few months knew doing so proved dangerous.

"What offends me is the time we're wasting here arguing when we should be finding Icarian and putting a stop to his plans once and for all."

"If you faced Icarian right now, he would kill you in less time than it took for you to draw a breath."

My chest heaved and my fingertips burned. "I'm stronger than you realize."

"Not strong enough."

"Try me."

A force suddenly exerted itself on my chest, and I flew backward into one of the giant bookcases on the other side of the room. Pain exploded across my back before I fell to the floor, where books rained down around my head.

"What the hell do you think you're doing?" I slowly rose to my feet, fists clenched at my sides, but I was talking to empty air. The Warlock Hag was gone.

"Teaching you a lesson." Her voice echoed off the walls, and I craned my neck upward, searching the spiraling wooden path lined with bookcases. She wasn't hovering up there either.

"How? By playing hide-and-go-seek?"

"By showing you you're not ready to face Icarian."

A piano suddenly appeared in the middle of the room and flew right at me. I cursed and leaped out of the way as it crashed into the bookcase behind me. By the time I skidded to a stop, a refrigerator shimmered into view and headed in my direction. I hauled myself over the staircase railing and darted up the landing. Two seconds later the appliance obliterated the spot where I'd been standing.

"Is this your plan for facing Icarian?" She mocked me as I bounded up the staircase like a rabbit, dodging the television, microwave, and oven she sent barreling toward me. The owners of the house she was teleporting all these items from were going to be extremely upset when they got home. "Running away?"

Not even close. "I've got a few tricks up my arm."

Her laughter told me I'd gotten yet another human phrase wrong, but I didn't care. She was talking, and that was all I needed. While I might not be able to summon ectoplasm, I had acquired new spells in my arsenal. Yesterday she taught me how to use my newly heightened senses to not only read emotions but to detect life. As I bounded over a leather couch she almost squashed me with, I scanned the direction her voice emanated from and found her.

The Warlock Hag appeared as a glowing silver ball of energy on the ground floor of the library. Now that I knew where she was, I could do something about it.

I dashed up the stairs, running at full speed for the spot directly above her, and flew over the rail. My skeletal dragon wings spouted from my back, and with one flap, I sped down toward her at breakneck speed.

The ball of energy gazed up at me one second too late.

I slammed into her with such force the library walls shook. The impact sent me flying upward and the Warlock Hag rolling to the middle of the room. I landed with a thud a second later while she, now completely visible, struggled to stand.

Even though I hurt in places I didn't realize were possible, I couldn't help the wry smile that teased its way across my lips. I'd finally gotten her to shut the hell up. "What did you think about that?"

"Clever." She stood and faced me, not realizing that a part of her disguise had failed her. A stray tendril of auburn hair snaked out of the bottom of her hood. Seeing the reddish lock made me miss Thad more than ever. "You tracked me with the energy of my life force."

I held my head up high.

"Yet such stunts will not aid you in a battle with a foe who wants you dead."

Were the words *good job* too hard to say? "But you *do* want me dead, and so does the Conclave."

"I don't *want* you dead, Aiden." She no longer spoke in the royal *we*, and her words came out kind and compassionate. Either she meant what she said or kicking her ass had knocked some compassion into her. "I want the instability of magic to stop. Too much is at stake."

"You know, the Conclave says that a lot, but you never tell us *what* that means."

"And I won't expound on it today either. Knowledge is a tricky thing. Possessing it can be a blessing and a curse."

She wasn't telling me anything I didn't know. I knew Icarian's endgame, and if I didn't stop it, the man I loved might pay the price.

"Your thoughts betray you." She glided toward me, her red lock still on prominent display. "Your mind turns once again to Thad Blackmoor."

I narrowed my eyes and gazed deep into her hood. "Invading my thoughts without proper provocation breaks the laws, you—"

"I did no such thing. Whenever you think of him, the air hums."

That wasn't all that hummed when I imagined Thad.

"Please keep those emotions to yourself." She spun around and glided away. "They're most… inappropriate."

"You can read my emotions?"

She shook her head. "No. You are broadcasting them."

How was the possible? From everything I'd read, necromancers didn't possess empathic powers. Emotions were the domain of the living. "I don't understand."

"Neither do I." She paused before a bookshelf, and a tome floated from the top shelf and opened before her. "Despite the fact that you have embraced the power of a necromancer, you not only still retain some of your fae abilities, but those gifts appear to have been somehow heightened. It doesn't make sense."

No, it didn't, especially considering that she told me my fairy had died during my transformation. If it was still alive within me, did that mean my inner vampyre was still there too? I couldn't sense it if it was. "Am I somehow becoming a vampyre fae necromancer?"

Her shoulders tensed. "I… do not know." The book shut and she spun around to face me. "What I do know is that you still cling to your memories of Thad. How you still possess them is beyond me, but I believe it is those emotions that are part of the problem. You need to divest yourself of them at once."

Like I'd ever willingly do that. "I love Thad, and I will *never* abandon that or him."

"Then you doom us all."

The urgency in her voice was strangely familiar. The last time I'd heard someone speak with such certainty had been—

"What is it?"

Could it really be?

"Aiden, answer me."

I cocked my head and stared at her. "Are you… the oracle?"

"I do not possess precognitive abilities."

She was telling the truth. Not only could I sense it, but I didn't detect the stench of rotting fish. Still, she was withholding information. I was as certain of that as I was of my love for Thad.

The Warlock Hag had a secret, and my gut told me learning what that was would make all the difference, so I nodded to the stray reddish lock that still lay outside her hood. "But I see that you are a redhead."

She glanced down at the stray strand and immediately flipped it inside her hood. "Our session is over for today."

Yes. She was definitely hiding something. "Good. I'm tired anyway." I turned and headed toward the door.

"Aiden, I know this is hard for you, but you must heed my advice."

I glanced over my shoulder. "And what's that?"

"In order for you to do what needs to be done, you need to abandon all ties to your previous life. A necromancer operates in death. Your love for Thad keeps you rooted in life. It weakens you and places us all in jeopardy."

She was wrong. My love for Thad gave me all the strength I needed. Instead of replying, I walked out of the library and down the hall, but I wasn't going back to my room.

I was going to find the answers I needed.

I STOOD in the middle of a corridor. To the right was the path that would take me safely to my room, where the Warlock Hag and the rest of the Conclave expected me to be when I wasn't learning necromancy. A thin red carpet safely marked the passage that took me past alabaster walls with indecipherable mystical signs etched across the frieze, heavy wooden doors that wouldn't open when I tried them, and small square windows that allowed me to see Earth leaning over the horizon. Instead of marveling at the magical cosmic beauty that surrounded me, all I could envision was Thad.

More than anything, I needed him right now. He was my best friend and the smartest person I knew. He'd make sense of my suspicions about the Warlock Hag and whether or not she was the oracle who'd appeared to me in warning.

If she was the woman in the mist, I didn't understand *why* she would be trying to help me when she appeared to hate my family and me so vehemently. Of course, the Warlock Hag might not be the oracle at all. She hadn't been lying when she admitted to not having precognitive abilities, but she hadn't told the whole truth either. It had been more of an omission, but what had she left out?

That was why I longed to have Thad by my side. If I had the power or the mystical know-how, I'd open up a portal as I once did to travel between Earth and Otherworld. I'd appear before him and we'd come up with a plan together. Unfortunately, magic more powerful than the abilities at my command kept us apart.

That didn't mean I had to figure this out alone, though.

I had Gerald, and I was confident that once I located him, he'd have the answers I needed. Even though he worked with the Warlock Hag, I suspected they didn't get along. Their obvious antagonism seemed proof enough of that. If I shared my suspicions about her with him, he might have some clue as to her motivation.

After all, if she was the oracle, that meant she was working independently of the Conclave, and after the way she had treated us, I couldn't trust *anything* she said or did.

That was why I had to find Gerald, but to do that, I had to either head straight or turn left. Either way, I'd be venturing into the unknown and taking my life into my hands.

According to the Warlock Hag, the passageways were enchanted. Only the Conclave could navigate the halls of the Veil without getting lost or activating a magical booby trap designed to destroy intruders. But I had to take that chance.

"So which way should I go?"

The hallway in front of me appeared to go on farther than I could see. Although candles nestled in their sconces lit the way, no doors or windows lined the gray stone walls in that direction. It had to be an illusion designed to keep me from venturing down that corridor.

The passageway on the left only went on about six feet before veering to the right. One doorway was visible from where I stood, and a small square window gazed out into the courtyard below, allowing a cool, refreshing breeze to wrap its arms around me in comfort. That trail certainly appeared safer, which was precisely why I wasn't going to take it.

"Here goes everything." I held my breath and stepped off the red carpet and into the corridor in front of me.

No alarms sounded, and no hidden booby traps activated. Perhaps the Warlock Hag had lied. Maybe protection spells didn't safeguard the hallways inside the Veil. If that was true, the Warlock Hag *couldn't* be trusted.

Two steps later, the grinding of stone preceded a brick wall slamming down behind me in a cloud of dust.

Well, that answered that.

Going back the way I'd come was no longer an option. To make matters worse, the long corridor that had previously stretched out before me now branched out in seven different directions. Each path looked identical to all the others, dimly lit and ominous.

My gut told me only one of those corridors would take me where I needed to go. The others would likely lead to a never-ending maze or a spell powerful enough to kill an undead necromancer. I had to find some way to use the spells the Warlock Hag had taught me to direct my path.

So I did what the Warlock Hag had been asking me to do. I closed my eyes and my senses to life and opened them up to death.

A deep chill settled across my flesh like permafrost, but strangely enough, I didn't shiver. I wasn't so much cold as I could sense an absence of warmth, as if every molecule of heat that had once been housed within my body suddenly vanished.

My heart no longer raced in my ears. Even when I was a vampyre, the sluggish beat kept tune to my low respiration, since my body didn't need to pump blood or circulate oxygen to survive. The blood I'd fed on had done that. Now even those bodily functions had shut off.

All this occurred when I simply opened myself up to death energy. What would happen to me when I fully embraced it as the Warlock Hag wanted me to do?

"Aiden, are you there?"

My eyes fluttered open, and I scanned my surroundings. Only long shadows and hissing torches surrounded me.

"Can you hear me?" The voice was faint but familiar.

"Aunt Millie?"

"Yes. It's about time you heard me." Her tone reminded me of an exasperated parent speaking to a child. *"I've been calling to you for hours."*

How could Drake's vampyre aunt be in the Veil? I studied the shifting shadows lining the corridor for her skulking form. "Where are you?"

"You're a necromancer now. You tell me."

I had no idea what that even meant. I might be a necromancer, but I'd yet to learn everything I was capable of doing. "I don't know how."

Her sigh practically resonated off the walls. *"You're thinking too much. Stop trying and just do it."*

Now she sounded just like the Warlock Hag, but perhaps they were both right. Magic wasn't something you could force. It flowed out of you as naturally as the air that left your lungs. Whenever I had summoned the flame of the fae or my vampyren form, I hadn't thought about it. I'd just done it as if I were reaching out to catch a falling object.

The moves had to be instinctual if I ever hoped to become what I needed to be to face Icarian.

So once again I shut my eyes, floating the last image of Aunt Millie to the surface of my consciousness. I could not only see her terror, but her emotion filled my mouth with something akin to rusty nails.

A second later my consciousness spread across the magical expanse.

I was no longer staring down the darkened corridor where I stood. It was the middle of the night, and I found myself in a forest surrounded by the other vampyren. They stared at me—well, at Aunt Millie, since I was gazing at them through her eyes—and stood tall as if ready to be given commands.

For the first time I truly understood the magnitude of my power, which went well beyond summoning ectoplasm. The Warlock Hag had told me the dead were mine to command, but I didn't understand what that truly meant. It didn't just mean I could tell them what to do. It meant they basically became extensions of me.

Dozens of questions flooded my mind, but only one bubbled to the surface: How was this even possible? Gerald had said time had been slowed down in the Veil. If Aunt Millie and I were conversing in real time, that meant the Veil and Earth were now in temporal synch. What did that mean?

That was when I noticed the structure that stood in the distance. It was Blackmoor Manor.

My fists clenched, and I spoke through gritted teeth. "What are you doing at the Blackmoors'?"

"We've been watching them ever since you left."

"Why?"

"Because they're in danger, and that means so is Drake."

Her announcement rattled me so much I almost lost the connection. "From who?"

"If I have to tell you that, then you haven't been paying attention the past few months."

Now I understood why Drake and Mason adored her so much. Even though Aunt Millie was conversing with a magical being capable of ordering her to drive a stake through her own heart, she took great joy in being as difficult and ornery as possible.

"Is Icarian there?"

"No, but the Blackmoors are up to something."

Of course they were, and that was one of the many reasons I loved them all. "Like what?"

"See for yourself."

As she drew closer, I noticed the strange bands of violet hovering over their house like a magical aurora borealis. Only the casting of a powerful spell reflected in the natural world. I had no idea what type of incantation they were working on, but my gut told me it involved rescuing me.

"There's something else."

Naturally. Like life wasn't already beyond complicated. I couldn't help rolling my eyes. Well, actually her eyes, which felt kind of weird.

"Don't you roll my eyes at me! I'm not the one who started this magical mess in the first place."

She was right. Aunt Millie and the rest of the vampyren were victims, so I took a deep breath. "What is it?"

"Something's coming. I can feel it. We all can."

That could only mean one thing: Icarian and his zombies were on their way—and I was stuck in the Veil. If my instincts were right, whatever Thad and his family were planning would come too late. I had to get to them by any means necessary.

"I'll be there as soon as I can."

"Where are you? We haven't been able to sense you."

"I'm in the Veil."

"You're where?" The vampyren gathered around her. *"You need to g—"*

The forest and the vampyren disappeared, and I opened my eyes to the corridor within the Veil. My connection to Aunt Millie hadn't just been lost. It had been severed, most likely by Icarian.

If he knew I was talking to Aunt Millie, then he most likely knew I had become a necromancer and would be able to stop him. I had to find Gerald and convince him to send me back to Havenbridge before Icarian lashed out at Thad and my family.

So I turned back to the series of corridors stretching out before me, and instead of thinking about what to do, I waved my hand in an arc, commanding my magic to find me a path that wouldn't lead to my death.

Dark currents of energy flowed out of all but one of the passageways. If I traveled down any of those corridors, I'd be facing death in one form or another. Death energy didn't radiate out of the second hallway on the right, so that was the corridor I chose.

Another brick wall slammed down behind me, but instead of another maze of corridors, a hallway no more than twelve feet long opened up before me. Wooden doors lined the left side, and a succession of windows no bigger than three feet wide cut into the ivory walls on the other, allowing me to see the tops of the trees that covered most of the floating island.

I'd made it out of the maze of magical traps. All I had left to do was locate Gerald.

Being able to sense death wouldn't find him, and I couldn't track him by homing in on his life force like I'd done with the Warlock Hag, especially not inside a castle with eight other living beings. There had to be some way to distinguish his life energy from everyone else's. What made Gerald different from the other members of the Conclave?

The answer came to me in a flash of fair skin, hazel eyes, and strawberry-blond hair that made my stomach flutter. "Thad."

He and Gerald had a personal connection that had existed prior to his ascension to the Conclave. They'd not only been friends, but Gerald had been Thad's confidant for years before Gerald's supposed death. In necromancy terms, Thad and Gerald's friendship meant their souls resonated with each other, and whether the Warlock Hag liked it or not, my soul still reverberated with Thad's.

I could use the vibrations of that force to pull me toward the only other person in the Veil who shared a link to the warlock I loved.

I closed my eyes again, this time bringing forth a mental image of Thad. His hazel eyes sparkled as he gazed up at me from his place on my chest, and his seductive smile sent a series of vibrations thrumming across my flesh. When Thad twined his fingers with mine, the shuddering pulses became stronger, more resonant, and reached deep into my soul.

It produced a visible wavelength that wrapped around me in gentle flowing waves—it almost felt like actually having Thad in my arms. I plucked those cords and the energy sang, sending magical pulses radiating outward and searching for a vibration similar to the one that rejoiced in my soul.

A hum pinged back to me from a few feet away. Its song was as vibrant as the tune Thad's memory played in my soul. I had no idea Thad and Gerald were that close.

I followed the vibrations down the hall, to the left, and through another maze of hallways that took me by glass mosaics depicting the history of the *homo magus*, statues erected in honor of past members of the Conclave, and more wooden doors that wouldn't budge.

The farther I traveled, though, the stronger the resonance became, and even though it played to a different key than the one in my soul, the music proved just as vibrant as the symphony Thad had created in my soul.

I arrived in front of a heavy wooden door that resembled all the others I'd seen so far. I took a deep breath and placed my hand upon the knob.

To my surprise, it opened.

"Gerald?"

I peeked inside, but he wasn't sitting on the blue chesterfield couch in the forward chamber or at the rectangular white-and-gold-leaf desk that sat between two expansive bookshelves along the far wall. I stepped inside and shut the door behind me as I gazed into the small hallway to the left that likely led to Gerald's sleeping quarters.

"Gerald, are you back there?"

No response drifted toward me from the back room. How was it possible for him *not* to be here? Based on the energy I'd detected, Gerald should have been in his room. It didn't make sense for the vibrations of the chamber itself to resonate so powerfully with energy connected to Thad, but it had and it still did.

Why?

I scanned the worn spines of the leather-bound books among the bookshelves for an answer. Judging by the cracked and dusty bindings, they contained ancient tomes of magic on subjects ranging from aerokinesis to vapor manipulation. Those were bizarre topics to find in a wizard's personal collection. They typically confined their arcane studies to texts that dealt with enhancing their already profound mental gifts.

The open books on premonition piled upon the desk, however, made sense. Gerald had been researching oracles and their abilities. Perhaps he hoped to use the magic at his command to find her, not realizing she was most likely closer than he imagined.

While knowing that our friend was still looking out for us gave me hope, it didn't explain the resonant energy that came from this room. Only the most powerful of bonds left behind such lasting echoes, and what I sensed went beyond the friendship Thad and Gerald had shared.

What puzzle piece was I missing?

My gaze immediately fell upon the narrow hallway leading to Gerald's bedroom, and instinct told me the answer was in there. I'd already entered Gerald's chamber uninvited. If I walked into his bedroom, I'd be violating more than his personal space.

I'd be potentially angering a friend.

I didn't have a choice. Icarian was gathering his forces, and they were likely headed straight for Thad. I dashed down the hallway and into his room. When I pushed open the door, I did a double take.

A picture of the Blackmoors rested on the bedstand, and along the left wall hung various images of Thad, his brothers, and his father throughout the years. In one photograph, a teenage Pierce draped his arm around a preteen Thad, whose scowl showed how much he didn't want to be in the picture. Even as a young grump, Thad still made my heart flutter. In another image, Mason, who had to be no more than three, wobbled toward his beaming father. There was a photo of Thad and his brothers dressed in their best for Yule, another of Thad sitting by himself while reading, and a half-dozen others capturing various moments of the Blackmoors' lives.

But the most surprising photo of them all was the family portrait.

Mrs. Blackmoor sat in a red chair with Mr. Blackmoor beaming behind her. His right hand lovingly rested on her shoulder, and Pierce, Thad, and Mason gathered around their mother with big smiles plastered across their faces. Thad told me it had been the last photo taken of the five of them before Priscilla Blackmoor succumbed to the cancer.

This same picture hung in the main hallway of Blackmoor Manor.

"Aiden?"

I tensed at the unfamiliar intonation and spun around.

It was the Warlock Hag. The metallic tone to her voice had vanished, and her hood no longer covered her head. It hung loosely around her beautiful features, and the same bright red hair from the photo on the wall cascaded around her thin shoulders.

"Mrs. Blackmoor?"

CHAPTER 12

I STOOD there for several seconds, completely incapable of speech. Although many questions crowded the tip of my tongue, the realization that the Warlock Hag was actually Thad's mother prevented me from giving any of them voice.

"Why don't we head back to the living area and sit down?" She turned to walk away before glancing back at me over her shoulder. "That is *if* you're capable of movement."

I wasn't entirely certain I could put one foot in front of the other. My entire world had been turned upside down. How was it possible for Thad's mother to be alive?

"Sit down and I'll get you some tea."

Her voice brought me out of my thoughts, and I was surprised to find myself standing in front of the couch in the forward chamber. When had I walked here from the bedroom?

"I'm sure you have many questions."

I did—far too many—but I still couldn't speak. Instead, I fell back onto the sofa as my mind did its best to make sense of everything.

Now that I knew the Warlock Hag was Priscilla Blackmoor, it explained why my spell had brought me to her chamber. Her room was practically a shrine to the life she once lived, and it was the resonating energy of a mother's love that my magic had picked up on.

After all, a parent's love was one of the strongest forces in the universe. I'd seen it at work most every day for the past few months in Mr. Blackmoor. His love for his children guided his actions and turned a strong man into a virtually indestructible warlock. He was always there for his sons, and he never abandoned them.

Unlike my father *and* Mrs. Blackmoor.

Flames of anger licked across my cheeks when the magnitude of her deception sank in. "Y-you're alive?"

She glanced up from where she had conjured up two cups of steaming tea. "I'd respond to that question if the answer weren't so obvious." Even though a thin smile spread across her hard features, the mocking lilt of her tone caused my lips to scowl and my heart to skip a beat. It was eerie how much she sounded like Thad.

"But how? You had cancer." I glared up at her. "Or was that a lie too?"

She handed me my cup and sighed. "No. I definitely had cancer, and my prognosis was bleak." She sat at the other end of the couch, cradling the cup in her hands. "And it broke my heart to see what my illness did to my family. They were falling apart, doing their best to find a cure. Oliver and Pierce searched for human remedies while my Thaddy…." She said his name with such tenderness, it was easy to see how much she favored him above all. "Well, he turned to magic, hoping to find some spell that would either dissolve the cancer or somehow make me immune to its effects."

I'd already heard all this. Thad had told me how relentlessly they'd searched for a way to save his mother and how they even contemplated locating the *immortalitas* spell. They had been willing to risk everything for her, and she repaid them by abandoning them. "But you didn't die." I waved at the room. "You came here?"

She took a sip of her tea. "I was just as surprised by that then as you are now. I may have been a member of a protector coven, but like everyone else, I had no knowledge of how one ascended to the Conclave. Evidently when one of the Conclave passes, as one did prior to my 'death,' the Gate chooses the replacement, and it chose me. After I took what I thought was my final breath, surrounded by my family, I woke up in this chamber, fully healed from cancer, and learned I had ascended to the Conclave."

"That doesn't make sense. Why choose someone who is dying to replace someone who just died? Wouldn't it be simpler if the Gate just kept the Conclave from dying?"

"We aren't gods, Aiden. We aren't meant to be immortal or all-knowing. Ascending to the Conclave is a duty bestowed only upon those the Gate feels are worthy. Once we have served our role, the Gate calls us back home and the process begins again."

Her recount didn't match what Gerald had told us months ago about his ascension. He had claimed his death was staged. Why were their ascensions to the Conclave so different? That was a mystery the Conclave would likely never clear up. They enjoyed their secrets, and based on Mrs. Blackmoor's wry grin, she took pleasure in them as well. "And you let Thad and everyone else think you were dead? Do you realize how much they grieved for you? The family almost fell apart after you were gone."

She glanced away for a second before returning her gaze to me. "I understand the pain my husband and sons have endured, but it was a choice I had to make. Our identities must remain anonymous for our protection as well as to protect the loved ones we leave behind."

"Bull!" I stood and threw the cup of tea into the wall, where it shattered into hundreds of pieces. If I were still a vampyre, I'd have already shifted and lunged for her throat. "I've seen what *good* parents do, and they don't let their loved ones hurt the way you did. Instead of choosing to let them know you were alive, you chose power over your family. *That* was the choice you made."

She didn't blink and didn't even seem affected by my outburst. Instead, she took another sip from her cup. "Don't confuse my actions with those of your father, Aiden."

I took a step toward her, and she arched an eyebrow in response.

"And don't misinterpret my rather calm demeanor to mean I won't knock you on your ass." Mrs. Blackmoor glanced at my clenched fists before leveling her gaze at me. It was her way of commanding me to stand down. When I did, she continued. "You have no concept of what I have done or why. You see the world through your rather limited perspective while I see it on a much grander scale."

I took several deep breaths before the desire to rip open her throat faded. The uncontrollable anger rising within me reminded me of the vampyre I'd once been. Perhaps it was still a part of me after all. "What do you mean?"

"You think I've chosen power over my family, but that isn't the case. I embraced being a member of the Conclave for one reason—to protect my family at all costs."

Who was she kidding? From the moment she first spoke to us, she'd set herself up as our adversary. "How can you say that? You've berated the Blackmoors ever since Yule. You almost killed Pierce and Mason. You were the driving force that ousted the Blackmoors as a protector coven. How do *any* of those actions show you *protecting* your family?"

"It's all about perspective." She placed her cup on the brass coffee table that materialized in front of the sofa and sat back. "I have it, and you don't."

I ran my fingers through my hair. Talking to her was just as aggravating as conversing with Pierce and Mason. "What does that even mean?"

"It means I know things you don't. In fact, I know things *many* don't, including the Conclave."

I had been right. "You *are* the oracle, aren't you?"

She smiled up at me as if I couldn't spell my own name. "I never claimed to be an oracle. That was what *you* made me out to be. But yes, I was the woman in the mist."

"But you said you had a vision and that it brought you to me."

"Correct, but I'm not an oracle." She swirled her hand as if she were stirring a pot, and fog suddenly formed in the room. "My active power is mist, and while that ability may seem benign, it is not. As I've grown stronger, so has my ability. Not only can I use it to blind an enemy or fill his lungs with vapor until he drowns, but I'm also able to command the mist to reflect scenes from the future and use that knowledge to keep my family safe."

"How does getting your family kicked out as a protector coven keep them safe?"

She took a deep breath before answering. "Because based on the future I have seen, the protector coven for the Order of the Black will die."

Without thinking, I grabbed her by the shoulders and yanked her to a standing position. "Thad and his family are going to die, and you wait until *now* to tell me?"

Her voice dropped to barely a whisper. "Release me immediately or you will understand how deadly I can truly be."

I let her go and stepped away. Based upon the scarlet flush to her cheeks, she had been a second away from keeping true to her word. I swallowed back the anger that burned a path down my throat as I worked to regain my calm. Losing my temper would get me nowhere with a woman of her power.

"I'm... sorry." I had to force the word out of my mouth. I'd obviously inherited a warlock's distaste for apologizing. "But I love Thad and the rest of your family. The thought of anything bad happening to them terrifies me."

She exhaled, clearly attempting to release her anger before it exploded out of her. It was something Mr. Blackmoor had done on countless occasions, and the gesture reminded me that despite her faults, she was a mother doing her best to save those she loved. "I understand. Why else do you think I sought you out and shared my visions with you? I needed you to embrace your transformation into a necromancer. From what we've *both* seen, it's the only way to stop Icarian and his zombies."

"You *knew* what the visions meant all along?"

She took a deep breath. "All except the blood drop. I still have no clue what it symbolizes other than a difficult choice you must make."

"Then why not just *tell* me?"

"And what would you have had me do, Aiden?" She pressed her lips into a white slash. "Pop into your bedroom and inform you that you were becoming a necromancer? I would have needlessly revealed myself to my family, which would only have distracted them from their mission, and shown my hand to the Conclave and possibly Icarian. There is a grand magical game being played here, and the only way to win is to play smart."

How did Mr. Blackmoor have anything in common with this woman? She was cold and ruthless, the complete opposite of the kind and loving man I'd come to know as my father. Sure, he could be grumpier than a bear woken up midhibernation, but he didn't place beating Icarian above the welfare of his sons.

"Is that all that's important to you? Winning?"

"You unfairly judge me for my actions because all you can see is the world from your—once again, very *limited*—perspective. Whatever moves I've made have been to secure the safety of my family."

I crossed my arms over my chest. "How does convincing the Conclave to remove them as a protector coven keep them safe? It places them in even *more* danger."

"No. It does not. A few months ago, while summoning images from the future in my mist, I saw the protector covens were locked in combat with a powerful magical being that could only be Icarian, and it was during that battle—" She took a deep breath and shivered. "—that the warlock protector coven was killed in one sweeping blow."

I couldn't imagine how horrifying it would be to see the deaths of her family unfold before her, and I also understood she would do anything to save them. Armed with that knowledge, I would have considered every available alternative to save Thad and the rest of my family. But was that even possible? Fate flowed like a mighty river. Nothing could alter its course. "I still don't understand how this changes anything. If the Blackmoors are supposed to—" I couldn't even think about it much less say the word.

"My family's fate is *not* set in stone. The only reason they were at the battle was because they were a protector coven, so by removing them from their station—"

"You removed them from the consequence."

"Exactly."

But if that was true—if my family was no longer slated to die—that meant someone else had to travel the path destiny had already set. Frost settled across my flesh as I returned my gaze to Mrs. Blackmoor's even stare. "And the Edwells? What will happen to them?"

She gathered her black robes around her and sniffed. "It was either my family or those sniveling weasels. What choice would you have made?"

My head spun. While she may have saved her family, she had condemned another to death. I understood the desperation. Just the thought of death reaching for Thad with its cold, uncaring hands had made me choose to embrace necromancy, which potentially threatened our blood tie. But I couldn't comprehend the indifference with which she treated the Edwells and their lives. They might be awful people, but they didn't deserve to die any more than the Blackmoors did.

"I would've found an alternative to sacrificing another family."

"There was *no* other way."

"How can you say that? You're a member of the Conclave. You know things that precious few of us do. With your power, you should have been able to find another course of action that saved more than just your family. I thought the Conclave was supposed to protect *all* members of the magical community, including the Edwells."

Mrs. Blackmoor bristled. "I won't have you or anyone else call my actions into question. I did what I had to do to save my family, and I'd sacrifice the Edwells or a thousand other covens to ensure my family's safety."

"That sounds like something Icarian or Bartram Kane would say."

If the scowl that marched across her face was any indication, I was definitely pressing my luck. "I'm nothing like them."

"Really? Bartram didn't care about the magical or human communities when he cast the *immortalitas* spell to save his son, and Icarian is willing to sacrifice anything, including magic or the lives of your sons, to prevent the Prophecy of the Three."

I instantly regretted the words as soon as they left my mouth.

Mrs. Blackmoor suddenly stood in front of me. Her narrowed eyes studied me closely. "What did you say?" When I didn't answer, she grabbed my shoulders and lifted my six-foot-four and over-two-hundred-pound frame off the floor. "Tell me what you know. Right. *Now.*"

If I didn't respond, I ran the risk of never being able to speak, much less breathe, again. I certainly couldn't protect Thad from my grave, so when she returned my feet to the stone floor, I filled her in on what I knew of Icarian's motives.

IT WAS Mrs. Blackmoor's turn to be speechless. She stumbled back toward the couch and lowered herself onto its cushions. "*That's* why Icarian has been trying to end magic? Because he fears my sons are the brothers from a prophecy no one has mentioned in over a millennium?"

"You know of it?" My heart raced. Maybe now I could finally learn what exactly the prophecy said. "Can you tell me about it?"

She waved my question away as if it were an annoying gnat. "I've never read it. All I know is that it was of grave concern to the first Conclave but hasn't been deemed a true threat for ages." She glared at me. "How do *you* know of it?"

I was glad Drake wasn't here. This wasn't going to go over well. "Icarian mentioned it to Drake during our last battle with him."

A storm raged across her expression as the coffee table in front of her cracked in two before flying into the far wall and exploding in a spray of wooden splinters. "That foolish little witch hunter should have revealed what he knew immediately."

"That foolish little witch hunter saved Mason's life and has been doing everything in his power to keep the rest of your sons safe."

"How?" She rose from the couch, trembling. The remaining furniture in her chamber bowed as her power continued to rattle the room. The bookshelves spilled their contents onto the floor as the furniture bent in half, the dishes clattered and shook as tiny fractures cracked across their surfaces, and her couch slowly folded in on itself. "By keeping this knowledge a secret? All he's done is expose Pierce, Thad, *and* Mason to more danger."

I crossed my arms over my chest and glared at her temper tantrum. Now I understood why Pierce and Mason flew off the handle so easily. "And what should Drake have done? Tell Mason and the rest of your family? What do you think your sons would have done with that knowledge?"

Her furniture snapped back into their usual positions, and her china stopped rattling. She stood tall and shook her red locks from her face. "They would have sacrificed themselves to save each other and all of magic."

"Yes. Unlike you, they wouldn't have allowed others to die in their place."

Her upper lip curled into a snarl, but she didn't bark or cause another object to almost self-destruct. Instead, Mrs. Blackmoor spoke in cool, measured tones. "Perhaps, but that doesn't change the fact that Drake

Carpenter should have revealed what he knew to the Conclave. We've been searching all of magic to understand Icarian's motives. Now that we know what they are, we can stop him." She pulled back her sleeves as if she were about to cast a spell. "I must summon the others at once."

"No." I dashed to her side, and though I was gambling with my own life, I clasped her forearm and forced her gaze to mine. "You can't do that."

She eyed my hand before withdrawing from my grasp. "And why is that?"

How could she not see the consequences of such an action? "Considering what you know of the Conclave's past, what do you think *they* would do if you told them why Icarian wanted to bring about the Spell Fall?"

She darted her gaze across the floor, no doubt recalling the Conclave's rather murky past. She knew better than anyone her colleagues' long history of sacrificing others for personal gain. They had banished my people to Otherworld and the shifters to Aeaea because they feared their potential threat. Even more, they'd used their enemies to protect the Crests of the Five.

They'd have no problem making the Blackmoors a convenient scapegoat.

Mrs. Blackmoor took a step back, her face slack. "They wouldn't. Would they?"

"Do you want to take the chance that they *wouldn't* agree with Icarian?"

She took a deep breath and gathered her robes. "I… do not."

"Good." That was one less thing for me to worry about, and I hadn't even addressed the fact that Icarian was likely on his way to Havenbridge with his horde of zombies. We needed a plan, and we needed one fast. "You and I have to figure out a way to stop Icarian on our own, without involving the Conclave or Thad and the others."

She nodded and took another deep breath. "It's the only way we can guarantee my family's safety."

She was finally using her brain instead of her magical brawn. "That's right, and they're in danger, if what Aunt Millie told me is true."

"You spoke to her? When?" After I told her what had happened during my search for Gerald, she regarded me with an arched eyebrow. "You successfully used a portion of your power as a necromancer."

Yes, I had, and obviously her nod was all the praise I'd get. "I might not be able to summon ectoplasm, but I might have just enough power to take on Icarian."

"No. As long as you love my son, you're straddling the line between life and death." She held out her hands. A brick-shaped golden box shimmered onto her palms. Flecks of silver twined around the edges, and a pentangle had been etched onto the lid. "But with *this*, we might be able to level the playing field."

"What is it?"

The cover opened. Resting on the red felt inside sat the missing crown of the Beast King. My breath hitched as I met her gaze. "*You* were the one who stole the Air Crest?"

"Obviously." She took it from the box and slid her fingertips across the circlet of gold. "Once I knew what Icarian was after and where this crest was located, I retrieved it before Icarian could."

I would have given her a kiss, but I suspected she'd knock me into the next universe. Instead, the constant dread that had been constricting my chest for the past few months eased its hold upon me. With the Air Crest in Mrs. Blackmoor's possession and within the protection of the Veil, Icarian would not be able to get his hands on it and bring about the Spell Fall.

"You get ahead of yourself." Her words brought me out of my thoughts, and her narrowed gaze told me that I'd been celebrating prematurely. Obviously I'd been broadcasting my emotions again. "We have *one* of the Crests of the Five. Icarian possesses two."

That wasn't necessarily true. "But you know where the Water Crest is. You told us that during Imbolc. If you get it, then we'll have two as well."

"If only it was as simple as you make it out to be. Extracting the Water Crest from its safe house would yield consequences you and the rest of my family would certainly find… objectionable."

"What do you mean?"

She studied me carefully, obviously trying to determine whether to let me in on this particular secret. A quick exhalation told me she'd arrived at her decision. "Drake Carpenter, the witch hunter who has so enthralled my youngest son and become a part of *my* family, *is* the Water Crest. If I remove it from his soul, he will die."

I leaned forward as if I hadn't heard her correctly. "Drake is one of the Crests of the Five?" Her nod practically pulled the carpet out from under me. That explained why Drake was immune to magic and why Icarian had been able to use the crests he did possess to get around Drake's immunity a few weeks ago. Unfortunately, it also told us something else. "And Icarian knows that, doesn't he?"

"Yes." Mrs. Blackmoor straightened her shoulders. "And I'm uncertain how Icarian intuited that information. I feigned ignorance as to the cause of Drake's magical immunity to keep the truth a secret from everyone, including the rest of the Conclave, but somehow Icarian figured it out."

And almost killed Drake as a result.

That was when it hit me. "That's why Icarian's on his way to Havenbridge with his zombies. He intends to use them to get the crest from Drake."

Her eyes narrowed. She clearly hadn't considered that. "It makes sense."

"Of course it does."

We jumped as a metallic voice suddenly boomed all around us as if God was speaking from a bullhorn. I recognized it immediately.

It was Icarian, and he had somehow found a way into the Veil.

CHAPTER 13

MRS. BLACKMOOR flung open the door to her bedroom and stepped into the hall. The torches that lit the corridor had been snuffed out, and a cold breeze blew through the castle.

"How did he get in here?"

She glanced over her shoulder. Her flinty gaze had rounded. "I'm uncertain. Penetrating our defenses should have been impossible. The incantation that keeps the Veil separated from the earthly plane has never before been broken."

"Why go through the trouble of breaking such a complicated spell?" Icarian's voice floated like a ghost around us. It wasn't malevolent or even threatening. Instead, he spoke to us as if we were old friends who'd run into each other on the street. It made the hair on the back of my head stand straight up. "It's easier to simply walk through the front door."

How powerful had Icarian become if not even a spell from the Conclave could stop him? That was a question I didn't really want an answer to. There was one question, however, I did need answered. If Icarian was here, had the Blackmoors survived his attack? "What have you done with my family?"

"I haven't caused any *permanent* harm." The cheerfulness in his disembodied voice made me shiver. "And I won't have to if you give me the Air Crest."

Mrs. Blackmoor's eyes flashed fire. She held the crown to her breast as she turned her gaze to me. "We can't let him take it. It will only increase his already formidable power."

That was definitely something we didn't need. "We have t—"

Low growls filled the corridor, accompanied by the stench of putrid flesh.

"I see the gifts I brought have arrived." Icarian's joyful tone had me imagining him clasping his hands and smiling at his gesture. He was as crazy as he was powerful.

Mrs. Blackmoor stepped farther into the hall, and I quickly followed her. We stood shoulder to shoulder, trying to pierce the veil of darkness that had engulfed the passageway, but I could barely see my hand in front of my face.

"Are the two of you afraid of the dark?"

Mrs. Blackmoor sniffed at Icarian's question. "Hardly." Three glowing orbs hovered above us. The magical spheres provided a cone of light that illuminated twelve feet before us, but even though I could hear the growls and shuffling of dozens of feet, our approaching enemy remained blanketed in the shadows.

Mrs. Blackmoor turned to me. "Are you ready to use your new abilities?"

"I hope so," Icarian replied with more eagerness than I cared for. It told me he expected me to fail, and I snarled at the air in response. "I've been waiting for this moment ever since I heard of your impending transformation. Let's see what you can do."

I wasn't certain what that was exactly. I'd been able to see Mrs. Blackmoor's life force, manipulate soul resonance, and enter Aunt Millie's mind, but I still couldn't summon ectoplasm—the most important part of my arsenal. I could only hope that being able to link psyches with Aunt Millie also meant I could force my will upon Icarian's undead army, but I couldn't let him see my doubt. Instead I puffed out my chest and channeled Pierce. "Bring it."

"I most definitely will."

I could practically see him nodding in anticipation.

The growling zombies hobbled into the mystical light. Dozens of pairs of milk-white eyes settled upon us. Their thin gray flesh looked like rotten meat, and it sagged off their bones as if they were wearing oversized clothes. They bared their teeth, which reminded me of broken tombstones, and snapped their jaws. The horde lurched forward, clawing at the air, ready to feast upon our flesh.

I held my hands outward as Mrs. Blackmoor had taught me, focusing my magic through my fingertips as I reached into their minds.

Eat. Kill. Eat. Kill.

Just as in my vision, the only thoughts that resonated in their hive-like mind were of death and destruction. It ripped through me like a windstorm filled with razor blades, which made it difficult to concentrate.

I winced through the pain. "I command you to stop."

The zombies ambled forward, their jaws still clacking and the distance between us shrinking.

Icarian chuckled.

"I said. *Stop!*"

Only six feet now separated us from being eaten alive as they continued their stumbling advance.

"Aiden." Mrs. Blackmoor rested her hand upon my shoulder. "Now would be a good time to do something."

As if I wasn't trying. I could hear them, but they either couldn't hear me or were ignoring me all together. I clenched my jaw, forcing every ounce of willpower into the word I next spoke. "Stop!"

It didn't work. Icarian's hold over them was too strong for me to break.

The zombies lunged, but before their decaying, oozing hands could grasp us, Mrs. Blackmoor summoned a wall of solid mist that acted as a barrier. The zombies pressed against the fog as if it were glass. They clawed at the obstacle in a frenzied attempt to reach us.

"I'd say that's cheating." Why did Icarian sound pleased rather than upset?

Mrs. Blackmoor ignored his irritating commentary and glared at me. "Your performance was unimpressive."

She was right. I was supposed to be the solution to defeating Icarian by taking control of his undead army, but how could I do that when they shrugged off my commands?

"I told you that clinging to your love for Thad would prove problematic. You must let it go. In order to command the dead, you must abandon your ties to life. It's the *only* way."

Was she right and Gerald wrong? He believed my blood tie to Thad would be the solution. I had to figure it out, quickly. If I didn't, if I made the wrong decision, the consequences would be devastating.

Icarian's voice broke my thoughts. "Are you ready for a surprise?"

A hand clutched Mrs. Blackmoor's robe and pulled her forward. She gasped as she almost fell into the snapping jaws of one of the zombies. It had eaten its way through her wall of mist and reached through the opening to claim its meal. What shocked me even more was that the zombie appeared to increase its mass as it ate.

I grabbed her by the shoulder and clutched the zombie's arm. The zombie snarled and gnashed in reply. While I might not be able to command them, I still had my strength. I ripped its arm from the socket and tore the still-grasping limb from her robe before tossing it aside.

"That shouldn't have been possible." She stared at the gathered zombies as they continued gnawing upon the mist, tearing bite-size chunks of it away as if it were cotton candy. As they feasted, they continued to increase in size.

"Ah, but it is." The smugness in Icarian's tone pissed me off. "And that's because they're…."

Mrs. Blackmoor froze and took two steps back.

I shifted my gaze from the horde back to her. "Unless they're what?"

"Magic-eaters," she whispered.

My stomach sank as Icarian shouted, "Surprise!"

Not only had Icarian brought the dead back to life as zombies, but he'd created a new magical species that consumed both flesh *and* magic.

That made them deadlier and more powerful than the vampyren, and without access to firearms, it also made them almost impossible to stop.

MOMENTS AFTER the zombies had eaten their way through the foggy barrier, Mrs. Blackmoor grabbed my hand, and the world shimmered around me. A second later we stood in the room with the blue marble tiled floors and the columns upon which the Conclave had perched when I first arrived in the Veil.

This time, however, the robed figures didn't stand in judgment upon their roosts.

"Where are the others?" Mrs. Blackmoor scanned the empty room. "They should be here."

I closed my eyes and cleared all thought from my mind. If I focused too hard, this wouldn't work. I had to let the magic guide me instead of trying to bend it to my will. When I opened my eyes, the silver ball of energy I'd tracked in the library had replaced Mrs. Blackmoor's corporeal form.

"What are you doing?" her ball of energy asked.

Instead of answering, I cast a spell to find other life forces in the castle. Mystical tethers coiled out of my fingertips. They coalesced and took the form of a pack of mint green bloodhounds that immediately sniffed the air and sprinted from the room.

My mind ran with them down the corridors, passing through wooden and brick barriers as if they didn't exist. When they crossed paths with the zombies who clamored to make them a meal, they dodged through their flailing arms and scoured the antechambers, the library, and every room within the Veil only to return to my feet, whimpering.

They found nothing.

"Aiden?"

The hounds disappeared, and I glanced at Mrs. Blackmoor, who was once again flesh and blood. "They aren't in the Veil."

"Impossible." She closed her eyes, no doubt using her own magic to search the area. "I would have detected their departure."

That wasn't necessarily true. After all, she had snuck out of the Veil and taken the Air Crest from the shifters. That meant there was at least one secret way in and out of this magical fortress, and Icarian had clearly found it.

Had the Conclave left when Icarian attacked, or—

"You're right." Mrs. Blackmoor turned her somber gaze to me. "We're alone."

Something struck the closed wooden doors leading to the room, and a chorus of growls and snarls grew louder with each passing moment.

I nodded toward the door. "Not for much longer."

"Icarian is likely right behind them." She pulled back her sleeves and faced the entrance, prepared to unleash magic that would most likely be useless.

"Wrong again!"

The grinding of metal followed the boom of Icarian's voice as the castle's ceiling peeled back like an onion. Man-sized stones fell from the crumbling structure, heading straight for us. A dome of energy summoned by Mrs. Blackmoor shielded us from the falling debris that crashed down around us like mortar shells.

A wave of zombies broke through the entrance, and they also poured into the room from the hole above. They scuttled down the wall like ants and gathered around us. Instead of swarming, they remained in the periphery, obviously obeying Icarian's command.

Many had grown just like the ones we encountered in the corridor, and some were almost as massive as I was. They'd clearly been eating magic.

"No one has to get hurt." Icarian hovered above us as a golden ball of light, appearing as he had when we last fought him and the witch hunters. "All you have to do is give me the Air Crest."

Mrs. Blackmoor sneered. "No."

The zombies shuffled forward, their groans growing louder.

"Do you really want me to let loose my army? Because even though they've already eaten, I will."

The smile in Icarian's voice made my skin crawl. "What have you done?"

"Would you like to see?"

No, I wouldn't. The gaping pit in my stomach told me he was referring to Thad.

I shut my eyes, forcing my consciousness to once again traverse the expanse and travel into Millie's, but when I opened my eyes, I didn't see the forest behind the Blackmoor mansion or any of the vampyren lurking about. I remained in the Veil.

Icarian was either blocking my abilities or something horrible had happened.

I glared at his golden form, trying to pierce the luminous barrier behind which he hid. The radiant light dimmed, becoming almost transparent in response to my mystical probes. Within the hollow shell, I detected an indistinguishable figure peering back at me. The shadowy slits of his eyes narrowed as he no doubt guessed what I was doing.

"No peeking." He waved a golden hand, and the barrier hardened and turned opaque as a wave of energy sent me flying backward and out of Mrs. Blackmoor's magical dome. I tumbled across the marble tile before crashing into one of the stone columns.

"Aiden?" Mrs. Blackmoor hovered by my side while keeping watchful eyes on Icarian and the growling zombies. "What did you see?"

Nothing that would tell us who Icarian was, but I did know one thing. The golden ball of energy wasn't Icarian's true form. He had somehow transmuted his corporeal appearance into a physical manifestation of his life force.

He clearly believed that protected him—that summoning the magical energy of his spirit would make him unbeatable—and he was right. The soul magic he harnessed made him invincible to most everyone else.

Except me.

I was a necromancer. Souls were *my* domain, and Icarian had made himself vulnerable to me.

"*What* did you see?" Mrs. Blackmoor grabbed me by my shoulders and shook me out of my thoughts.

"Nothing. I couldn't quite penetrate his defenses."

"Of course you couldn't." The giddy chirp to Icarian's voice revealed he believed my deception, and I needed it to stay that way. He couldn't know I had figured out his defenses until I could use that information to my advantage. "The magic I wield is beyond even that of the Conclave."

"And what have you done with them?" Mrs. Blackmoor sneered up at the ball of light.

His golden form shrugged. "I've… removed them from the playing field."

That wasn't good. If Icarian could overwhelm the most powerful of us all, what could the rest of us do?

"You killed them?"

Icarian gasped as if that was the most ridiculous question ever asked. "Not at all. That would create anarchy, which would be counterproductive to my plans."

"And what about Thad and my family?" I took two steps forward, ignoring the warning growls of the zombies swaying around us. "What have you done to them?"

"Only what was necessary."

I clenched my fists, trying to siphon the ectoplasm I needed to bring him to his knees. "And what does that mean?"

"I'll show you." Golden arrows of light flew from Icarian's soul, streaking through the room. When they struck, the world around me exploded with golden light.

CHAPTER 14

WHEN THE light faded, we had been whisked away from the Veil and stood amid the barren, bloody landscape from the vision Mrs. Blackmoor had shared with me. Huge holes where the earth had exploded with corpses dotted the terrain, broken fragments of headstones littered the soil, and the enormous crack I'd created with my fist split the land.

The surroundings looked exactly as they had when I was last here.

This shouldn't be possible. This environment existed only in a prophetic vision. But I was once again standing on the blood-soaked ground. That could only mean one thing.

This place was real.

"Aiden, look!"

I expected to find Icarian looming in the distance with his army of undead magic-eaters clamoring for us, but Mrs. Blackmoor's pointing finger led my gaze to a series of tombstones about fifty yards away. More than two-dozen figures sat motionless upon the ground, their wrists and bodies bound in glowing chains to the grave markers behind them.

My breath hitched as I scanned the line of captives, praying to the Gate for Thad and the rest of my family not to be among their number. When I caught a glimpse of strawberry-blond hair, a cry tore itself from my throat. "Thad!"

I sprinted across the red soil, ignoring Mrs. Blackmoor's protests. Her alarm didn't concern me. All that mattered was getting to the man I loved, taking him in my arms, and never, *ever* letting him go.

I screamed his name again, but he didn't stir. His entire body drooped forward as if he were unconscious or—

I refused to allow my brain to even finish the thought.

He was okay. He *had* to be okay.

"Thad, I'm here." I skidded to his side and fell to the dirt. His clothes had been almost ripped to shreds, and the angry red slashes that cut across his chest, arms, and legs made me snarl. Icarian and his army would pay.

I gently lifted his chin with my thumb, hoping the movement would rouse him, but his eyes remained closed. I felt for a pulse. It was slow and ragged, and tears slid down my cheeks in response.

He was alive. Thank the Gate he was alive. Now I had to free him.

I grabbed hold of the glowing restraints and pulled. Nothing happened. I had to free him as quickly as possible before Icarian made his grand entrance. I rose, wrapped my hands around the glowing links, and yanked. They refused to break, so I planted my feet in the bloody earth and gave it everything I had. Sweat poured down my shaking arms, and the veins in my biceps bulged almost to the point of exploding through my skin.

The chains never budged.

"Aiden?" Mrs. Blackmoor stood behind me, her eyes searching the sky. "We must be prepared. Icarian is close by."

How could she focus on anything right now other than her son, unconscious and bleeding in front of her? "I don't care. Thad comes first."

"No, he doesn't." She lifted me from my kneeling position and dangled me off the ground. I wasn't accustomed to being so easily manhandled, and the low growl in the back of my throat communicated that. "You must focus."

A dead calm swept through me like an Arctic wind, and my flesh tingled in response. "Unhand me."

Mrs. Blackmoor winced as energy I hadn't meant to summon crystallized across my flesh. She dropped me and glanced down at her hands, which looked as if she had touched a hot stove. "What did you just do?"

I wasn't certain, and right now I didn't care. I returned my attention to Thad and kneeled beside him once again. No matter how many times I shook him or called his name, he failed to respond. The only sign of life was his labored breathing, so I did the only thing left for me to do.

I pressed my lips to his, took his ragged breaths deep into my lungs, and held them there. His life force rattled inside me, filling me with more warmth than a fire fairy could ever create on his own. It had been that way since the moment I met him. He'd taken a cocky fae prince and shown him what it was like to truly feel alive, and it was a gift I intended to share.

I stroked his cheek, outlining the curve of his jaw with my fingertips as I slowly exhaled our shared breath back into his lungs. Just as Thad had breathed new life into me with his love and his presence, I intended to fill him with every single molecule of air in my lungs until it soothed his battered flesh and his wounded soul and brought my warlock back to me.

"Aiden," Mrs. Blackmoor gasped. "He's awake."

I opened my eyes to the most glorious sight in the world. Thad's beautiful hazel eyes peered at me from half-closed eyelids, but his fluttering lids told me he struggled to fight his way back to consciousness. Whatever Icarian had done to him had sapped him of his strength and had brought him to the brink of death. It hovered around him like a hungry wolf, but it would not claim its prize while I was here.

"Don't worry, Thad. I'm right here."

Holding his face in my hands, I mounted his lips once again, filling him with the breath remaining within my lungs. I nibbled his lips and stroked his cheek, using my touch and our passion to reignite the spark he needed to find his way out of the darkness.

Thad's eyes fluttered completely open. He sat up straight, his smile cutting a wide swath across his fair, yet bloodied, complexion. He had never looked stronger, more full of life, than he did right now.

"Aiden! You're back!" He moved to wrap his arms around me, but the chains held him fast. "What the hell?"

"Stay still. You could injure yourself further." I'd clearly breathed a bit too much life into him. He thrashed, trying to get loose and completely ignoring my warning. Why was I so surprised? He rarely listened to me.

"Get me out of h—" Thad's gaze drifted over my shoulder, and the breath I'd worked so hard to give him completely exited his body. "M-Mom?"

Mrs. Blackmoor stepped beside me and smiled down at her son. "Yes, Thaddy. It's me."

He darted his eyes back and forth between his mother and me, obviously trying to decide if this was real or another attack by Icarian. When he finally settled his gaze upon his mother, shock fell upon the shore of anger before hope washed it all away.

A stream of tears fell from the corners of his eyes and down his bloodstained cheeks. "Are you—? Am *I*—?

"I'm alive." She kneeled beside him and brushed a stray reddish lock from his forehead. "And so are you."

He fell into her embrace, sobbing, and buried his face into her neck. "How... is this... possible? I... was there... when... you died."

"I know." She cooed in his ear the way my mother used to when I was a sprite and had a nightmare. She stroked his cheek and ran her hands through his thick locks. "I'll explain everything once we free you and get you out of this place."

She motioned to the chains, and I prayed with every fiber of my being that her magic would be enough, but it wasn't. The chains remained where they were.

"Impossible." She rose, and tendrils of mist snaked from the ground. They wrapped around the chains, squeezing with all their magical might, but still nothing.

Icarian's magic was stronger than even a member of the Conclave's.

"Where's Dad and the others?" Thad glanced around, searching the battered faces for his family, but his bindings kept him from moving his neck more than an inch in either direction. "Are they okay? Icarian's zombies attacked us at home."

I stood and scanned the crowd. All the protector covens were there, including the Edwells, and there were even some people I didn't recognize. Their tunics, however, marked them as shifters. Obviously Kale had contacted his people and brought in the cavalry, which included the Beast King, who was also bound in chains. Unfortunately, their added power hadn't seemed to make much of a difference.

Everyone looked to be in worse shape than Thad. King Caspian had a hole in his shoulder. I didn't even want to venture a guess as to what had caused it. Edith Stonewall's nose appeared broken, and an angry bruise had turned her flesh a deep purple. Edith's mother slumped next to her, her bruised flesh visible through her ripped blouse and pants.

When my gaze settled on Mr. Blackmoor, who lay six feet away, my breath hitched. His shoulder jutted out at a grotesque angle. His head lolled to one side, his lip had been busted open, and blood from a gash over his left eye poured down his face. He had no doubt fought his damnedest against the magical onslaught that brought all of them to their knees, and so had Mason, Pierce, and Kale, who were unconscious and wounded as well.

The only one missing was Drake. His absence didn't bode well for any of us.

"Your family's here." I nodded to where everyone but Drake lay. Their chests moved up and down, so I knew they were alive. "They're hurt but still breathing."

Upon seeing her wounded husband, Mrs. Blackmoor rushed to his side. "Oliver!" She tried to wake him with gentle caresses and kisses upon his lips. His eyes didn't open, and I hadn't expected them to.

I had breathed Thad back to consciousness. I had no clue how I had done it, but every magical instinct I possessed told me I had the power to drag everyone out of the waters that separated life from death.

I just had to figure out how.

"Aiden?" Thad gazed up at me from his restraints, and my heart sighed. Even though it had only been hours since he last saw me, it had been weeks since I last drank in every glorious dip of his flesh.

I crouched down next to him and fluttered my fingers across his skin. Even bloody, he was the most handsome man in the world. "Yes?"

"Your father."

My thoughts froze. "Wh-what about him?"

"He's here."

"What?" I stood up, scanning the area for King Oberon. "How?"

"I summoned him to help us get you back."

That explained the violet energy I'd seen floating over Blackmoor Manor. Thad had managed to pierce the veil separating Earth from Otherworld.

"And how did that work out for you?"

Icarian's voice thundered all around us and shook the ground like the earthquake that had leveled Havenbridge. Now that he was here, it was time to show him what I could do.

I GATHERED my thoughts while Mrs. Blackmoor and Thad scanned the skies for Icarian, but they wouldn't find him. He was playing hide-and-go-seek again, and I was done playing his games. This time we'd play this my way and by my rules. I stood and faced the reddened sky.

"What have you done with my father and Drake?"

My words earned me audible gasps from Mrs. Blackmoor, who obviously hadn't realized they weren't among the unconscious.

"I'm keeping them someplace... safe, until our business is concluded. Consider their absence an insurance policy so that you do as I ask and hand over the Air Crest."

I bared my teeth while Thad rattled the chains that kept him confined. "You can attack Havenbridge and send however many armies you want against us, but we'll never give it to you."

As evidence of Thad's claim, Mrs. Blackmoor placed the relic in her robe.

"Really?" For some reason Icarian sounded surprised. Did he truly believe we would just hand what he needed to end magic over to him? "Even after you've seen how easily I defeated the protector covens, a handful of shifters, and the kings of both Otherworld and Aeaea?"

"You don't scare me." Surprisingly, the words I spoke were true. While I'd been intimidated by Icarian's power for weeks, my apprehension had vanished. "I'll find my father and Drake, and I'll make you pay for everything you've done."

Icarian's chuckle filled the sky. "How will you find them? Do you even know *where* we are?"

I didn't, but it felt strangely like home. This place, however, lacked the natural splendor and beauty of Otherworld.

"You don't, do you? You're not a very good necromancer."

Though the tone of his voice indicated amusement, I sensed the truth. It flowed off him in halting waves. I made him nervous. Bringing me here, wherever *here* was, had to be a test—one he believed I had failed.

I'd show him what failure truly looked like.

Mrs. Blackmoor's taunts brought me out of my thoughts. "Do you really believe snatching me from the Veil and bringing me *here* somehow gives you the upper hand?"

"I have the upper hand wherever I go." Based on the tone of his voice, Icarian most likely held his chin high. "Just look at my defeated foes behind you. But this isn't about them. I brought you here so we could chat and, if needed, I could release my army without exposing magic to humans."

His words and actions didn't make sense, and judging from the furrowed brows of Thad and Mrs. Blackmoor, they agreed. Icarian had basically declared war on magic, he had spoken the *immortalitas* spell and created an army of undead magic-eaters, yet he worried about exposing magic?

I was missing something, and it was time to find out what that was.

"You've attacked my family and you expect us to chat?" Mrs. Blackmoor asked.

In response, Icarian's zombies materialized across the barren landscape. They groaned and their white eyes went mad with evident hunger, yet still they remained where they were. Icarian's sway over them was strong. That would change.

I could feel it as strongly as my love for Thad.

Whatever I sensed amid the death and destruction around me tugged upon my chest as if I was made of metal and the nightmarish landscape was one big magnet. Something stirred within me.

A dense fog rolled over the dead land. It progressed like a steamroller across the bloody soil and flattened the jutting gravestones between the zombies and us in a series of grinding crunches. Somehow she increased the density of her mist and made the vapor as solid as steel. My gut told me her display of strength would prove fruitless. It would be my power that made the difference.

Icarian laughed as if his best friend had told the funniest joke in the world. "Oh, Priscilla. Your sense of humor still gets me every time. And here I'd begun to think your time with the Conclave had pickled your wit."

She arched her eyebrow at the air around us and glanced over at me. I nodded in agreement. Icarian clearly knew her, which meant she knew the man behind the disguised voice. All we had to do was get him to slip up and reveal his true identity.

That had to be my focus right now, and not the strange sensations that pricked across my flesh like a thousand needles.

Icarian tsked at us. "Stop giving each other those meaningful looks. You're not going to figure out who I am. Well, at least not until after there's nothing you can do about it."

His tone was too casual, as if he were talking about plans for a vacation and not either eliminating magic or killing someone I loved. Whoever Icarian was, he'd clearly lost his hold on sanity.

"Now, how about we end this silliness?" Icarian once again appeared as a golden ball of light about twelve feet away from us. "Give me the Air Crest and we'll be one step closer to bringing this chapter to a close."

Mrs. Blackmoor clenched her fists. "You'll have to kill me to get it."

"Mom, no!" Thad strained to get free to protect her.

"Don't worry, Thad. I don't want your mother dead." He was telling the truth. The air didn't smell like rotting fish.

She snorted, standing next to Thad. "Just my sons?"

"Don't be absurd. I have no intention of wiping out your family. Eliminating one is all that is required."

"Then take me and be done with it."

I whirled around and glared at Thad. "No. That's out of the question."

"No, it's not." Thad's stern gaze met mine. "If it saves those I love *and* magic, I have to."

"I'm glad you see it that way." Icarian glided toward Thad.

Mrs. Blackmoor's scream of fury halted him in his tracks. "Stay away from him!" The mist she had created earlier churned and sped toward Icarian. She clearly intended to grind him to dust as her power had done to the gravestones. Icarian had other plans. Golden light exploded from his form, slicing through the advancing fog.

After dissipating her power, Icarian turned his focus to Mrs. Blackmoor. "I merely wish to end the greatest threat to magic, and you still resist?"

"By committing murder?" I placed myself directly between Icarian and Mrs. Blackmoor. Even though she didn't need me to protect her, I couldn't let a psychotic magical being get within striking distance of my future mother-in-law, no matter how unpleasant she might sometimes be. I had to keep her and Thad safe and keep Icarian from getting his shimmering hands on a third crest.

"I would *never* do such a thing." He hesitated, his golden form glistening like a mini sun in the bloodred sky. "Doing so breaks the magical laws by which we are all bound."

His answer awoke a rage unlike any I'd ever experienced. It burned hotter than the fire of the fae and more caustic than vampyren bile. Instead of shoving it down, I embraced it. When I did, I sensed the enormous amounts of mystical energy floating on invisible currents all around me. "And reciting the *immortalitas* spell doesn't?"

Icarian sighed and hesitantly nodded. "True. I did do that, but only because necessity demanded it, and it yielded… unexpected results."

I had been right all along. He hadn't meant to almost level Havenbridge, and that revealed an important fact about him. "So you lost control of the spell, is that it?" His radiance flickered. I'd struck a nerve, which was what I hoped for. I needed to keep him distracted while my paranormal senses inspected the magical forces around me. "Perhaps you're not as powerful as you'd like us to believe."

"Aiden, your attempts to rile my temper are both obvious and futile." His voice never strained. It was almost as if he'd separated his emotions from his actions. "But I assure you, I am far more powerful than anyone realizes."

The stench of rotting fish filled the air. Icarian wasn't as powerful as we'd originally believed. That meant his power had to lie with the crests. If we separated him from the two he possessed, we might be able to take him down.

"Stop it!" Mrs. Blackmoor smacked me upside my head while Icarian snorted.

"You really need to gain control over your new powers." He rose high in the sky and glanced down at us. "Broadcasting your intentions to your enemies isn't the wisest move to make."

I rubbed the back of my head and glanced over at Mrs. Blackmoor's stern gaze. She was clearly ready to send her mist after me.

Fortunately neither of them realized I'd done that on purpose. Thad was a different story. His perceptive hazel eyes beamed, and a smile crept across his delicious lips. He knew exactly what I'd done and why because he could read me as easily as I read him. Revealing my thoughts to Icarian was the only way I could test if I was right. Judging by how high Icarian hovered in the sky, I was definitely on the right track.

"You must tell me how you acquired this ability to broadcast your emotions. It's not a skill associated with a necromancer or a fire fae." Icarian's relaxed tone revealed he didn't suspect I'd opened myself up to the swarming energy all around me. It funneled into me like a river feeding an ocean, and I gritted my teeth as it crested inside me.

I took a deep breath, hoping the strain in my voice would be interpreted as fear. If Icarian figured out what I was doing, he'd stop me. "How about some quid pro quo?"

"Interesting." He hovered a few feet closer to us. "What would you like to know?"

"Everything you've done has been because of the Prophecy of the Three, right?"

Thad cocked his head to one side. "With what?"

Icarian nodded and motioned for me to continue.

"Tell us what the prophecy says."

Mrs. Blackmoor's sideways glance revealed she understood what I was doing, and her quickly retreating smile indicated she approved. Her powers of perception were just as keen as Thad's. "That's right. You claim to be trying to save all of magic from some alleged threat you perceive my sons to be, yet in my time on the Conclave, the topic has never once been discussed. If this were truly a cause for concern, why not bring it before the Conclave and let us deal with the matter?"

"Because the Conclave fails to act. It debates."

He was right about that. For the past few months, the Blackmoors had complained of the Conclave's inability to take action.

"So we're supposed to take you at your word?" Thad asked. "When you've spent the last few months creating havoc in the name of some secret agenda?"

Icarian's golden light flashed once. He was continuing to lose his cool, and with any luck, he'd give me the opportunity I needed. "I'll tell you what I know."

"No." Mrs. Blackmoor shook her head. "I want to see it for myself."

"Fine." In response to Icarian, a black leather-bound book shimmered into view before us. "But afterward, I expect Aiden to tell *me* what I want to know."

My heartbeat raced as I reached for the book. Within its dusty pages, I'd find the information that would explain why Icarian had thrust the magical world into chaos, but before I had a chance to take it, the tome drifted away from my grasp.

"Agree to my terms." Icarian spoke in measured tones. "Now."

I glanced up at him and nodded. "You have my word. Once I understand the prophecy, I'll share everything I've got."

The book floated into my hands and opened itself to the last page. Written in big cursive letters at the top were the words *The Prophecy of the Three.*

A man of great power and might
Shall find endless love at first sight
And from that blessed union be
Planted seeds that number in three.

The first shall grow hearty and strong
And never quite learn right from wrong.
His reach will extend to on high
Claiming dominion of the sky.

The second shall grow cold but wise
Consuming knowledge with his eyes.
His intellect shall triple and
Spread like water across the land.

In inky dark the third shall bloom,
A harbinger of light or doom

For if his gift is black as night,
He may descend to claim his right.

Together then the world shall see
The power of the brothers three,
And when that day comes, as it's writ
The heavens and earth shall be split.

Against their foes, they'll be at odds
Establishing themselves as gods.
Humanity will be mere sheep;
Nothing more than souls to reap.

For this could be the end of days
A single choice—preserve or raze?
This is how it will come to be—
The prophecy of brothers three.

The book shut and disappeared the moment I finished reading out loud.

"I don't understand." I glanced over at Thad and Mrs. Blackmoor, whose face had drained of all color, before turning back to Icarian. "You're afraid of a poem?"

"It's *not* a poem. These are the last words of Pythia."

Thad and Mrs. Blackmoor gasped at Icarian's announcement. They had clearly heard of this person.

"Who is Pythia?"

"Sh-she was a High Priestess in ancient Greece." Mrs. Blackmoor drew in deep, ragged breaths.

Thad gulped. "Also known as the Oracle of Delphi."

I immediately understood why Icarian feared her divination. I might not have remembered the name Pythia, but I was familiar with the Oracle of Delphi. Every single one of her premonitions—the Trojan War, the fall of the Grecian empire, and the decimation of the *homo magus* by the witch hunters—had come true.

If Pythia had envisioned this future, that meant—

I darted my gaze to Thad, who scanned the ground as he processed the information.

"Now do you understand why the Blackmoors must be stopped? The Conclave has possessed this information for over a millennium, yet they've done nothing to safeguard our community or prevent this apocalyptic event from occurring. When I realized what the Blackmoor brothers were becoming, I took it upon myself to rectify the oversight and save us all." Icarian closed the distance between us. "Surely you must see that."

Thad shook his head in response, unwilling to believe in the possibility.

I didn't want to believe it either, but I did want to continue this discussion as more and more energy funneled into me from the dead landscape. "I refuse to believe the oracle is referring to Thad or his brothers."

"It can't be," Thad muttered, more to himself than anyone else.

"Are you blind to the similarities?" Icarian practically shook in exasperation.

"Why?" I was pretending to be especially dense. "Because Thad is one of three brothers?"

"It's more than that, and you know it." Icarian's words came down like a hammer striking an anvil. "The prophecy basically describes the Blackmoors. Oliver Blackmoor is a man of 'great power and might' who was spell bound to Priscilla." Mrs. Blackmoor gazed off into the distance and shook her head.

He ignored her gesture for him to stop—and the building energy spreading through my limbs. "And their children, 'which number in three,' are the result of that extremely rare union."

"Coincidence. Nothing more."

Icarian scoffed at me. "And what about the description of the brothers? Pierce can fly and commands lightning. He has 'dominion of the sky.' Mason's shadow-weaving abilities are 'black as night,' and you know as well as I do that Thad is both 'cold' and 'wise.'"

Thad winced as if he'd just been pronounced guilty of a crime.

"More coincidences." I batted his words away while moving to stand next to Thad. In response to my presence, he sighed and nodded up at me. He'd be strong, and I'd be his strength. "We have no idea how many other brothers might have similar powers."

Icarian drifted closer. He was almost in range. "No other family has experienced the inexplicable power growth of the Blackmoors. The Conclave would know of it."

A chill traveled down my spine and Thad sucked in his breath. He'd come to the same conclusion I had. There was only one way Icarian could possibly know what the Conclave knew, and suddenly everything made sense.

Ebenezer Kane had been a prisoner within the Veil, yet he escaped. The Crests of the Five had been hidden from the rest of the magical community, but they had been found. Icarian had bypassed protection spells on Otherworld and Aeaea, and commanded shadow weavers, sorcerers, shifters, and even witch hunters, which were all feats that no one else could have accomplished—*unless* Icarian *was* one of the Conclave.

Only one question remained, and I intended on finding that answer even though the pit opening up in my gut told me I already knew. "You speak of the Conclave as if they're all-knowing. They aren't. Most of their information comes from either the Blackmoors or the protector covens."

"Still you fail to realize what this prophecy means." If Icarian were flesh and blood right now instead of a ball of energy, he'd no doubt be frothing at the mouth. "If Pierce, Mason, and Thad are the brothers from Pythia's vision, then that means they represent the next magical evolution of our species. They are destined to wield powers that will make them gods."

Mrs. Blackmoor shuffled away as if the information was too much for her, but I knew better. She'd dropped her defenses and let me see her emotions. She was getting into position. Thad curled into a ball in anticipation of the onslaught.

I crossed my arms over my chest and glared at him. "Gods aren't real."

"Not yet." He shook his golden fist at my inability to see the world the way he did, and I couldn't be happier about that. It meant I hadn't lost my sanity. "But Pythia's prophecy was a warning of such an event: 'Humanity will be mere sheep. Nothing more than souls to reap.'"

"You're forgetting one thing."

Icarian focused his attention entirely on me. "And what's that?"

"The kind of men Pierce, Thad, and Mason are."

He sniffed. "You mean the fact that Pierce is a brute who thinks only with his fists or that Mason is a mischievous imp who causes more trouble than he solves?"

My heart sank. He clearly had no love for Mason or Pierce. "And what about Thad?" I took two steps forward, further closing the distance between us.

Icarian's heavy sigh spoke of the tremendous guilt he carried as he turned his attention to the man I loved. It verified my worst fear, and the anger within me crested, waiting for the moment when I would unleash its gathered fury.

"I'm sorry, Thad, I really am, but your intellect distances you from your emotions and often makes you cold and aloof," he answered, oblivious to the curl to Thad's upper lip or the change in my demeanor. I widened my stance and stood up tall. "Imagine what having godly abilities could do to someone who prefers knowledge to people? What could such power do to a raging brute like Pierce or a trickster like Mason?"

It was time. "The same thing possessing magical relics does to a shortsighted old fool."

I released the ectoplasm I'd siphoned from the barren land around me right into Icarian, and he immediately recognized his mistake. By bringing me to what I now understood to be the realm of the dead, he'd exposed me to the very power Mrs. Blackmoor had been trying to get me to summon. Unfortunately, being here also placed those I loved in danger.

The magic of this place fed off the living. I had to end this battle quickly and get everyone home.

My sage green energy cracked the golden shell he'd erected to conceal his identity and protect himself from attack. Its radiance flickered as stress fractures cut jagged lines across the casing. In a few moments I'd gaze upon the face of the man who pretended to be my friend but who was, in fact, my enemy.

In a blinding explosion of gold and green, Icarian's golden sphere faded, and the gray eyes of Gerald Wa fixed their angry gaze upon me.

CHAPTER 15

"YOU WERE my friend." Thad's words came out as a choked sob. I crouched next to him, placing my arm around his shoulders as he wept into my neck.

"It may not seem like it," Gerald said, "but I still am."

Thad stiffened in my embrace. "We weren't friends. I was a means to an end."

"No, that's not true. I never wanted you to be the one to pay the price." He gestured to Pierce and Mason. "It's always been one of them I was truly after."

"That's your example of friendship?" Thad lunged out of my embrace, but he didn't get far thanks to Gerald's magic. "You want to kill one of my brothers!"

Gerald took a deep breath. "I want to spare *you*."

"And I want you to go to hell."

Gerald fell back two steps in response to Thad's venom, and his gray eyes flashed steel. "Don't make me reconsider that decision."

The fury within me fed my power like a magma flow, and I charged. A steady barrage of ectoplasm blasted out of my fingers as if I'd turned into a volcano. Equally furious, Mrs. Blackmoor stood behind Gerald, pelting the dome of light he had erected to protect himself from her mist and the sapphire beams of energy that flew out of her clenched fists.

Gerald's moving lips told me he was trying to communicate with us, but I couldn't hear a word. The continuous clash of magic created thunderous explosions that vibrated the ground beneath my feet.

If we kept up the onslaught long enough, we might be able to take him down for good.

"Enough!" Gerald's right hand glowed with scarlet energy while his left pulsed a deep emerald. He had activated the Fire and the Earth Crests he held in his grip. In response, a storm of fireballs fell from the sky, obliterating the land all around us. I leaped to the right and rolled into a ball as a fiery meteor, bigger than Thad's automobile, struck the ground where I once stood.

Roots exploded from the soil on my left, reaching out for Thad with wooden limbs. If they wrapped around him, they'd tear him apart.

I rushed to his side and released a stream of ectoplasm, causing them to wither and turn to dust. More roots dug their way out of the ground, swiping at us from every direction.

I did my best to destroy them, but there were too many. For every limb I annihilated, another two took its place. It would only be a matter of seconds before they overwhelmed us.

A gust of wind swept across the land, gathering the roots up in its blustering fury and ripped them from the soil. As they sailed off in the distance, I glanced over my shoulder to see Mrs. Blackmoor wielding the Air Crest. She had saved us, but before I could thank her, the firestorm Gerald had summoned vanished.

He stood behind us. His hands still glowed crimson and emerald, but anger no longer blazed across his steely gaze. His eyes were now hooded in regret, especially when he noted the scowl on Thad's face.

"I never meant for it to come to this."

Who was he kidding? He'd been attacking us for months. "How else was this supposed to end? Did you think we'd be grateful for your betrayal?"

He sighed. "I had hoped once you learned my motives that you might...."

"Understand?" Mrs. Blackmoor peered down her nose at him, but the indignant fire in her gaze flickered when she clutched her chest and winced. The death energy that surrounded her was sapping her strength. If being here was already affecting her this way, what was it doing to Thad and my family?

"I suppose that was a foolish fantasy."

That was foolish, and that wasn't the kind of man I'd believed Gerald to be. Clearly, I had been wrong on so many fronts.

"That was why I revealed my motives to Drake. I had hoped he would tell his family or the rest of the Conclave. I believed that if everyone knew what I had surmised about the Blackmoors and the Prophecy of the Three, that this could come to a... peaceful end."

No. What he had hoped for was that Thad or his brothers would offer up their lives to save magic and bring peace. "What you wanted was a simple solution. You wanted Thad, Pierce, or Mason to save you from the evils you committed in the name of protecting magic." Gerald flinched and glanced away. "You wanted to use their inherent goodness against them."

"I wanted this to end." Gerald's shoulders slumped. "When this first started, when I released Ebenezer from his cell, I had no idea he'd become enthralled with Mason's power and attempt to claim it as his own. I envisioned he'd eliminate the threat quickly and it would be done."

"Those threats are my sons!" The ground underneath Gerald exploded in response to Mrs. Blackmoor's wrath. The force catapulted him into the red sky, but Gerald quickly recovered. He held out his arms, slowed his ascent, and hovered over us.

"You don't think I know that, Priscilla?" Gerald glared at her, obviously incensed by the attack. "You've been a member of the Conclave for just over a year. You know we must protect the welfare of the *entire* community. Our concerns are greater than any individual, *including* your sons, and that's why I didn't inform the Conclave of my suspicions. I kept you in the dark because I wanted to spare you the heartache of having to debate which of your sons should die to save magic, so I took the task upon myself. I carried the burden of the greater good upon my shoulders instead."

I'd been wrong. Gerald hadn't lost his mind. He held the misguided belief that he'd be the savior of magic, that no one else was up to the task. That didn't make him crazy. It made him a victim of pride.

"Is that what you were doing when Ben destroyed my home, or when he resurrected Sersie and razed Aeaea? What about when you struck up a deal with the witch hunters? Were you fighting for the greater good then too?"

Gerald took a deep breath and turned his gaze to me. "I had to improvise. Ebenezer had mucked up my plans, and since he seemed incapable of removing a Blackmoor from the equation, I realized I needed a plan B, so I sent him after the Crests of the Five and turned to the Spell Fall as the solution."

Did Gerald even realize the depths of his sins? "So you sent Ben after the Earth Crest? That means Drake's aunt Millie, a woman you claimed to love, died because of *you*."

"It wasn't supposed to happen that way." His voice trailed off as if he'd left the present and traveled to the past. "Ebenezer was only supposed to steal the Earth Crest, not kill her. Harming her was never a part of the plan. But when she fought back, he mortally wounded her. I couldn't just let him leave her there to die, so I...."

"You ordered Ben to turn her into a vampyre?" Mrs. Blackmoor spat out the question as if it were venom.

His eyes met ours. They were feverish and overbright, and his fingers twitched around the crests. "It was the only solution that made sense. If I did nothing, she would be gone. For good. There was no way I could live with that on my conscience, so yes." He took a step forward and thrust out his chest. "I ordered Ebenezer to turn her." He focused his gaze upon me. "Just as I ordered him to turn you."

My nostrils flared, and my muscles clenched as fire not only scorched my flesh but consumed me from the inside out. For months I'd lamented my transformation into a vampyre, and I'd blamed Ben. He hadn't been entirely responsible. He'd been acting under orders. He hadn't killed and changed me because he saw me as an obstacle to gaining Thad's love, as I'd once believed.

The reason was far crueler. I'd been turned to ease Gerald's guilt, and that realization caused my entire body to erupt into black flame.

I HAD no real concept of what was happening. One second I was listening to Gerald's explanations, and a second later I had launched myself into the sky, raining lances of black fire at him.

His wide eyes indicated he had no clue what was going on, but that didn't stop him from erecting a golden sphere to deflect the bombardment. The flaming weapons struck the barrier, embedding their fiery points into the shield, which slowly began to melt. "What power is this?"

The words flew out of my mouth as if I'd always known the answer. "Weapons forged from the funeral pyres of the dead." More burning lances crashed into Gerald's magic as knowledge I'd not previously possessed filled my brain. The black flames fed not on oxygen but on light and life, just like this land did.

Even more arcane knowledge funneled into me as the power of necromancy engulfed my body. This time, though, the surging energy didn't melt my flesh as it had done a few weeks ago, and I understood why.

Back then, I hadn't truly embraced the power; I had merely opened myself up to it, which had been my mistake. The death magic couldn't take hold. It fought against the vampyre and the fae and melted them away in its attempt to fill me anew, but it had only been able to bestow partial gifts instead of the full abilities I now wielded.

In my anger and need to protect Thad, I had done the one thing Mrs. Blackmoor had been trying to get me to do. I crossed the line from life to death. I left behind the vampyre and the fae that had lain dormant within me. Their abilities, those that had mixed with the necromancy, that had allowed me to not only sense emotions but to briefly broadcast them, faded away.

Unfortunately, the blood tie that tethered me to Thad grew slack. The longer I stayed on this side and the more death magic I generated, the faster the connection would fray.

There was only one thing left to do: end this as quickly as possible.

While I continued to bombard Gerald with black flames, I funneled more ectoplasm from the realm around me and unleashed it in one concentrated blast. The energy slammed into the barrier in an explosion that rocked the red sky and sent Gerald tumbling toward the ground.

My dragon wings sprouted from my back, and they carried me to him as I rained black fire and hurled corrosive ectoplasm upon his traitorous head.

"Enough!" A beam of golden light exploded from his hands, briefly blinding me. When the glow faded, Gerald stood below me. He clutched his shoulder in pain. One of my flaming lances jutted from his flesh. "Bravo for drawing first blood, but it will be your last."

Who was he kidding? The wound bled freely, and if the weapon wasn't removed, it would consume him until his spirit shriveled up and died. Perhaps if I offered him a way out, he'd take it. "It's time to end this. Don't make me hurt you again."

"You've only succeeded in doing what I have allowed you to do."

I snorted. "You think too highly of yourself. The crests you've stolen have augmented your powers. Without them, you're nothing."

"Am I?" Gerald shook his head as if he couldn't believe the depths of my stupidity. With a grimace, he snapped the lance from his body and tossed it aside. That shouldn't have been possible. "It's true the crests enhance my abilities, but even so, I've yet to unleash my full power upon you in deference to the friendship we once shared."

What more could Gerald do?

"Once I heal, that reprieve will end."

"Aiden!" Thad hollered from below, where Mrs. Blackmoor stood guard over him and the others. The zombies that had been waiting impatiently to devour living flesh and magic charged across the barren land, heading straight for my love, my family, and my friends. A giant wall of fog rolled in as a barrier thanks to Mrs. Blackmoor, but it wouldn't last long and neither would she. She was expending too much magical energy, and the land around her was absorbing it and her life force at a quickened pace. If I didn't do something soon, the zombies would consume her and then everyone I loved.

"Go ahead." Gerald nodded toward where his army had converged on the mist, ripping into it with their gray teeth and growing in mass with each bite.

"You can stop me…." He began to glow and fade away. "Or save them. The choice is yours."

It wasn't a tough decision. I couldn't take Gerald down at the expense of everyone else. Unlike him, I had a fully functioning conscience. I cast one final snarl at him as he disappeared. I had no doubt we'd see each other much sooner than either of us cared for. With one powerful flap of my dragon wings, I sped toward my family.

Mrs. Blackmoor's wall already had huge holes through which the zombies attempted to gain access to their meal. Since she couldn't fight back with her own magic, which would only make the undead more powerful, she took the only available route. She refortified the barrier as quickly as possible.

She just couldn't do it fast enough. There were too many, and she was one warlock. I had to even the odds.

I unleashed a steady stream of ectoplasm upon the zombies closest to the wall, and the extraplanar energy dissolved the biological matter they were composed of. Fortunately I harnessed the only type of magic they couldn't consume, but that didn't stop the rest from surging forward and taking their fallen comrades' places.

Still, I bought Mrs. Blackmoor some time to strengthen the foggy rampart and for me to assemble an army of my own.

I shut my eyes and let the power within guide me past the swirling thoughts of the zombies who refused to obey my commands. Even though Gerald wasn't present, his influence over them proved too strong, so I reached out farther, sending my consciousness searching for the ones I needed the most.

"Aiden?"

I had successfully linked with Aunt Millie again. She and the rest of the vampyren were flying through the night sky over Havenbridge.

"Where are you? Icarian's armies attacked—"

"Be silent." She immediately complied, which wasn't like her. I was clearly getting better at being a necromancer. Thank the Gate for small favors. "I need you to come to me. Now."

"But how—?"

I imagined the fiery portal I had used as a fire fae to travel between Otherworld and Earth. A second later a pinwheel of black flame formed in the sky before Aunt Millie and her army. They flew through it, and moments later, a loud *whoosh* precipitated the appearance of spinning blades of black flame in the red sky above.

Aunt Millie and the vampyren exited the tunnel. They emerged with talons flexed and prehensile tongues rattling. They were ready to do battle at my command.

I pointed toward the zombies. "Kill as many of them as you can."

Without a word of protest, the vampyren flew into action. They descended upon our foes, slicing through their corpses with their claws or beheading them with their prehensile tongues.

Mrs. Blackmoor nodded in appreciation of the assistance while Thad beamed up at me, giving me his warm, broad smile that still made me want to strip him naked. I took that and the stiffening in my groin to mean our connection still held fast. I had to hurry before it vanished completely.

I waved my hand and dozens of flaming black knives floated above my friends and family. It was time to set them free. I brought my raised hand down, and the fiery blades streaked downward, striking the chains Gerald had used to restrain, depower, and keep everyone unconscious.

As I suspected, the ebony fire consumed the golden restraints.

"Finally!" Thad sprung to his feet the second he was free, and I landed by his side.

I pulled him into my embrace, burying my face in his neck and relishing in the feel of his warmth against mine. Being with Thad again made me feel invincible, as if I could take on a hundred Geralds without batting an eye. "I missed you so much." I leaned back and gazed down into his honey-colored eyes and ran a big finger across the pink lips I couldn't wait to devour. Unlike his mother, he didn't appear to be affected by this place at all. It had to be our connection as our blood tie once again grew taut. "I worried I might never see you again."

"Nonsense." He caressed my cheeks and pressed the full weight of his body against my own. "I never once doubted I'd hold you in my arms again."

Those were exactly the words I needed to hear. They told me that no matter what, our blood tie could never be severed, not by Gerald or death. Thad was mine forever, and I was forever his.

That was our destiny.

CHAPTER 16

As I held Thad, whispering to him that I'd never let him go, the vampyren destroyed the last of the zombies while Mrs. Blackmoor used her magic to rouse our friends and family from Gerald's spell and heal a majority of their wounds.

Expending so much energy nearly did her in. Luckily, the land of the dead was mine to command. I was able to return some of the energy being here had stolen from her. Color returned to her pale cheeks, and she stood up straighter. She gave me a nod and a smile, but she knew as well as I did that it was only a temporary fix.

We had to get everyone home.

One by one, our friends and family woke up, extremely dazed and barely able to stand, but as they started to take notice of Mrs. Blackmoor standing next to Thad and me, a murmur slowly spread among them until it grew into a cry of surprise and celebration.

"Mom!" Pierce and Mason shouted at the same time as they flew into their mother's arms. They sobbed into her shoulder, clutching at her back and her arms as if they were trying to make sense of what they could see and feel.

She kissed their foreheads and caressed their cheeks. "Yes, boys. It's me."

"But how?" Mason asked through wet eyes.

"It's a long story."

"Well, it's one I would love to hear." Mrs. Proctor stood by her husband, beaming, tears streaming down her face. I could no longer read her emotions, but I didn't need the ability to tell she was glad to see her friend alive.

"How about you give me a shot at explaining?" Mr. Blackmoor's words were thick as he walked toward his wife. A smile, broader than any I'd ever seen before, spread wide across his lips. "My beautiful, smart, powerful wife was the Warlock Hag."

Everyone glanced down at her black robes as if noticing them for the first time, and their mouths fell agape.

His response, however, produced a different expression across Mrs. Blackmoor's countenance. She frowned. "*What* did you just call me?"

He moved his sons aside and pulled her into his arms. "Never mind." He ran his big hand across her cheek and smiled before delivering a deep, openmouthed kiss that rouged both their cheeks. "I'm just glad I was right."

"But *how* did you know?"

Mr. Blackmoor rested his forehead against hers and sighed. "After we fought the witch hunters and were arguing about the Edwells, you asked me, 'When will you ever learn?' I can't remember how many times you've asked me that in the more than twenty years we've been married."

"Maybe one of these days you'll actually have an answer." She giggled like a schoolgirl, which took me by surprise. I'd grown accustomed to the hard-as-nails warlock who kicked ass and smiled while doing it. Evidently being in her husband's arms and reunited with her family brought out her softer side. It was a change I could definitely live with.

Mr. Edwell wobbled forward on his squat legs and cleared his throat. "While this reunion has been... delightful." He forced a fake smile across his plump lips that earned him a set of scowls from *every* Blackmoor, including Mrs. Blackmoor. It was yet another development I heartily accepted. "Will someone please tell me where we are and what the hell is going on?"

Mr. Stonewall nodded. "Those are answers I would most certainly welcome."

Everyone's eyes suddenly shifted to me.

"This," I said, waving to the barren world around me, "is the land of the dead."

The faces of most everyone blanched in reply. They also realized the danger of remaining where death magic reigned supreme.

"We must leave immediately," Mrs. Proctor announced.

"How did we get here in the first place?" Mason asked, oblivious, as always, to the mood change around him. "The last thing I remember was the undead appearing in our living room. We tried to fight them off, but our spells didn't work. They only grew stronger and kept coming."

"We can discuss this in Havenbridge," Mr. Stonewall replied with a nod to me. He was ready to be taken home.

"No. I want answers now." Mr. Edwell waddled forward, also ignorant of the predicament. Why wasn't I surprised? "How is being here even possible? Are the zombies gone for good? And what about Icarian? Where is he?" He then pointed a chubby finger at the vampyren who huddled away from us. "And why the hell are there bloodsucking monsters standing a few feet from us?"

I stepped out of Thad's embrace and sneered down at him. "Those *monsters* saved your life and the lives of everyone here, so shut up before I order them to take you out for a bite."

The vampyren hissed in appreciation while Mr. Edwell gasped and stepped back. "You wouldn't!"

"Try me."

Thad grabbed my hand and forced my gaze to his. My riled temper immediately calmed, but staring down into his golden gaze only made my heart race. Even as one of the undead, I'd never felt more alive. "I think it's time for you to take us home and tell us *everything*."

He was right. In fact, it was past time.

"Wait a minute!" Mason's strained voice suddenly filled the silence. He stood on his tiptoes, surveying the crowd with wide eyes. In the excitement of seeing his mother alive, he hadn't noticed the one thing I knew would set him off like a nuclear explosion. "Where the hell's Drake? I'm not going *anywhere* without him."

He was right. We couldn't leave without Drake. He was here somewhere, and since he was the Water Crest, we had to find him—fast. I took a deep breath, and instead of taking everyone home, I explained why we couldn't leave by telling them everything, from Gerald's betrayal to the Prophecy of the Three.

WHEN I finally finished speaking, shock stole the words from the many gaping mouths around me. I certainly understood. To learn that one of our own, someone we believed in and cared about, could violate our trust proved almost too much to bear, yet we couldn't let the weight of treachery keep us from moving forward, from doing whatever we had to do to set things right, save magic, and keep my family safe.

Those were the words I intended to say before Mason went off.

"Gerald is Icarian *and* he has *Drake*?" His tanned face flushed, and he clenched his fists. In response, the shadows coiled around him like rattlesnakes ready to strike. "I'm going to kill him!"

Mr. Blackmoor placed his hand on Mason's shoulder and gave it a squeeze. "We'll find Drake. I guarantee it."

"Damn straight!" Aunt Millie parted the crowd with her presence and marched over to Mason. Even though she had tried to kill him on multiple occasions, Mason flew into her arms and held her tight. All had seemingly been forgiven, especially since the boy they both loved was in danger. "Don't you fret. I'll do whatever I have to, to get my Drake back."

Her words caused shoulders to tense and gazes to bounce. Clearly the protector covens were still judging her and the other vampyren on their past instead of their most recent actions. I couldn't say I blamed them. While under Ben and Gerald's command, they had committed heinous crimes, but sadistic psychopaths no longer controlled them, and if I had my way, no one else would be able to do so again.

"She's right." Mr. Blackmoor gave Aunt Millie a reassuring nod. "We all will."

Even though they were putting their lives in danger by remaining here, the rest of the protector covens agreed without hesitation. I couldn't help but smile. Despite Drake's witch hunter lineage, he'd finally been accepted as one of us. After everything he'd been through to protect Mason and the rest of magic, it was the least he deserved, even if the scowling Edwells didn't agree.

What they thought on the subject didn't really matter to anyone but them.

"And what of the Lord of the Fae?" Caspian, who had been crowned the shifters' new Beast King a couple of months ago, took a regal step forward. Two burly shifters in tunics stood on either side of him. They were King Caspian's personal guards, and their gazes darted across the landscape, clearly attempting to locate any approaching threat. "And the rest of the Conclave?"

Mrs. Blackmoor stepped out of her husband's embrace for the first time since they were reunited. "We'll find them all."

"But how?" Mrs. Proctor asked.

It was a good question, and no one had a ready answer for it. Drake, my father, and the Conclave could be held captive anywhere in the never-ending expanse of red gloom, and the notion frightened me. Gerald had warned me that he wasn't done, that he had been pulling his punches. Would we be able to find them before Gerald made his next move?

"As always, you ignore the severest threat of all." Mr. Edwell plodded forward with his wife and daughter on either side of him, their jaws clenched.

Mr. Blackmoor arched an eyebrow in warning. "And what would that be, Leopold?"

"Your sons!" He pointed an accusing finger at Pierce, Mason, and Thad. I had to fight the desire to break his fat digit in two, but Thad slipped his hand into mine, which quickly cooled my raging temper. Even though the flames of anger burned the apples of Thad's cheeks, he was right. We had to remain calm. Attacking the Edwells would only prove Mr. Edwell's point. "You all heard what Aiden said about the Prophecy of the Three. The Blackmoors are the biggest threat, *not* Gerald."

Mrs. Edwell nodded. "They should be dealt with immediately."

Arcs of electricity sizzled from Pierce's clenched fist as he stepped forward, but Mrs. Blackmoor's outstretched arm stopped him in his tracks. "And what measures should be taken, Agnes? Should we kill one of my children? Would that be sufficient, or would you prefer if we sacrificed them all?"

Mrs. Edwell swallowed hard under the weight of Mrs. Blackmoor's emerald glare before glancing down at her husband, who had broken out into a cold sweat.

"You allow your emotions to get the better of your, Priscilla." As always, Mr. Stonewall spoke with cool, measured tones. "While I disagree with the Edwells' approach to the subject, we cannot simply dismiss the prophecy or the warning it provides. Doing so would be illogical."

Mrs. Blackmoor turned her piercing glare upon him. "Watch yourself, Lawrence. I am still a member of the Conclave."

"You are also the mother of the warlocks in question." King Caspian slid across the soil like the cobra he turned into. Since he was a shifter and not a *homo magus*, he could speak as freely as he wished. Neither Mrs. Blackmoor nor the Conclave held any jurisdiction over him or his kind. "You cannot be objective on the matter. Therefore, dealing with the situation must be removed from your hands."

"I couldn't agree more." Gerald materialized above us in an explosion of golden light that transformed the red sky into a ruddy orange. The wound I'd inflicted earlier had healed, which surprised me. It should have taken Gerald days if not weeks to recover from the flaming black lance. "Which is why I have placed that responsibility in mine."

"Your hands are red with the blood of those you have killed and betrayed." Mrs. Blackmoor pulled the Air Crest out of her robe, and her hand pulsed with the energy of a small sun. She clearly meant the gesture to be intimidating, but Gerald wasn't fazed. He glanced down at her with smiling eyes, as if he possessed knowledge no one else did.

"I've killed no one."

"You killed me." Aunt Millie's words echoed in judgment.

For half a second, the Gerald I remembered floated to the surface. He gazed at the woman he once loved with eyes hooded in regret, but two blinks later the emotion had been replaced by a blank affect. "I'm through debating the matter. You've all been made aware of the prophecy. You know what I seek to do. Either magic must end or one of the Blackmoor brothers must die. I leave that decision to you."

"There's always an alternative to chaos and murder." Mr. Stonewall's stern voice surprised me. In the months that I'd known him, the logical wizard had never allowed his emotions to get the better of him. Today appeared to be an exception. Not only did his words come out strained, but his blue eyes blazed like sapphires against his dark brown flesh. His family gathered around him and clicked on their powers. "You must be stopped."

Mr. Edwell rushed to his side. "You can't be serious. You're taking arms against the Conclave."

"Gerald no longer represents the Conclave I follow." In response to Mrs. Proctor's words, her family nodded and stood ready to fight at her side.

"This is suicide."

"No, it's not, Mrs. Edwell," Kale said as the shifters morphed into their animal forms, flashing tooth and claw. "This is doing what is right."

The vampyren hissed in agreement.

"You wanted to be a protector coven, Leopold." Mr. Blackmoor shifted to stone as his family and I joined the growing army against Gerald. "This is what we do. We protect magic and guard the Gate from *anyone* who threatens it."

Mr. Edwell exchanged glances with his wife and daughter before letting out a defeated sigh. "Fine." His hands glowed with scarlet energy. "But my family and I better make it out of this alive."

His reply made Mrs. Blackmoor wince.

"I'm disappointed in all of you." Gerald shook his head and let out a sigh. "But the choice has been made, and it is you who must live with the consequences—just like the Conclave."

"What did you say?"

"You heard me, Priscilla." He winked at her as if they shared a secret. "Just like I tried to do with all of you, I attempted to convince our colleagues into seeing the merits of my plan. Unfortunately for them, they couldn't be persuaded."

A golden mass of energy popped into existence like a giant bubble. It floated in the crimson sky before Gerald. Inside the sphere, seven hooded and robed figures, two in black, three in white, and two in gray, lay motionless in the amber liquid that encased them. My stomach lodged in my throat.

Somehow he was using his augmented powers to siphon their magic into him. That had to be how he healed so quickly. He was using their mystical energies to replace what he had lost, but he was risking the lives of the most powerful *homines magi* on the planet in the process.

"Gerald, you must stop! You're killing the Conclave."

Everyone around me gasped.

"If the Conclave dies, the fault lies with them." He locked his steely gaze upon mine. "And you."

It took me a few moments to register the gravity of his words. When I did, the heavy weight of despair crushed my chest. While his motives, however misguided, might have once been to save magic from a prophecy he deemed to be inevitable, he had now crossed the line. He was willing to kill those who once governed the magical community not to save his species but to save himself.

His actions continued to grow more heinous, and as I gazed at the pulsating waves of power that wrapped around him, energy that thrummed from the crests that symbolized life and the energy gleaned from the impending deaths of the Conclave, I understood why. He was caught within a riptide of magic and emotion he couldn't control, and it had destroyed the logical wizard we'd all come to know and love.

Gerald Wa could no longer be saved.

Ectoplasm flickered to life in my palms. "We'll do whatever it takes to stop you." The low hum of powers clicking on immediately followed my words. The warlocks, witches, wizards, shifters, and vampyren at my side were ready to fight.

"You're certainly welcome to try."

My dragon wings lifted me skyward, and Pierce, Adam, the vampyren, and Kale in his eagle form took to the air with me as we sped toward Gerald. I fired a stream of ectoplasm, Pierce let loose spindles of pink lightning, and Adam unleashed a gale-force wind. Our powers collided with the golden aura surrounding Gerald in a thunderous explosion, but the barrier didn't fall.

Kale clawed and pecked at the shield while the vampyren converged. Some attempted to slice through the field with their claws, while others used their paranormal strength to pummel the mystical wall.

Safe behind his magic, Gerald grinned. "Is that all you've got?"

"Not even close," Mrs. Blackmoor called from below as everyone on the ground prepared to strike.

We flew out of the way as they unleashed their active abilities and spells. The air sizzled as their combined powers struck Gerald's defenses in a detonation of light that spread across the sky like the approaching dawn.

When the radiance faded, Gerald's barrier remained, and he flashed us a devious grin. "My turn."

Kale reverted to his human form, and a second later he, Pierce, and Adam plummeted to the ground. I sped toward Kale and swooped him into my arms while commanding the vampyren to catch Pierce and Adam.

"Fucking bastard!" Pierce complained once Aunt Millie set his feet upon the red earth. His voice was weak, and his legs wobbled as the land around him siphoned his magic and life force. A quick glance around revealed that the living magical users, with the exception of Thad, were being similarly affected. "He shut off our powers."

Of course he had. It was the same trick he used on us a few weeks ago. This time, however, Gerald's ploy hadn't been as successful as his last attempt. I still had access to my necromancy, and the vampyren hovered around me. It appeared that Gerald's ability to nullify magic didn't extend to the undead—or Mrs. Blackmoor.

Fog swirled around her as an emerald fire lit up her gaze. Activating the Air Crest likely made her immune to his incantation and to the draining effects of this land. "We still have enough power to kick your ass."

"Not for long." Gerald's hands glowed scarlet and emerald. The mystical energy flowing from the Conclave gushed out of their unconscious bodies until the cocoon that held them captive imploded, and the Conclave was gone.

"H-he killed them?"

I couldn't find the breath to answer Thad. All I could do was nod as Gerald absorbed the energy created by their deaths.

CHAPTER 17

THE SILENCE that followed was deafening, and it took several beats to comprehend the fact that the governing body of magic, the most powerful warlocks, witches, and wizards in the world, had been destroyed by one of their own.

The absolute relish with which Gerald had consumed their power made the situation even more horrifying. In his quest to protect magic, he had done the very opposite. He had potentially thrown the magical community into a state of chaos even worse than the prophecy he feared.

That was when everything clicked. The visions Mrs. Blackmoor had shared with me bubbled up to the surface—the zombies, the barren blood-soaked earth, the floating tombstone, and more importantly, the blood drop.

It had been the answer all along. The blood drop *had* to fall.

"You bastard!" Before I could stop her, Mrs. Blackmoor launched herself at Gerald, the Air Crest in her grip leaving a trail of yellow energy like a comet zooming across the sky. She struck the barrier separating them with such force that the ground beneath our feet trembled.

Gerald didn't seem to notice. He was too busy staring at his hands as if he were looking at them for the first time.

Mrs. Blackmoor struck the mystical field with the crown, clearly hoping to use its power to break the incantation. "Drop this protection spell at once."

"If you insist." Gerald's hand shot out of the barrier and wrapped around her neck. While she choked and flailed in his grasp, attempting to use all the magic at her disposal to free herself, Gerald plucked the Air Crest from her hand. Then he tossed her to the ground.

I caught her before she struck the earth and flew her to her husband. She balled her fists into the fabric of his shirt, tears of frustration streaming down her cheeks. "Without the crest, I can't cancel out Gerald's spell. My magic... is gone."

I still had mine, and if I was right, that was all we'd need.

"That's right." Gerald activated the third crest, and his already radiant aura grew brighter than the sun's corona. "Now there is no one who can stop me."

He was right, but he was also wrong.

"Think again." My wings sprouted from my back and lifted me in the air. Aunt Millie and the rest of the vampyren followed, but if this was going to work and if I was going to keep everyone else safe, I needed Gerald's undivided attention.

"Stay."

Their snarls told me they didn't like it, but they had no choice but to obey.

"You think *you* can stop *me*?" Gerald laughed so hard I wouldn't have been surprised if he tumbled from the sky. "You may be able to summon extraplanar energy, but I have three of the Crests of the Five. Your ectoplasm will never get through my defenses, and neither will those annoying fiery spears."

He was probably right about that. Gerald had amassed so much mystical strength, he'd become virtually indestructible, but there was one fact he was forgetting, and it would be a lesson he would never forget.

I planned on staking my life on it. All I had to do was piss him off.

"You may be strong, but you're not stronger than the forces that gather against you." Mint green waves of energy rippled out of my body and extended outward, reaching deep into the bloodred soil below. The ground heaved and split, sending fissures snaking across the earthen crust.

"What the fuck are you doing?" Pierce screamed from below. His angry words mirrored the shocked expressions and ticked-off sneers that gazed up at me as the upheaval knocked everyone off their feet.

The only one who didn't appear worried was Thad. Even though he struggled to ride the tectonic shifts I caused across the land of the dead, his beaming face told me he trusted me as unconditionally as he loved me. I was the luckiest vampyre fae necromancer in the world. I hoped when this was finally over, he would be able to forgive me.

"What forces?" Gerald's question refocused my attention on him. Pulses of scarlet, emerald, and amber energy flickered across his form. He was clearly siphoning even more power from the three crests he held, but it wasn't enough. In order for this to work, I needed him to summon the fourth.

"Forces you never truly understood."

"Impossible." A grin slid across his features. "I've forgotten more about magic than you ever knew."

"So then you just forgot that I'm a necromancer and this is the land of the dead?" The ground below exploded in a shower of red earth and rock that sent everyone scrambling for cover, but they didn't have to worry. The energy I manipulated responded to my commands. The falling debris never even got close to my family and friends, and with the influx of power, I was able to also slow down the draining effect the land had on everyone else.

Gerald shrugged. "And you intend to do what? Destroy the earth upon which your loved ones stand?"

"I'm not after what's on the ground. I want what's *in* it."

A gaping hole fifty yards wide yawned open beneath us, and hundreds of zombies streamed out of the gap like ants from a disturbed mound. Their vacant white eyes scoured their surroundings for their meal of flesh and magic, and when they set their gazes upon Thad and everyone else, they snapped their jaws in anticipation before surging forward.

Eat. Kill. Eat. Kill.

"No. Not them."

The zombies stopped as one and gazed up at me.

I pointed to Gerald. "Him."

Gerald let out peals of laughter as the zombies turned around and gathered underneath where he hovered in the sky. "Oh, Aiden. Is this really your plan? I'm impressed that you're *finally* able to command the undead, something any necromancer worth his salt should have been able to do from day one, but as long as I'm up here, there's relatively little your undead army can do to me—unless your cadre of magic-eaters can suddenly sprout wings."

"You're right. About everything."

He nodded. "Of course. I always am."

And he was. He just didn't know how right he'd been.

I should have been able to control the zombies all along, but my fear of losing Thad paralyzed me. It made me incapable of harnessing the power I needed to bring this to its foretold end. But my concerns had been unwarranted.

The love that Thad and I shared, the blood tie that bound us together whether I was a fae, vampyre, or necromancer was the key. Gerald's advice about holding on to that love, which he hoped would *prevent* me from stopping him, would do the exact opposite.

"These zombies *do* need wings." I snapped my fingers and leathery wings sprouted from their backs, carrying my undead army straight toward Gerald.

His eyes practically popped out of his head. He clearly had no clue of the extent of my abilities, because his knowledge came from the books he read, not from the magic that coursed through my veins. Not only could I reanimate the dead, but I could alter their forms to suit my needs, something he didn't appreciate as my flying zombies converged upon him. They took chunks out of his golden aura, ripping apart his barrier as if it were paper. The excess power he had consumed made them grow three times their mass, but there were limits to what even they could devour.

Gerald's only hope to stop them was to do exactly what I wanted.

"You think you've beaten me? Well, you haven't." Gerald sent all the magic he had acquired into the barrier, and the zombies closest to him grew fatter with power until the energy they ate became too much for their bloated husks.

One by one they exploded, returning to the ashes that spawned them.

Sweat matted Gerald's silver hair to his forehead, and he smiled at me. "Clever, but fruitless nonetheless."

I crossed my arms over my chest. "You think so?" The ground exploded once again, and another hole opened up as a new wave of zombies came crawling out of the ground. "Because I've got more. Do you?"

A scowl twisted Gerald's features. Though he was still more powerful than I was, I'd managed to deplete his reserves. If I kept this up, I'd weaken him enough to make him drop his barrier and eat ectoplasm. "Yes, I do."

Another golden cocoon materialized with Drake and my father inside. I let out a sigh of relief when I noticed their chests rising and falling. Upon seeing the unconscious body of Drake, though, Mason practically detonated.

"Give me back my boyfriend!"

His tanned face burned red, and if Gerald hadn't shut off Mason's powers, I had no doubt he'd be filling the sky with shadows as he had when he fought Gerald during Imbolc. That was exactly the kind of reaction I was hoping for.

"Predictable." I snapped my fingers again, and my zombies once again descended upon Gerald, but this time I added blasts of ectoplasm to the mix. "How did I know you were going to bring Drake and my father here? You think absorbing my father's fae magic and the power within the Water Crest inside Drake will make you stronger?"

"What?" Mason practically foamed at the mouth. It took both of his parents to hold him back.

Gerald exploded with energy again, obliterating my new wave of zombies. "Of course it will."

Now it was time for a gamble I hoped Mrs. Blackmoor could forgive me for. "Like the power you absorbed from the Conclave? It didn't work the way you planned, did it? You destroyed every *single* one of them and you still don't have enough power."

Gerald turned his mad gaze below. "But I haven't taken *all* their power yet, have I?" An unseen force yanked Mrs. Blackmoor from where she stood to within the magical cocoon alongside Drake and my father. "Thank you for reminding me."

Pierce bellowed in anger and sprinted across the field along with the rest of his family. "If you touch a hair on her head, I'll kill you."

It was working. Pierce and Mason were pissed. Their fear for their loved ones had reached a boiling point. Now it was time to send all three brothers over the edge.

"You'll never win, Gerald." I flew toward him, colliding with the energy barrier between us and striking it with the ectoplasm burning from my fists. The shield had been weakened during the last two onslaughts, and its light shimmered. In another few seconds, I'd break through. Gerald clearly realized once that happened, my ectoplasm would destroy him. No matter how much power he might possess, he was still composed of matter, and extraplanar energy destroyed anything alive. "You believe your wizard logic to be infallible, but the truth is you've misunderstood the prophecy all along."

"I've misunderstood nothing!" A powerful blast of arcane energy slammed into me, sending me spiraling to the ground. When I struck the earth, shards of agony ripped through me as most of the bones in my body shattered. The pain almost made me pass out, but I couldn't. I wasn't done. Yet. Even though every movement caused my broken bones to crunch and splinter even further, I stood and glared up at Gerald as he funneled one last blast into his glowing hands.

This was it.

"Aiden, no!" Thad's fearful scream broke my heart as he sprinted toward me. He wouldn't get here in time, but that was okay. This was how it was meant to be.

Gerald was finally mad enough to kill me.

I HAD no clue when Gerald's first burst of energy struck me. All I knew was every time another wave hit, I flew through the air and landed with a moist thump. Blood covered my body, but I couldn't tell if it was mine or the result of bouncing across the blood-soaked terrain.

It didn't really matter. I was dying. My right leg had fallen off somewhere during the initial onslaught. I remember hearing the crunch of bone and the sound of ripping flesh before it felt like someone shoved a red-hot poker in my thigh. A second later, the limb was gone. With my luck, one of my zombies was chowing down on it.

Was that irony or coincidence? I could never quite tell the difference.

Another blast hit me in the chest, but I didn't experience any pain, just a pressure that shoved me backward another twenty feet. I hit the ground hard enough that the red firmament above started to spin.

I hadn't noticed how beautiful the sky was here in the land of the dead. Sure, it wasn't the streaks of gold that glinted across the canopy in Otherworld or the different shades of blue in the heavens above Havenbridge. Still, the varying shades of red weren't as ominous as I'd thought the first time I saw them. The deep, rich color and odd texture were actually soothing. They reminded me of the red fluffy blanket Thad and I used to cuddle under during the winter months. We'd wrap its downy folds around our nakedness and tangle our bodies together.

I was going to miss that.

No. I was going to miss Thad and the life we were supposed to live together.

A shadow hovered over me. It was difficult to make out, mostly because my eyelids were getting extremely heavy, but as the figure descended, I noticed a pair of gray eyes.

Gerald had come for one last parting blow. It would be one he wouldn't live to regret.

"I don't understand you, Aiden. You're not stupid, yet your most recent behavior can only be categorized as such." He floated a few inches above me, and the rage that had previously overcome him had abated. Warmth had returned to his previously cold and distant gray eyes, as if he truly cared about my well-being. He reminded me of the Gerald I once knew, the wizard I'd called my friend.

"I'm... smarter... than you think." Every word I spoke hurt, but I had to say them. I wanted to be the one who told him he'd lost. After everything I'd been through, after sacrificing a future with Thad, I deserved that much.

"Because you made me angry? Because you made me bring you to the brink of death?"

"Yes."

"I see. You believe by forcing me to attack you that Thad would somehow save the day the way he did against Ben, the way Pierce did in Aeaea, and the way Mason did during Imbolc."

It was that and so much more, but he still didn't see it.

"Well, that's not going to happen." He motioned to his left. Since I couldn't turn my head, he lowered himself to the ground and helped me out. Thad, his brothers, and the protector covens stood a few feet away, outside a field of golden energy Gerald had erected around us.

"Hold on!" Pierce shouted as he pounded upon the barrier.

"That's right." Mason kicked and punched. "We're coming."

Tears streamed down Thad's cheeks. "Don't you give up, Aiden. I love you."

And I loved him. Seeing the fear etched across his pallid features made me want to reach out and comfort him. I'd take him in my arms, lay his face against my chest, and let the beating of my heart soothe him as I stroked his hair and told him everything would be all right.

Even if I could, he wouldn't believe me. He didn't know what I knew.

"As you can see, Aiden, this time, the cavalry will *not* be coming, because I'm more powerful than ever. I not only have the magic of the Conclave and three of the crests, but when I'm done with you, I'll rip the Water Crest from Drake and drain every last drop of mystical energy from Priscilla Blackmoor *and* your father. Of course, they'll die, but what does that matter? Their deaths will grant me the collective powers of the Conclave as well as access to the fifth and final crest."

"To bring... about... the Spell Fall?"

"*Why* would I end all of magic now that I'm the most powerful being that has ever existed?"

I was glad he admitted it not just to me but in front of Thad and his brothers. He'd become the god he feared the Blackmoors would be.

"I'm going to end the threat of the Blackmoors once and for all by eliminating the *entire* family." He scratched his chin. "I might even wipe out all the protector covens and start from scratch."

It made me sad that the Gerald Wa I knew no longer existed, but it made what came next a lot easier to bear.

When I spoke, my words came out all at once instead of through a series of ragged breaths. "You'll have to kill me first."

"Is *that* what you want, Aiden?" Gerald filled his palms with energy so powerful the radiating waves of heat started to melt my flesh.

"No!" Thad screamed from the barrier. "Please don't do it!"

I blew him a kiss before turning my gaze to Gerald's. "It's the only way."

Blinding light filled my vision as pain ripped a hole in my chest. With strength I didn't realize I could muster, I craned my head forward, and I saw it—a single blood drop falling from my wound.

It was done. My eyes refused to stay open and the world around me filled with shadows, but with my final breath, I revealed a truth that made Gerald gasp.

"You just brought about... the Prophecy of the Three."

MY EYES fluttered open, but I wasn't lying on my back or staring up at the bloodred sky as I'd been when Gerald killed me. I was upright, and I was standing next to him. He couldn't see me, though. Something lying on the ground before him held his focus.

It was me, or what used to be me. All the blood and gore made it difficult to tell. I turned my attention from my corpse to the body my consciousness housed. I'd become transparent, and a field of blue surrounded my incorporeal form. This had to be my spiritual energy, the form all dying matter took before crossing through the Gate into the astral plane.

From what I'd been told, most spirits were immediately whisked through the Gate upon death, so how come I was still here?

It had to be the last remnants of the power I wielded as a necromancer. Even though I knew my death had been destined, I hadn't wanted to miss Thad and his brothers beating the snot out of Gerald.

Now it appeared I'd have a front-row seat.

"Gerald Wa." Pierce hovered above the dome of energy Gerald believed protected him. He was about to learn nothing would save him from the fury about to be unleashed. "Drop your spell and face your judgment."

Gerald's face turned whiter than his hair. "H-how is this possible? I voided your powers."

Lighting streaked from Pierce's body into the sky above him in a thunderous crash. "You've voided *nothing*." The angrier Pierce got, the faster the lines of crackling energy continued to fork from him into the heavens above. It was almost as if he was transferring his essence into the sky instead of channeling the energy from the heavens into him. "You've only succeeded in bringing about that which you feared the most."

When Gerald took two steps backward, I smiled. I'd been right.

All this time he'd been attempting to stop the Blackmoor brothers from coming into godly power, but he never once thought about *why* they would need to.

It hadn't been to enslave the masses.

That wasn't who they were. Gerald had forgotten that. Yes, Pierce, Thad, and Mason had amassed astounding abilities over the past few months, but he'd overlooked the reasons why. They were responding to the foes they faced, the enemies that threatened their loved ones. Their powers were linked to their hearts, to their need to protect, and to their capacity to love.

By destroying the Conclave and absorbing the powers within the crests, Gerald had turned himself into a threat that only the brothers from the prophecy could defeat.

"No. I read Pythia's words. You and your brothers will destroy us all." He pointed to Pierce, who no longer levitated above the dome as a flesh-and-blood warlock. He had funneled himself into the heavens, where his energy dominated the sky. "Just look at what you've become."

"We've become what you have made us." Mason appeared behind Gerald in a cloak of darkness. The shadows he commanded no longer coiled around him. He was now a living and breathing shade.

Gerald unleashed a barrage of magical energy at Mason, who didn't attempt to avoid the attack. Instead, the shadows comprising him opened like a black hole and sucked the energy inside.

"N-no. This can't be happening."

"But it is happening, Gerald." Thad stood on the other side of the dome of magical energy that still separated them, but just like his brothers, Thad had become the very power he wielded. Thick sheets of ice had replaced his flesh, and when he placed his hand upon Gerald's golden barrier, it immediately froze. A second later the dome shattered. He crossed over to where Gerald cowered, and every step Thad took froze the ground around him. "Because you betrayed us."

Pierce's voice boomed like thunder. "You turned on your kind and all of humanity."

"You killed your friends." Mason's shadow body glided across the soil. "You've threatened to murder innocents in order to hold on to the power you've stolen."

The brothers spoke as one. "We cannot allow that to continue."

"Do you even hear what they're saying?" Gerald turned to address the protector covens, shifters, and vampyren who stood in the periphery watching. "They're talking as if they're gods, believing they have the right to stand in judgment. Just you wait and see. In a few months or even days, *you* will be where I am, and they will either subjugate or destroy you."

"You fail to see the truth." Thad appeared in front of Gerald as a swirling mass of snow. "Instead you seek to cast blame or incite fear."

"We are not your judges," Pierce thundered from up above.

Mason nodded to the spectators. "They are."

Gerald glanced from the brothers to his former friends, whose scowling, angry faces delivered their verdict.

"So it is decided." Pierce's voice rolled like thunder across the heavens. "What you have stolen must now be returned." Lightning streaked from the firmament, striking Gerald dozens of times until the energy from the Air, Earth, and Fire Crests returned to the talismans. With their power restored, a single bolt of lightning sent them sailing from Gerald's grip and soaring off into the sky.

"The power you killed for must now be sent back to the Gate." Thad's snowstorm forced open Gerald's mouth before cramming its full fury down his throat. His body bloated and shook as the force of the whirling wind and ice likely shredded his insides. A moment later, the storm ripped out of his mouth, nostrils, and ears, tearing free the golden mystical radiance he had siphoned from the Conclave. The mass of energy swirled in the air for a few seconds as if expressing its gratitude, before fading away.

Mason's shadow form enveloped Gerald until he was nothing more than a black blob. "And the gray magic you were born with shall be stripped from you forever."

When the shadow slipped free, Gerald fell to his knees, tears streaming down his cheeks as he faced the brothers from the prophecy. "Well, what are you waiting for? Kill me and be done with it."

"We are not your executioners, Gerald Wa." The brothers once again spoke as one.

"You're not going to kill me?"

"No."

"They're giving that honor to me."

Gerald's eyes grew wide as Aunt Millie plunged her hand through his back and out his chest. When she withdrew her limb along with Gerald's heart, he fell face-first into the bloody soil.

It was finally over. The man I loved and the warlocks I'd called my brothers had defeated their most powerful enemy. Now it was time for me to leave them all behind and journey into the Gate.

A swirling white light opened up in front of me. It was the Gate, swinging its door wide open to welcome me back to the astral plane. Its sparkling beauty filled my eyes with tears and my heart with the peace only going home could evoke. The pull it exerted was strong, but I didn't want to go. I had so much to live for, and my life with Thad had only begun, but my time here was over. My body had expired, and my soul needed to move on, to find rest, and to await the day Thad joined me on the other side.

I blew Thad a kiss before turning around and heading toward the light.

"Aiden Teine."

The brothers' voices stopped me in my tracks, and I glanced over my shoulder. "You can see me?"

"Of course we can."

Their answer caused Mr. Blackmoor and the others to arch their eyebrows as they glanced around the barren landscape. Apparently Thad and his brothers were the only ones who could see *and* hear me.

"You sacrificed yourself to save those you love. Your gift will not be forgotten."

I dashed to Thad, fully intending on swallowing him in my embrace one last time, but my spectral arms passed through him. Being a ghost royally sucked right now.

A smile carved itself across his icy lips. "You're dead, Your Highness. You can't embrace the living."

I laughed. Not even possessing godly power prevented him from teasingly calling me stupid. Damn, I was going to miss his taunts and his kisses and his naked flesh against mine. "So I've noticed."

"Now I shall return the gift you gave to me." Thad crossed over to my body, creating patches of ice as he walked.

"What gift?"

In response, Mason's shadow form spread across the land, gathering the limb that had been separated from my body during Gerald's attack. His silhouette draped across my corpse, and a single bolt of lightning struck the cloak of darkness. When Mason removed the cloak, my leg had been reattached and my wounds had been healed.

Thad knelt at my side. "When Gerald had restrained me and I hovered near death, you used your necromancy to grant me the breath of life. Now I return that breath of life to you." He pressed his lips to mine and exhaled.

A red tether shot from my physical body and fastened itself to my spectral form. Jolts of electricity shot through my previously numb limbs as the thread of magical energy yanked me forward. I didn't need anyone to tell me what type of magic this was because I felt it in my tingling toes and fingertips and in the sudden fluttering in my chest.

The cord represented the manifestation of our love, the blood tie that bound us together.

A moment later my eyes fluttered open. I was once again lying on the ground with Thad smiling down at me. The ice that had coated his flesh had vanished, and he gazed down at me with those gorgeous hazel eyes that warmed my soul.

"Welcome back."

I BASKED in the warmth of Thad's hazel gaze for several moments, soaking up the love that beamed down at me, until I couldn't help myself.

I wrapped my big hand around his neck and brought his mouth back to mine. The moment our lips touched, the fire Thad's gaze had sparked in my soul spread across my flesh. I embraced the heat like it was the first day of summer after a long, cold winter, and that was exactly what the past few months—hell, even the past few days—had been.

Dark, ominous clouds had spread across our lives for so long, I was beginning to wonder if we'd ever see the light of day again, but dawn had finally broken across the blackened sky. Even better, Thad was in my arms again. His lips were pressed to mine, and my tongue twined around his, and if I had my way, we'd taste each other's kisses for at least a week. Except we'd also be naked.

"You really want me to barf, don't you?"

And alone.

Mason's snarky comment forced us to break our kiss. He stood a few feet away, a cheesy smile stretched wide across his lips and his arms wrapped around Drake. Judging by how tightly Mason held him, Drake would likely not get a moment to himself for the next month or two, and I couldn't be happier. I was just glad to see Drake conscious, free from Gerald's prison, and reunited with his aunt Millie, who stood by his side.

"Aiden?"

I gazed up into a pair of green eyes that resembled my own. "Dad." I had to fight the desire to fly into his arms, but King Oberon had never been one to show emotion even before he banished me from my home. "I'm glad you're safe."

A second later I found myself engulfed in his embrace, my feet dangling off the ground. Normally I'd hate being so easily overpowered, but right now I didn't care. I wrapped my arms around him and squeezed tight.

"I'm so proud of you," he said once my feet made contact with the ground.

"Y-you are?"

He put his hands on my shoulders, and though he smiled, tears fell from his eyes. "I've been a fool. Everything you are, everything you became, led you to this point—to save us and all of magic." He took a deep breath. "Do you think you can ever forgive me?"

I swallowed back my emotions. I honestly never thought this day would come. When my father and my people had turned their backs on me, I figured I'd never see Otherworld again. Maybe that was no longer true, and that realization made my eyes sting and my tongue thick. "Of course."

"Just in case you were wondering, I'm proud of you too." Mr. Blackmoor pulled me into his customary papa bear embrace before holding me at arm's length and giving me his once-over. "I'm so glad to see—" His voice broke as it always did when happiness stole his words. After breathing through his emotions, he muttered, "That you're safe."

I was pretty happy about that myself, even if I didn't quite understand how it happened. "I have your sons to thank for that."

Pierce waved my words away before pulling Kale close. "It ain't no thing."

"Are you kidding?" Kale glanced up at him, his golden eyes beaming. "The three of you brought Aiden back to life."

Yes, they did, which begged the question: "*How* did you do that?"

"I don't really know." Mason glanced at his brothers, who shrugged in reply.

"So how did you know you *could* do that?" Mr. Stonewall asked.

Thad leaned against me, and the warmth of his body made me wish everyone would go away. "We didn't. At least not really. It's kind of hard to explain."

"Please try."

In response to his father's request, Thad exhaled. It was what he did when he was trying to find an answer that evaded him. "It was like we had tapped directly into the Gate and were able to draw whatever powers we needed to do whatever was necessary."

His comment caused mouths to drop.

"And do you still have access to such unlimited magic?" King Caspian arched his eyebrows and studied Thad closely. He wasn't the only one. The protector covens darted their gazes from Thad and his brothers to each other.

I could understand their apprehension, especially after what we'd just experienced with Gerald. Possessing such powerful magic had driven him insane. That, combined with the Prophecy of the Three, would make anyone nervous. Still, their reactions irritated me. Thad and his brothers had just saved us all. They'd used their enhanced abilities not to harm anyone but to protect us.

"No," Thad replied. "The link's been severed."

When Pierce and Mason nodded in agreement, everyone except King Caspian loudly exhaled. He narrowed his eyes. "But could you access them again?"

Thad and his brothers exchanged glances followed by a long silence, which in itself was an answer. They weren't sure, and only time would tell if they would need to harness those abilities again.

"What happens to us?" Aunt Millie left Drake's side and stood with the army of vampyren that had gathered along the fringes of where we stood. The menacing monsters that had plagued us the past few months had morphed into insecure children. Well, everyone except Aunt Millie. She returned the dubious stares with her head high, unlike the other vampyren, who glanced around nervously and shuffled their feet.

"I'm not sure," Mrs. Blackmoor admitted with a sigh. "While your assistance definitely proved invaluable, your past actions can't be overlooked."

"They were being controlled. They can't be held responsible."

"While that might be true, Aiden," she replied, "it's not an excuse."

"I would agree," King Caspian added with a nod. "Their kind was partially responsible for destroying Aeaea, and as the Beast King, I demand they pay."

"You mean the way the shifters paid when Sersie controlled them?"

King Caspian tensed in response to my question, and so did his royal guards. They were only a few seconds away from morphing into their beast forms and charging, if their twitching muscles were any indication.

The ever cool-headed Kale interceded. Being the liaison between his people and the rest of the magical community wasn't easy, but in the few short months he'd served in that role, he'd managed to maintain a tentative peace between the species. "I believe what Aiden is trying to point out is that none of us have room to judge the vampyren. Sorcerers, mad wizards, and unstable warlocks have manipulated and used us all."

He was right. Every magical species, including the fae, had contributed to the problems of distrust in the magical community. Everyone nodded, and Caspian and his guards withdrew their scowls.

"So we just let the vampyren roam free?"

Although the prospect clearly upset Mrs. Proctor, I had an idea that might ease her nerves. The vampyren were magically bound to follow my orders, after all.

"Yes and no."

Thad glanced up at me from his place on my arm. "What does that mean?"

"You'll see." I planted a kiss to his lips.

"What does *that* mean?" Mrs. Blackmoor arched a tentative eyebrow. Even after everything we'd been through together, she still looked at me as if I were a problem she had to solve. Hopefully one day she'd get over it, but if she didn't, that was no skin off my lips. I loved her son. Nothing was going to change that.

I gestured toward the vampyren. "You must obey all magical law. You cannot reveal the existence of magic, and you cannot harm someone who is not trying to harm you."

The vampyren snickered, and Aunt Millie flashed me a huge grin. "We'll follow magical law, but not because you tell us to."

"What?" I turned from her smug gaze to Thad's. "Am I not a necromancer anymore?"

Thad slid his hands into mine and kissed my chin. "Nope. You're not a vampyre either. I only brought the fire fairy back to life."

More emotions than I could express clogged my throat, so I did the next best thing. I used my kiss to show my appreciation and give him a preview of what he had to look forward to tonight.

"And you think this is a proper solution?" King Caspian's strident tone interrupted our kiss. His lips formed a thin white line. "To take them at their word that they'll follow magical law? What makes you think they will?"

Aunt Millie sneered. "How about the fact that I haven't torn open your neck yet?"

King Caspian hissed, while most everyone else hid their smiles behind their hands.

"So is that it?" Kale asked. "Is this nightmare finally over?"

Our battle with Gerald certainly was, but we still had a long road ahead of us. With the exception of Mrs. Blackmoor, the Conclave had been wiped out, and it was anybody's guess what new problems that would cause. Whatever happened, the magical community was going to have to rebuild both its governing body and the trust Gerald had shattered.

And the grin that slithered across King Caspian's thin lips told me he might be a problem.

CHAPTER 18

I SLEPT for two days straight after returning to Blackmoor Manor. Apparently dying and being resurrected took its toll on a body, so I crawled into bed with Thad, and instead of doing what we really wanted to do, we held each other and passed out.

It was exactly what we both needed.

Having him in my arms and feeling his naked body pressed so perfectly against mine cast its powerful magic across my flesh, into my heart, and throughout my soul.

We'd faced so much and literally battled death—again—to be together. But more importantly, we'd beaten it for the *second* time. Nothing was capable of separating us, and though we might have proclaimed that to whomever would listen, we had undeniable proof yet again.

Our love, our blood tie, connected us no matter what might try to come between us, and after two days of rejuvenating our bodies and our souls, the warm rays of sunlight that fell across my naked flesh urged me to celebrate the bond that tethered us.

Past time, if the hardness in my groin was any indication.

"I see someone's finally up." Thad wiggled his butt against my erection.

I pressed a kiss to the back of his neck, inhaling his crisp, musky scent. Damn, how did Thad always smell like sex? "Have I told you I love you?"

Thad spun around in my arms, and despite some restless moments of sleep, not a single strand of hair was out of place. For someone who was still among the living, he sure slept like the dead. "Not in the past eight hours."

I rolled on top of him and swiped my tongue across his lips. "That's completely unacceptable."

"I would agree." He wrapped his arms around my shoulders before sliding his fingertips along the contours of my back. Whenever he did that, I shivered in pleasure.

I pressed my hardness against him and wiggled my eyebrows, hoping Thad would get my not-so-subtle hint.

"As much as I would love to make a sweaty heap with you, we don't have time. We have to get ready for the party, remember?"

I groaned and fell into his neck. I'd completely forgotten about the party Mr. Blackmoor was hosting at the manor. He wanted to celebrate defeating Gerald and his wife's return from the dead with the protector covens, and while it had sounded like a good idea when he mentioned it after we departed the land of the dead, standing around and making small talk was the last thing I wanted to do.

What I *really* wanted to do was Thad.

"Can't we just stay in bed and do naughty things to each other?"

"Only if you want to upset my mother. She *is* the guest of honor, you know."

I definitely didn't want to do that. Mrs. Blackmoor terrified me more than Gerald. With a huff, I rolled off Thad and fell onto my back. "Fine, but I intend to file a formal protest."

"So noted, Your Highness."

I rolled my eyes as Thad flashed me a big grin before throwing the sheets off his naked body. Great. He'd gone from teasing me to torturing me. It wasn't fair. Just glimpsing his naked flesh and his gorgeous manhood made me hungrier than when I'd been a vampyre.

Thad nodded to the closet. "Pick out something to wear while I brush my teeth."

"Really?" He never let me choose my outfit.

"I figure sacrificing yourself for the good of all magic deserves a special reward."

I leered at his butt and licked my lips. "Can I choose an alternate prize?"

"You can have *this*," he said, wiggling his muscled mounds at me, "*after* the party."

"It had better be a *short* party," I grumbled to myself as Thad disappeared behind the bathroom door. Since I clearly wasn't getting any, I stomped from the bed to the closet in search of an outfit Thad would find acceptable and that appealed to my more colorful fashion sense.

After tossing shirt after collared shirt aside, I found a bright yellow polo that reminded me of a garden rose. Naturally, I paired the top with green shorts. A yellow rose wasn't a yellow rose without its green stem. How could Thad possibly object?

Still, it was probably better to be safe than sorry, so I pulled the items off their hangers and headed toward the bathroom. The sound of rushing water told me Thad was still brushing his teeth, but when I pushed open the door, I found Thad staring at his reflection.

"Are you okay?"

He didn't answer. He continued staring at himself as if he didn't know who he was looking at.

"Thad, what's wrong?"

Through the reflection, he drifted his gaze to me and let out a sigh. I dropped the clothes and pulled him to my chest. It was what I did to ease his troubling thoughts, to remind him that my arms would forever protect him from all his worries. I combed my fingers through his hair before kissing the top of his head, and I waited. When Thad was like this, he couldn't be rushed. He had to process and take the time to find just the right words.

"I guess I'm just scared."

"Of what?"

"Of everything really."

Fortunately I'd grown fluent in Thad over the past few months and had a general idea of what was on his mind. "Is it Gerald? Are you afraid that his threat's not really over?"

Thad peered up at me and shook his head. "No. I know he's gone. There's no coming back from what my brothers and I did to him."

Or from Aunt Millie yanking his heart out of his chest. "Then what?"

"I've been having… nightmares."

I wasn't surprised, considering everything. "About?"

"The prophecy and about what my brothers and I were able to do."

I could understand that. Nightmares plagued my dreams every night after I'd been turned into a vampyre. More often than not, I woke up clutching at the sheets in panic after dreaming about hunting down Thad. In those dreams, the bloodlust had been unstoppable and the vampyre I constantly sought to control couldn't be reined in, but my fears had been just that—fears.

My monster had never been a threat to Thad because I would never let it.

"You're not a danger to me or anyone else."

He scrunched up his lips. "How do you know? Did you not see what I became?"

"I did, but I also saw you and your brothers return those powers when you were done. You're not Gerald, Thad. You're *you*, the sexiest, smartest, *strongest* warlock I've ever met. Only someone with a truly good heart could give up such extraordinary power, and that's exactly what you and your brothers did."

"But what if we… tap into them again?"

I shrugged. "You'll do what needs to be done and then send the magic right back to the Gate."

"But the prophecy said—"

"Thad, listen to me."

He took his bottom lip between his teeth and nodded.

"I know this prophecy is scary. It sure terrified me the first time I heard about it. I even vowed to do everything in my power to keep it from happening, but that was a mistake. I allowed my fear of the unknown to dictate my actions instead of using what I *did* know to guide me." I rubbed my thumb across his trembling upper lip. "And what I do know is that you're a good man and an even better warlock. You do what's right not because it's expected of you but because it's the right thing to do. That's why this prophecy doesn't frighten me anymore. So what if you can occasionally tap into godly power? Sure, it makes you a magical badass, but it won't change who you are on the inside. I believe in you, and I trust in you. You'll *always* do what's right. No matter what."

Thad rose on his tiptoes and crushed his mouth to mine. He blew hot pants of breath across my flesh, triggering my passion to swell between us. When he wrapped a hand around my hardness, a moan escaped my throat. "You just earned yourself an early reward."

"What about the party?"

He worked his grip up my length in a slow, leisurely tug. "To hell with it. There's nothing wrong with being fashionably late, right?"

"Not at all, my liege." I swept Thad off his feet and carried him back to bed.

When I set him down, he quickly crawled backward on the mattress, beckoning me with his finger, and even though I wanted nothing more than to pounce on the flesh I couldn't wait to kiss and lick and nibble, I hovered above him, admiring the creamy color of his skin, the rouge my kisses brought to his cheeks and lips, and the longing evident in his blown pupils. I had no idea how I'd been so lucky as to have this man fall in love with me, but his love was a gift I gladly accepted. I held it close to the hearth he'd made of my heart, and so many emotions surged up from within that I couldn't stop them from leaking out the corners of my eyes.

"Aiden, are you okay?" Thad wiped the tears away with his slender fingers.

I was more than okay. Thad loved me, which was a miracle to me. He needed to not only know that, but to feel it the way I did. He couldn't doubt how special he was, how lucky *I* was to have him, and how confident I was in the goodness that lived in his heart. I swallowed hard and nodded. "I just love you so much."

"I'm glad you do." He wrapped his arms around my neck, bringing my bigger body against his. The moment our flesh touched, I gasped as tremors of pleasure rippled across my skin. "Because I love you too, so *very* much."

The words sent a rush of heat straight to my groin before an aching need engulfed me in a searing wave. It demanded to be appeased in a way it hadn't before, and only Thad's gorgeous, muscled body could satisfy the craving. I caressed his sides, his chest, and his face with my roving hands. I nibbled and swiped my tongue across his lips before stealing his breath and replacing it with my own. "I need you."

He wrapped his legs around my waist and thrust upward. "I'm yours to take."

Just the thought of sliding into his warmth made me growl, but that wasn't what either of us needed today. My body required—no, *demanded*—something we hadn't done before.

"Not this time. I need *you* to claim me."

"Really?"

The arched eyebrow wasn't a surprise. Ever since we'd been together, I assumed the more active role because, well, because I really couldn't help myself. Whenever Thad brought up the idea of topping me over the past few months, I'd agreed. Why wouldn't I? I loved being naked with him. But when Thad's clothes came off, the beast within me took control and I pounced.

Thad had never complained. He enjoyed when I made love to him. I know I sure as hell loved when his body wrapped around mine. But after everything he'd been through—hell, after everything we'd *both* been through—I needed to surrender my body to him, to show him that though our powers might have changed, nothing between us had. If anything, our love had only grown stronger, more resilient, and it was time to take the next step.

"Are you up for it?"

A wicked smile slid across his expression as he grabbed a handful of my ass. "I most *definitely* am."

I dove back upon his lips. I slipped my tongue inside, drinking in the sweetness as my mind sizzled with the anticipation of having the man I loved inside me. I trailed a blazing path down his chin to his chest. I slithered my tongue around his nipple, eliciting low, breathy moans and whispered words of encouragement. When I gently placed the hardened flesh between my teeth, Thad arched his throbbing hardness against me before placing his hand on my head and guiding me farther south.

His urgent response spurred me on. I traced my tongue down his chest and through the concave of his stomach before descending toward the trim patch of red below. I swirled my tongue through the nest of hair, delighting in the musky scent that filled my nasal passages and fanned the flames of my desire.

I fluttered my tongue across the engorged head, lapping up the sweetness it produced, before sliding its length into my mouth.

Thad grabbed my head and bucked. "Holy shit!"

His cock pulsed, coating my tongue with more slick liquid that I greedily consumed as I bobbed up and down his shaft. Thad clawed at the bedsheets, cursing and writhing, as I increased the suction. I slid my tongue along the hardened flesh while pumping my fist in frenzied circular motions.

Every swipe of my tongue across his musky flesh, every low moan I tore from his body, and every wild thrust of his hips only fed my need to have Thad fill me with his love.

"Please stop," Thad gasped, gently tugging himself from my mouth. "If you keep going, I won't be able to claim you for another thirty minutes."

I couldn't wait that long, so I straddled Thad's groin. His hardness pressed against my crevice, and I arched against his warm flesh. "I need you inside me so bad."

Thad yanked open the bedstand drawer and produced a bottle of lube. He handed it to me, and with a click of the cap, I poured a generous amount onto my palm before coating the both of us with the slick liquid.

I took him in my hand and guided him to my entrance. "Are you ready?"

"Are you serious?" Thad's eyes were wide, and he clawed at my thighs like a wild animal. It was pretty hot, knowing he couldn't wait to claim the love I willingly offered. "It's been too long."

That was the damn truth. It felt like months since we last shared our bodies, and I didn't intend to wait a moment longer, for anything. As far as I was concerned, this was just the first step we had to take. I rose on my knees and placed Thad at my opening. Once he slipped inside, once there was nothing more between us, the fears Thad still carried in his chest would dissipate and become less important than the bond we shared, the one that tethered us together through life and death.

The one that told the universe that the blood that coursed through our bodies originated from the same beating heart.

I lowered myself onto Thad, wincing at the sharp sting as my body made room for his girth, and when the full length of him rested inside me, every nerve ending sizzled to life across my skin. I pawed at his chest as he began to slowly move his hips up and down. Every time he withdrew, my body clung to him, refusing to let their missing part go, and when he plunged back inside in one mighty stroke, my body rejoiced and my skin thrummed in celebration of his return.

Thad's rhythm grew faster, more urgent, so I leaned forward, bracing myself against the headboard while Thad gripped my hips for balance. He slammed upward in steady, mind-blowing collisions that sent wave after never-ending wave of bliss coursing through my body. I moaned through each upthrust that massaged the bundle of nerves within. Each time he collided with my internal button, streaks of light shot across my vision until I was panting.

"God, Aiden. I don't know how much longer I'll last." Thad spread his hands across my chest, twirling my nipples between his fingers as I rode his bucking hips.

Neither did I. This felt too great, too wonderful, and I wanted it to go on forever, but the growing hardness inside me combined with the short, rapid thrusts told me that wasn't going to happen.

I tilted my body forward until my lips once again met Thad's. He sucked my tongue into his mouth as he pistoned even faster and his breath grew more ragged. I brought my body back down, meeting his upthrust with my downward movement. The intense friction caused him to grip my hips as sweat slid down his face and chest.

I wiped his perspiration from his body and took myself in hand, stroking to the feverish pace Thad set. He ran his hands over me, clutching my chest, my thighs, and my shoulders as he pummeled me, forcing every inch inside until he groaned and his body went rigid. His cock doubled in width as it pulsed, filling me with everything I needed. He clutched my ass and my hip, burying himself deep as I continued to ride him through his orgasm and straight toward mine.

With one final tug, I coated my hand and Thad's chest with four milky volleys before collapsing on top of him in a wonderfully sticky mess.

"That was unbelievable," I finally managed to force out between halting breaths.

Thad kissed my forehead and then my lips before grinning up at me. "I had no idea you were such a good bottom. We're definitely doing *that* again."

"Yes, my liege."

Someone banged on our door, hard. "Are you guys done yet?"

It was Pierce, and he was being his normally pleasant self.

Thad snarled at the closed door. "Go. Away."

"Okay. I'll just tell Dad that you're not coming because you're too busy… coming."

"We'll be down in fifteen," I called to Pierce as I climbed off Thad.

"I'd make it quicker than that," he snickered. "Or else Mom will be the one who comes up here the next time."

Thad bolted off the bed as if it were on fire. "We'll be there in ten."

AFTER AN extremely quick wash with a hand towel, we dressed and bounded down the stairs to the sound of a ringing doorbell. The first guests had arrived, and Mr. and Mrs. Blackmoor strolled toward the door.

I had to do a double take to make sure I wasn't seeing things. Mrs. Blackmoor had traded in her black robe for a yellow dress that accentuated her slim figure, and her full, gorgeous auburn hair flowed off her shoulders instead of being confined in a thick hood. She looked stunning.

Mr. Blackmoor, who was dressed in a purple short-sleeved button-down and dark denim jeans, didn't look too bad himself. Of course the huge grins that practically cracked their faces in two only made them look more radiant.

"It's about time you boys decided to give it a rest."

Thad's face turned at least four different shades of red. "Mom!"

"What?" She attempted an innocent grin that only made her look guiltier, while Mr. Blackmoor chuckled at her side.

The doorbell rang again.

"Don't tease them too much," he said, pressing a kiss to her lips. "If we didn't have this party today, we'd still be upstairs doing the same thing."

"Oh my God!" Thad put his hands to his ears. "I'm *not* hearing this."

"How can you *not*?" Pierce walked into the corridor with Kale in tow. They wore jeans and matching T-shirts that said *I'm his*. Pierce glanced at his smooching parents and grimaced. "They've been at it nonstop. It's gross."

"Give us a break," Mr. Blackmoor replied. "My sexy wife and I have a *lot* of time to make up for."

Pierce and Thad groaned as the doorbell rang two more times.

"Are you guys deaf? The doorbell's rin—" Mason skidded to a halt next to his parents and gagged. I was pleased to see he'd returned to his usual annoying self. Although he was glad his mother was alive, Mason hadn't coped well with her deceit. He and Pierce had been angry, almost resentful, but obviously they had worked most of it out while Thad and I had slept. "Are you two *still* going at it?"

Pierce leaned against the wall. "I think I'm going to be sick."

"You boys need to grow up," Drake announced as he opened the front door.

The Proctors stood on the front porch. Each one of them carried a dish of some sort, and they immediately snagged Mason's attention.

He peered through the glass covers and practically salivated. "What did you bring?"

Miranda sneered. "Back up, Roach Boy. If you get your cooties on my apple pie, I'll deck you."

Mason started. "You bake?"

"Of course I do." She held up her chin and pushed past him.

While their parents exchanged greetings, Mason followed Miranda like a dog looking for a treat. "I didn't know you were so domestic."

"She's actually quite good," Adam added as he hugged Pierce and then Kale. "She's even better than Mom, but don't tell her I said so."

"Too late." Mrs. Proctor flashed her son a playful glare.

Charlotte elbowed her brother. "You're in for it now."

"It was nice knowing you." Mr. Proctor patted his son's shoulder before we all filed into the kitchen, where food was placed on serving platters and Mason bounced around from dish to dish. Miranda followed him around the countertop, smacking his hand every two seconds.

The doorbell rang again, and a few minutes later, Mr. Blackmoor escorted the Stonewalls and the Edwells into the kitchen, which had reached capacity. After they set up their dishes on the spacious marble countertop, the group spread out among the kitchen, hallway, and dining room.

I stood off to the side, taking it all in. Seeing everyone together made me long for my family in a way I hadn't in quite some time. Although my father had been invited to the feast, it wasn't customary for the king of the fae to remain on Earth. Hopefully, when the new governing body was formed, the boundaries that kept us apart might disappear.

As it was, they were starting to vanish already.

For the first time, the families didn't separate into their respective covens and glance disdainfully at one another. Instead, they talked *to* each other, and occasional bouts of laughter overpowered the hum of pleasant conversation.

Could the animosity finally be over?

"It's pretty amazing, isn't it?" Thad slid next to me and wrapped his hand around my bicep.

It was more than amazing.

Mr. Edwell, who chatted with the other High Priests, told a joke that earned him hearty laughter and a pat on the back from Mr. Blackmoor. Mrs. Stonewall actually looked interested in the conversation she was having with Mrs. Edwell instead of looking as if she wanted to gnaw her foot off to escape. Mason sat on one of the barstools, telling Miranda and Charity a story that didn't make them look like they wanted to kill him.

It was a miracle.

Despite his efforts to destroy all of magic, Gerald had brought everyone together instead. I guess there really was a silver lining to every situation.

"I hope I'm not too late."

Aunt Millie stood just outside the kitchen, holding a large casserole dish. Her presence caused a slight interruption in the flow of conversation, but surprisingly enough, the roll of voices continued while Drake bolted from his chair to her side.

"I'm so glad you made it!" He took the dish from her hands and gave her a peck on the cheek she puffed out for him.

"At my age, I'm glad to make it just about anywhere."

"I think someone's forgetting she's a vampyre."

Aunt Millie shooed my words away as I walked over to greet her. "I'll have no more of that talk," she said as she patted my cheek during our hug. "As far as I'm concerned, I'm back to being my old arthritic self."

Yeah, right. While she wasn't fooling anyone, we all got the message. She wanted her life to return to some semblance of normalcy, which was why Mr. Blackmoor was going to help her buy back her house.

As if on cue, Mr. Blackmoor stood by her side. "Millie, I'm so pleased you could make it."

After she thanked him for including her in the festivities, Mr. Blackmoor announced, "It's time to eat."

The words were met with eager nods, and after we all piled food onto our plates, we exited the manor and headed toward the party tables, which had been set up on the lawn and draped with white cloths.

For the next few hours, we ate and we talked and we laughed. The differences between us continued to melt away until we were no longer witches, wizards, or warlocks. No one cared that she sat next to a witch hunter, that a vampyre passed the bread, or that a former vampyre fae necromancer looked, according to Pierce, like a giant parrot in his green-and-yellow outfit.

We'd become a family, and we were stronger than ever.

Even though the magical world was in a state of chaos, I wasn't worried about what might be coming our way. If some other threat waited to fill Gerald's shoes, we'd beat it just as we'd done all the other enemies who foolishly believed they could take us on. That, however, was a problem we wouldn't face until tomorrow, or next month, or even next year.

For now, all I needed to know of the world existed around this table and in the warlock at my side. That was what made this moment perfect.

"Thad?" I asked, leaning over and whispering in his ear. "I need to ask you something."

He leaned into me and flashed me a smile that made my belly flop. "Okay. What is it?"

"Will you do me the honor of becoming my prince?"

Thad sat up, his eyes wide. "Are you— Was that—"

When I pushed my chair back and got down on one knee, everyone suddenly stopped talking. "On the day we met, you saved me from more than just a banshee. You saved me from knowing a life without true love, and it's a gift you continue to give me every day—in the way that you kiss me or touch me or even say my name. Your love has given me the strength to face death and conquer it, because for me, there is no life or even an afterlife without you, so Thaddeus Blackmoor, will you please make me the happiest man across all the magical planes and agree to be my husband for the rest of our lives—and beyond?"

Tears poured out of the corners of Thad's eyes as he fell to his knees in front of me. He caressed my face before covering my cheeks and lips with a flurry of the sweetest kisses imaginable. "Yes, Your Highness. Of course I will."

The backyard filled with cheers and applause as the most delicious shiver traveled across my spine. I traced my fingertips across Thad's jaw, around his chin, and down the neck I loved to kiss before pressing my lips to his. I held him tight as I inhaled his answer deep into my rejoicing soul.

"I just have one condition." The slant to his lips told me he was about to be difficult. I wouldn't have it any other way.

"Whatever you want is yours."

"You have to promise to grow old with me and not die on me anymore. At least not until we cross into the Gate together."

That was exactly the future I wanted. "You've got it, my liege."

For bonus content from

THE WARLOCK

BROTHERS OF

HAVENBRIDGE

check out

www.havenbridge.me

JACOB Z. FLORES lives a double life. During the day, he is a respected college English professor and midlevel administrator. At night and during his summer vacation, he loosens the tie and tosses aside the trendy sports coat to write man-on-man fiction, where the hardass assessor of freshman-level composition turns his attention to the firm posteriors and other rigid appendages of the characters in his fictional world.

Summers in Provincetown, Massachusetts, provide Jacob with inspiration for his fiction. The abundance of barely clothed man flesh and daily debauchery stimulates his personal muse. When he isn't stroking the keyboard, Jacob spends time with his daughter. They both represent a bright blue blip in an otherwise predominantly red swath in south Texas.

Blog: jacobzflores.com
Facebook: www.facebook.com/jacob.flores2
Twitter: @JacobZFlores
Pinterest: www.pinterest.com/jacobflores2
Goodreads: www.goodreads.com/author/show/5142501.Jacob_Z_
Flores
Google Plus: plus.google.com/u/0/+JacobFlores9595/posts

JACOB Z. FLORES

SPELL
BOUND

THE WARLOCK BROTHERS OF HAVENBRIDGE: BOOK ONE

The Warlock Brothers of Havenbridge: Book One

Mason Blackmoor just can't compete with his brothers, much less his father. They represent the epitome of black magic, strong, dark, and wicked, and though Mason tries to live up to his respected lineage, most of the spells he casts go awry. To make matters worse, his active power has yet to kick in. While his brothers wield lightning and harness the cold, Mason sits on the sidelines, waiting for the moment when he can finally enter the magical game.

When a dead body is discovered on the football field of his high school, Mason meets Drake Carpenter, the new kid in town. Drake's confident demeanor and quick wit rub Mason the wrong way. Drake is far too self-assured for someone without an ounce of magical blood in his body, and Mason aims to teach him a lesson—like turn him into a roach. And if he's lucky, maybe this time Mason won't be the one turned into an insect.

Not surprisingly, the dislike is mutual, and Drake does nothing to dispel Mason's suspicion that the sexy boy with a southern drawl is somehow connected to the murder.

If only Mason didn't find himself inexplicably spell bound whenever they are together, they might actually find out what danger hides in the shadows.

www.dreamspinnerpress.com

JACOB Z. FLORES

BLOOD TIED

THE WARLOCK BROTHERS OF HAVENBRIDGE: BOOK TWO

The Warlock Brothers of Havenbridge: Book Two

Thad Blackmoor's heart is as cold as his icy magical abilities. He considers emotions a waste of his time and prefers to study the arcane, using the sacred books of his coven to grow in his craft. He aspires to supersede his father and elder brother Pierce in power, and now that his younger brother, Mason, has tapped into the rare warlock power of darkness, he needs to work harder than ever.

But Thad's ambitions are halted when he saves Aiden Teine, a fire fairy, from a banshee. Thad's immediate attraction to Aiden catches him off guard and thaws his cold heart for the first time. As Thad, Aiden, and his brothers investigate the connection between the banshee attack and the vampyre and shadow weaver who almost killed them, Thad tries to dodge Ben, a sexy warlock who won't let him be after a one-night stand.

Their search for answers leads them to the Otherworld, where something even more insidious is at work—something Thad will need more than logic to stand against.

www.dreamspinnerpress.com

JACOB Z. FLORES

SOUL STRUCK

THE WARLOCK BROTHERS OF HAVENBRIDGE: BOOK THREE

The Warlock Brothers of Havenbridge: Book Three

Like the electricity he commands, Pierce Blackmoor streaks through life on raw power and pure sexual energy. His conquests on the battlefield and in the bedroom form his foundation, but that bedrock crumbles when his younger brothers' abilities surpass his own. Pierce finds himself at an all-time low, and clawing his way back to the top becomes his only concern.

Pierce's plan to reassert his dominance, however, takes a backseat when he wounds Kale Aquilo, an emissary of the Beast King, lord of all shifters.

Kale's beguiling nature shoots like a lightning bolt straight to Pierce's soul, and when the soft-spoken Kale relays that a virus is killing his people, Pierce abandons his quest for power to do something he has never done before—protect someone other than himself.

As Kale, Pierce, and his brothers struggle to find the root of the magical virus spreading plague across Aeaea, the shifter island, they face a gauntlet of old and new foes. Soul struck, Pierce and Kale must uncover the truth behind the conspiracy gathering in the shadows.

www.dreamspinnerpress.com

JACOB Z. FLORES

SPELL
FALL

THE WARLOCK BROTHERS OF HAVENBRIDGE: BOOK FOUR

The Warlock Brothers of Havenbridge: Book Four

Love and trust made them soul mates, but destiny might have other plans.

Ever since Drake Carpenter fell in love with warlock Mason Blackmoor, his life has been one supernatural battle after another, but Drake doesn't mind… much. To be with Mason and experience the magical connection they share, Drake would face entire hordes of vampyren, shifters, or fae—and he has. Luckily Drake is immune to magic, though no one can explain his natural ability to negate almost any enchantment. With Drake's own family gone, Mason is all he has. So why is Drake experiencing disturbing dreams about Mason that terrify him?

A new threat looms on the horizon, and a revelation about Drake's identity and the true origin of his bond with Mason shatters everything Drake believes. If Drake, Mason, and all of magic are to survive the coming Spell Fall, the most destructive curse in sorcery, Drake must deal with the truth and fight his way back to Mason—because their enemies are gaining strength, and they intend to reach the boy Drake loves first.

www.dreamspinnerpress.com

JACOB Z. FLORES

Please REMEMBER *Me*

Successful lawyer Santi Herrera couldn't be happier with the direction his life is taking. Not only is he on track to becoming a partner in his law firm, but he's planning his wedding to Hank Burton, a south Texas contractor who has made a name for himself despite his humble beginnings. The introverted lone wolf Santi and the friendly, outgoing Hank complement each other perfectly. From the moment they laid eyes on each other, they were hooked, and as far as Santi and Hank are concerned, a happily ever after is their destiny.

But fate deals them a devastating new hand.

A construction accident leaves Hank with severe head trauma and brings him precariously close to death. When he finally awakens, Hank doesn't remember Santi or the love they shared for the past three years. Santi faces the greatest challenge of his life. Can he respark a flame his lover can't recall? And can he stop the diverging paths that fickle fate charts between them?

Santi has faith in the love he and Hank shared and in the words his father once spoke to him: "It's never too late to fall in love. All over again."

www.dreamspinnerpress.com

A One Fine Day Novel

What happens in Vegas doesn't always stay in Vegas.

Cody Hayes is having one epic morning-after. The hangover following a Vegas bachelor party is nothing new to him, and neither is the naked man in his bed.

His apparent marriage is a different story.

Carefully plotting every detail of his life carried Julian Canales to a Senate seat as an openly gay man. A drunken night of Truth or Dare isn't like him… and neither is marrying a man he just met. He'd get an annulment, but the media has gotten wind of his hasty nuptials. If Julian's political career is going to survive, he has to stay married to a man who's his opposite in every way.

Now he must convince Cody that all they need to do is survive a conservative political rival, a heartbroken ex, their painful pasts… and an attraction neither man can fight.

www.dreamspinnerpress.com

FOR MORE

OF THE
BEST
GAY
ROMANCE

DREAMSPINNER
PRESS
dreamspinnerpress.com

www.ingramcontent.com/pod-product-compliance
Lightning Source LLC
Chambersburg PA
CBHW070107260626
47160CB00004B/1359